"I gave up on us.

"The last thing I wanted was to upset you," Jack said softly. "I didn't think— You sounded so calm on the phone. It was easy to convince myself that we'd grown apart, that you wanted it, too."

"I guess I was in shock."

"You cried." A flat statement of regret.

"Yes."

"I am sorry. You don't know how sorry."

"That," Bridget whispered, "was a long time ago. Apologies aren't necessary."

"Apologies are absolutely necessary," he whispered, "for our future."

She stood inches away from the only man she'd given her heart to. Truth was she had forgiven him. No, she'd never blamed him. It was as Auntie Penny had said when she told her they'd broken up. *It's sad to hear, but, my dear, you weren't meant to be together.*

She'd believed her aunt for twelve years, but now...had they both—no, all three—been wrong?

Dear Reader,

Christmas has come early this year! Here's your chance to have holiday cheer while soaking up the sun. This story marks the start of my new trilogy, The Montgomerys of Spirit Lake. You might remember that Spirit Lake was the setting for my previous Heartwarming trilogy featuring the Greene family.

The Greenes were a great bunch, and Mel appears again in this story. But he keeps a low profile because it's all about Jack and Bridget, the eldest Montgomery sister. And Jack's newly adopted girls. And Bridget's sisters and mother. And the customers at the restaurant they operate. And pretty soon, it's the whole town. That's the way Christmas snowballs, right?

I would love to hear from you. Harlequin Heartwarming has a daily blog where you can find me and the rest of your favorite authors. You can find me on Facebook under M. K. Stelmack Author, or visit my web home at mkstelmackauthor.com, where I have excerpts and pics and links to more.

Happy reading! And let me be the first—as I'm sure I am—to wish you all a very merry Christmas.

Best,

M. K.

HEARTWARMING

All They Want for Christmas

M. K. Stelmack

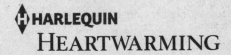

HARLEQUIN
HEARTWARMING

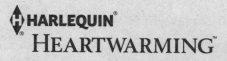

HARLEQUIN®
HEARTWARMING™

ISBN-13: 978-1-335-88988-1

All They Want for Christmas

Copyright © 2020 by S. M. Stelmack

Recycling programs for this product may not exist in your area.

This edition published by arrangement with Harlequin Books S.A.

For questions and comments about the quality of this book, please contact us at CustomerService@Harlequin.com.

Harlequin Enterprises ULC
22 Adelaide St. West, 40th Floor
Toronto, Ontario M5H 4E3, Canada
www.Harlequin.com

Printed in U.S.A.

M. K. Stelmack writes historical and contemporary fiction. She is the author of A True North Hero series with Harlequin Heartwarming, the third book of which was made into a movie. She lives in Alberta, Canada, close to a town the fictional Spirit Lake of her stories is patterned after.

Books by M. K. Stelmack

Harlequin Heartwarming

A True North Hero

A Roof Over Their Heads
Building a Family
Coming Home to You

Visit the Author Profile page
at Harlequin.com for more titles.

To parents of daughters.

CHAPTER ONE

BRIDGET MONTGOMERY AND her two sisters stood around the kitchen island heaped with baked dishes from what looked like half the Spirit Lake population. Auntie Penny would have packed the lot off to the community kitchen. No outside food at my *restaurant* or my home.

Dead. Auntie Penny. The two didn't belong together.

"Why did everyone think we need food?" Krista said. "We hosted the reception. At the restaurant. Just the leftovers from that filled the fridge there." She tapped her lips and eyed a cupcake stand that had somehow survived the trip home with all the iced confections in place. "Mind you, those are begging to be eaten."

"Giving food is a deep cultural gesture of gratitude and goodwill," Mara said. She inhaled. "Is that lentil dal I smell?"

Bridget had worked in a restaurant for the

past dozen years, and all she could smell was food. She exchanged a dubious glance with Krista. Were Mara's other senses taking over as her sight failed?

"Maybe," Krista ventured.

Mara sidled along the island, sniffing like a scent dog. "There it is. How about we have it for supper?" She lifted a stack of three lasagnas in aluminum foil pans—three!—which Bridget swiftly took, then reached for a ceramic baking dish.

"Bingo!" Mara swung her load away, her elbow catching on the cupcake stand.

Burdened with the heavy lasagnas, Bridget could only watch as Krista launched herself across the island to snag the stand, but not before a half-dozen cupcakes toppled to the tile floor.

Reflexes honed from a dozen years of spills on a public dining floor kicked in for Bridget. "Don't move," she ordered Mara and then used the lasagnas to plow an opening between the coffee machine and toaster—creating another accident waiting to happen—and joined Krista at Mara's feet to pick up cupcakes.

"I'm sorry," Mara said. "I saw the cupcakes, but then I just…didn't."

"No worries," Krista said. "Now I've an excuse to eat one." She licked the icing—white with blue snowflake sprinkles. Very Christmassy. A week into November and for the first time in almost forever Bridget couldn't summon up any Christmas spirit. Not even a single "ho-ho-ho." And to think that back in July, she'd sung the entire "The Twelve Days of Christmas" to a disbelieving breakfast crowd. For the fun of it.

"What are you? Four?" Bridget snapped. "You'll clean off the icing and leave the rest."

Krista kept looking at Bridget as she picked up a second upended cupcake and gave the festive top a long, slow lick.

Bridget retaliated with a deep eye roll. Was she the only one who saw how much Mara's eyesight had deteriorated in a year? And why was Mara going through this alone? Then again, what did any of them know about what the others were dealing with? Three sisters, three separate roofs.

Bridget dampened a dish towel under the kitchen tap and handed it to Mara. "There's icing on your—"

"I know. I can see that far." Mara whisked the towel from Bridget's hand and wiped at the icing on her skirt. She must hate this fussing, must feel humiliated. Bridget fumbled for something to say.

Krista set the mauled cupcakes back on the stand, as if no one would notice her tongue tracks. She really was four. "Couldn't we just give the food away at the restaurant?"

"Outside food is not permitted," Bridget said, "and besides, most of this food is from Auntie Penny's customers. I can't serve Mel and Daphne's lasagna back to them. No, we have to find a place for it all."

Krista opened the fridge. It was full. She opened the freezer drawer underneath. The same. "I'm out of ideas."

"Isn't there a deep freezer downstairs?" Mara asked.

"Let me guess," Krista said. "Full."

Full of pies and cakes made of raspberries and saskatoon berries and rhubarb. As well as casseroles, soups and stews. And a cold-storage room lined with canned pickles, pickled beets and asparagus tips, jams and jellies, salsas and sauces, chutneys and marmalades. For Auntie Penny, cooking and baking had been therapy, and in the months before she'd visited Deidre, the Montgomery sisters' mother, she'd undergone a lot of sessions.

Bridget's gaze strayed to the kitchen window, where it was already dark outside at five thirty.

And cold. Bridget clapped her hands. "I know. I'll get out the coolers—and I have the big storage chest on the back deck. We'll put everything in there."

"Are you sure it's cold enough?" Krista said.

"This is Alberta, not Ontario. It's November. Yes, it'll be cold enough."

"Won't raccoons get in it?" Mara said.

"And you," Bridget said, "have spent too long on Vancouver Island. Raccoons haven't reached here yet."

Krista split the top off a third cupcake. Really? "Basically, you're saying that Alberta in the winter is only good for freezing food outdoors."

"Alberta is way better than—" Bridget stopped when she saw the growing grins on her sisters' faces. The two always knew how to get under her skin. Common genes. She was adopted. Stranger genes. Still, she had loved Krista and Mara since meeting them at age six. Was forever grateful to her sisters' parents for getting her out of foster care.

"You have to remember," Mara said, "that

when the three of us came as kids, it was always during the summer. Yes, we were here for high school, but we moved on. You stayed. Spirit Lake is your home."

"Not ours" was the implied add-on. Putting her sisters back on planes, each heading in a different direction, meant she'd drive back to a house full of food and no one to share it with.

She could picture Christmas Day. Eating chocolate-cupcake bottoms and lasagna straight from the aluminum pan. Texting her sisters. Watching a holiday movie where singles meet for their happily-ever-after. Checking to see if it was still too early to go to bed.

BRIDGET HOVERED HER thumbs over her phone screen, trying to think of another way to say "Thanks, we will miss her, too." Mara sat on the kitchen floor among oversize coolers, calling out to Krista the size and shape of each dish she was ready to pack.

They'd not wanted Bridget's help. Just as well, with messages still popping up hourly. She'd answered no fewer than five hundred messages in the past three weeks with at least a few words. No using emojis out of respect for Auntie Penny. *Never saw a smiley face I didn't want to scream at.*

Thank you, Bridget typed. Your words mean so much. She hadn't used that one in a while.

She scrolled for anything from Jack. Out of curiosity. She'd personally messaged him the news, resisting the temptation to call. He and Auntie Penny had been close. As close as they could be when he moved from one place or another on the other side of the world. Bridget was merely the girlfriend he'd dumped a dozen years ago. Publicly, a girlfriend. Secretly, between them and Auntie Penny, his fiancée.

He had texted back almost immediately. How are you?

Fine. A stupid thing to say, considering she then unloaded the circumstances of her aunt's death. A fatal car crash while in Arizona visiting her sister, Deidre.

Can I call you? Now?

He was somewhere in Venezuela—she knew from Auntie Penny. Only a difference of two hours. She typed Please, but then erased it and typed Thanks, but I'm okay when she could barely see the screen through her tears.

His reply took longer. Maybe he was re-typing. Or he had to pause while he inoculated children against malaria or patched up wounded villagers or dug a well or whatever crisis he was single-handedly resolving. We'll talk soon.

Talk? What did he mean? When? Which she'd deleted because it came across as needy, and went with Sounds good.

No reply. Probably for the best. She would've been a sobbing mess, another humanitarian emergency for him to deal with.

Two weeks ago, she'd notified him of the celebration-of-life date as part of a mass message, and he'd replied two days later, Talk then.

She'd quickly answered with Love to hear from you and then scolded herself for putting in the word *love*. It sounded at once breezy and weighty.

He hadn't called today. Had she really thought he would? More than three hundred guests, and the absence of even his voice was as much of a huge gaping hole as when he'd chosen not to come home to her twelve years ago.

If she couldn't handle his absence, what about Auntie Penny's?

Her phone screen was peppered with teary emojis and messages of prayers, thoughts, hugs and the open-ended "If there's anything we can do…"

Mara was up to her elbows in the cooler while Krista munched on shortbread from a cookie tin, content as always to let someone else do the work.

"Stay," Bridget said loudly, surprising herself. "Stay awhile…for Christmas."

Her sisters exchanged their telepathic looks.

"That's more than a month away," Mara said cautiously.

Almost two months actually, and her sisters had never stayed longer than six days since graduating from high school. But there was plenty of room. Mara could keep the guest room upstairs, and Krista could stay in the one downstairs.

Krista's mouth twisted into the beginnings of a refusal.

"You're between gigs, anyway," Bridget said hurriedly. Krista was in the fashion biz. To be honest, Bridget didn't know exactly what her youngest sister did, and she wasn't sure she'd understand if she was told.

"Yes, but that means I need to hustle to get another one. Rent doesn't pay itself."

"I'll pay," Bridget blurted. How, she had no idea.

Five years ago, Auntie Penny had mortgaged the house to the hilt to finance do-or-be-closed-down renos to the restaurant. Then the economy had seriously nose-dived and everyone decided to eat their omelets at home instead of at Penny's. Each year had gotten worse. Before leaving for Arizona, her aunt had handed her an envelope "for us to discuss when I return," which Bridget interpreted as ugly budget stuff. She'd dropped it into the mail sorter by the fridge. She was now too scared, and too tired, to read it.

Still, surely, she could rustle up a couple thousand to cover rent.

"I believe you. It's just that—" Krista plucked at the dangly bits on her bracelet "—it's just that…people are expecting me back."

Bridget sat up. "You're seeing someone."

Krista fiddled with her mermaid pendant, a present from Auntie Penny when she was a kid. Bridget was floored Krista still had it, considering a six-month lease was her idea of a long-term commitment. "It's not going so well. And then this thing with Auntie Penny happened… He said—he said that I need to get back or I can just stay here."

"He doesn't own Toronto. He can't tell you to stay away."

Krista gave Bridget a meaningful look. Bridget sucked in her breath. "You're living with him."

"Yes." A single word, heavy with worry.

"Tell the jerk you're taking his advice."

Krista rubbed the pendant over her lower lip, a thinking gesture. Bridget pressed for the advantage. "Right, Mara? You're the psychologist."

"As of two months ago. I'm hardly an expert."

"You don't have to be to know this guy has got to go."

"He's got to go because you want Krista to stay," Mara clarified. "And before you ask, I already have automatic withdrawal for my rent, so you don't need to give me a cent."

Mara might not need money, but she needed help. "So then," Bridget said, "you're both staying."

Her sisters offered up silence, which wasn't an outright refusal.

"Look. I know you guys have your own

lives. I just— Couldn't we do this Christmas together?" She was slathering on the pity-pleading as thick as the snowflake icing.

Mara caved first. "I can't stay for that long. Maybe another two weeks."

Bridget looked at Krista, who said, "Philip wanted me back yesterday."

"Tell Prince Philip you'll be back when you're good and ready."

"Bridget! Stop bullying me. I'll say it my own way."

"But you are going to say it?"

"Later."

"And you'll stay for Christmas?"

"Only if Mara does."

"Fine." Mara thunked a lid tight onto a cooler. "Until after Christmas. But promise not to ask us to stay longer. I can't refuse you anything."

Bridget jumped off the couch and twirled into the kitchen. "Yes, yes, yes! This will be the first time in seven years we're together on the actual Christmas Day."

"We were all together three years ago," Krista said.

"Yeah, but you brought that dude who never got off his phone," Bridget said.

"He did when you threw it in the snow-bank," Mara reminded her.

"I don't regret it. You can't be with a guy who smiles at a screen more than he does—"

There was a knock at the front door. A taxi was pulling away from the curb.

Bridget threw on the porch light. A man in a parka stood there with two kids muffled in winter gear. She gasped. Was it…? No, it couldn't be.

He threw back his hood. It was.

Talk soon. She'd never imagined he'd meant in person.

JACK HOLDSTROM WANTED nothing more than to stretch out and sleep. The kitchen table they were all sitting at seemed good about now. The girls looked ready to join him. Dark smudges under their eyes stood out even on their brown skin, and their braids were fuzzy from thirty-two straight hours of traveling. So far in such a short time. The wait at Immigration in Toronto had taken the longest, and they'd missed their connecting flight west to Calgary.

His arrival was totally unexpected, and from the way Bridget was sitting, tight and rigid, unwelcome. Mara and Krista, lined up on either side of Bridget, weren't much better. Penny must not have told her about the adoption of the girls. She had said that she would in her own good time. Which she'd run out of.

Bridget nudged a platter of cupcakes toward the girls. "Do you want one?"

He translated. Isabella told Sofia to say no, and Sofia gave way to her older sister with a reluctant shake of her head. Isabella gave Bridget a silent, stone-faced refusal. Isabella must be so exhausted she was no longer thinking straight. He'd never seen her refuse food before.

Bridget chewed on the inside of her cheek hard enough to pull on the side of her face. Her tell signal for when she was troubled. Was she worried about his girls? With the same coloring as Isabella and Sofia, she looked the part of a concerned mother. Far more than him, with his light brown hair and blue eyes.

Hurriedly, he said, "I think they're just tired. I know I am. Do you mind if we head straight for bed?"

"Where?" Bridget said.

"Uh, wherever will work."

"There's no room here."

"There's Auntie's room," Mara said quietly.

"But that's— I mean, all of her things—" Bridget looked at the girls. "All of you in the one room?"

If she had any idea of what the girls had endured, she wouldn't have bothered with that question. Still. It was good to know that he had brought the girls someplace where the concept of three people in one room seemed like overcrowding amounting to a human-rights violation.

"That'll do us just fine for now."

"For now?"

If he hadn't been so tired, Jack might've chosen his words more carefully. "Until we figure out who is sleeping where in the house moving forward."

Bridget's eyebrows rose, along with her voice. "Moving forward?"

Yes, Bridget had just lost her aunt but she had to face facts, and not pretend that she didn't understand why he was there. "Bridge. Your aunt wrote me. She said she gave you a letter, too. It's in the will. I'm entitled to half the house."

He might as well have announced someone else's sudden death. She looked wildly at Mara and then Krista, who appeared every bit as confused.

Then Bridget's expression cut to one of fierce certainty. She bunched her napkin and threw it on her plate. She bumped against her chair and the island to get to the mail sorter by the fridge. She tore open a manila envelope and set to reading the sheet inside. Jack recognized the writing on the back of the letter. It was Penny's.

It probably contained much the same message as his letter. *I'm sure you think my gift is unusual and overly generous. No, I haven't lost my marbles yet... I have a simple, logical reason. Come home for Christmas, and I'll explain to you and Bridget when we're all together in the same room, maybe around the kitchen table, drinking my famous cider, your girls tucked warm and safe in bed.*

"The restaurant," Bridget said faintly. "You get Auntie Penny's share of it, too."

"I'm not interested in it. We can negotiate that." He'd sign it all over to her right now if it would wipe that horrible sadness from her face.

She slowly refolded the letter and tucked it back into the envelope, then fingered the shredded top of the envelope.

"I get it."

Bridget had whispered the exact same

words into the phone all those years ago, when he'd called to say that he'd changed his mind about their future together. He had never hated three words more.

BRIDGET LEFT MARA and Krista to sort out sleeping arrangements for the so-called guests. She could hear them in Auntie Penny's room, kitty-corner to hers—drawers opening, the flick of a bedsheet and plumping of a pillow, calls for fresh toothbrushes and towels.

She sat on the edge of her bed, her aunt's letter open on her lap under the glow of her bedside light. Bridget could only glance at bits at a time, as if the words emitted their own brightness. *Joint ownership with Jack. I'm as fond of him as I am of you. You two were close...work out something. We'll talk at Christmas when we're all together.*

Except there'd be no Christmas together. Though Auntie Penny might've had a premonition when she wrote that letter, how could she have known she'd crash her rental on an Arizona highway not five miles away from her sister's place?

Deidre had called Bridget with the news three weeks ago—the first time her mother had talked to her since Bridget's thirty-first birthday in April. She arranged the cremation and the ashes to be sent north, but she hadn't come for the funeral. "I already said my goodbye."

As executor of the will, Deidre would have to say more than goodbye. "I'll sort that out soon," she'd said.

"Suit yourself," Bridget had replied. How would Deidre sort it out from Arizona? Bridget realized she hadn't specifically invited her mother north. She would call tomorrow and do her duty, though she'd no idea where Deidre would sleep. Wait. Had Auntie Penny told Deidre she was giving half the house to Jack? Was that why she hadn't come, because she knew that with Jack there'd be no room? Everyone had known except her. Because she hadn't bothered to read the letter.

Noises from across the hall died away, and there was a discreet knock on her door. Mara appeared. "They're settled in."

Yeah, for good.

Mara sat down beside Bridget and nodded at the letter. "Did she explain why?"

"Jack needs a good home to raise his daughters. She didn't say why it has to be this one." Bridget crushed the edges of the paper in her hand. "She planned to talk to me when she got back. The real reason required a face-to-face, I guess."

Mara made a sympathetic noise. She was good with those. "The will must confirm its legality, I suppose."

"Will-shmill. Auntie Penny told us both, so I have to respect her intentions." But what *were* her intentions? To give Jack a house of debt? As mercenary as it sounded, Bridget hoped Auntie Penny had stocks or savings that could get them through the next bit. She had already cashed in savings to stave off the bank in the summer. "My rainy-day fund," she'd said. The situation now was more like Noah's forty days and nights.

Mara nudged her shoulder against Bridget's. "Having integrity is such a drag."

It was more than integrity. It was the girls. Jack had never acted as if he wanted a family and now here he was with two girls straight out of nowhere. She couldn't blame him. The younger seemed so sad, the older looked cornered and both of them so...*hunched*. They pulled on a deep, inert part of her being, the part where she'd buried the first six years of her life before her parents had rescued her from foster care. No way would she be the one to throw these girls out of the home they'd come halfway around the world for. Even if it was a home built on rocky financial ground.

"Do you know where the girls are from?" Mara asked.

"Venezuela, I guess. That's where he was."

"I'm sure we'll learn more tomorrow." Mara sighed. "The little one is cute. She showed me her missing front tooth."

"The other one is loose. She was wiggling it with her tongue at the table."

"I hadn't noticed."

"Probably because you were polite enough not to stare. I had a harder time."

Mara did the shoulder nudge again. "And at Jack?" She spoke softly so there was no danger he'd hear. Krista rooting in the kitchen freezer for ice cream was louder than their conversation.

"No," Bridget said quickly. She winced. Too quickly. Mara had always been able to read people, her sisters especially, and now that she was armed with her papers, she was all kinds of deadly.

"I admit that it's weird to have the guy I once dated living under the same roof. But it's not like I haven't seen him since he left." Seven times in the past twelve years to be precise, when he'd come back to visit his parents or raise money for whatever humanitarian project he was involved in. And every time, she'd swear her heart was mended, and then he'd take off to some forsaken place and rip a hole in it she'd have to stitch back up. He'd last come home three years ago for his father's funeral. Also victim of a car accident, west of town.

"It's just that it'll take a bit to get used to, and you know how I am with change."

Mara made another patient, sympathetic noise. Bridget, as the oldest, should've been the sibling to lead the charge into unknown territory. Instead she'd waved goodbye to her sisters and parked herself in Spirit Lake, picking up courses online or at the local college on an as-needed basis. Visits with her sisters or vacations had never extended beyond a week. Somewhere along the way, her sisters gave up on Bridget traveling and came out to Spirit Lake instead.

"The house will be extra crowded now," Mara said. "Do you still want Krista and me to stay?"

Bridget clamped her arm around Mara's shoulders. "You're not going anywhere."

Mara wrapped her arm around Bridget's

waist and squeezed back. Sister squeezes were the best, like putting on an old, favorite Christmas sweater. "Krista and me, we didn't tell Jack that we'd planned to stay until after Christmas. I don't know how he'll feel about that."

"Too late," Bridget said. "He should've told me he was coming. Besides, if he's happy enough to stuff himself and the kids into a room for one night, another few nights won't matter."

"Almost two months is not a few nights."

"The girls can take this bed. It's a double, right? I'll take the sofa bed downstairs."

"You really are determined that we stay for Christmas."

"We're all we've got," Bridget said.

"There is Mom," Mara said.

"And where is she?"

Mara gave a one-shouldered shrug, exactly as she'd always done when Bridget had pointed out Deidre's shortcomings. "We are adults now," she said quietly. "We're allowed to make choices."

Adults who carried hurts from childhood, deaths and a stupid heartbreak from a dozen years ago. Okay, maybe one adult who carried all that.

"You're staying for Christmas," Bridget re-affirmed. Then she remembered the odd little family—as odd as hers—across the hallway, and added, "Whether we like it or not, we're all staying for Christmas."

CHAPTER TWO

THE GARBAGE HADN'T been taken out. Bridget noticed as soon as she opened the back door of the restaurant. She was pretty sure she'd asked someone to do it, but in the flurry of packing and storing food, she'd forgotten to double-check.

She might as well empty out the front trash, too. She shrugged out of her jacket and kicked off her boots. She could hear Mano clattering around in the kitchen.

"Morning, Mano," she said and kept moving for self-preservation. Despite twenty years cooking breakfast, Mano was not a morning person.

He was chopping peppers. "The garbage wasn't taken out."

"Dealing," she said, clearing the swinging door to the front. Great. Three tables weren't set, one of them where Mel and Daphne always ate. She'd asked Mara to set up the front just to get her out of the chaos of the kitchen yesterday, but she'd forgotten these. Or not seen them.

Bridget beelined for the bathrooms. Sink needed a scrub and...she flushed the toilet. Yeah, that, too. She changed out the garbage bin and the paper-bag liners in the two stalls and headed for the garbage can under the till, then back down the hallway.

As she passed the kitchen entrance, Mano called, "There's no room in the fridge."

Bridget stopped. "What's the solution?"

"I'm not the boss."

"Neither am I."

Mano stopped chopping. "Yeah," he said softly. "You are."

Bridget scrunched her fists on the plastic garbage bags. She was and she wasn't. Jack, who hadn't worked at Penny's a single day of his life, was now as much the boss as she was. She'd poured her heart and soul into this restaurant for all her working life, yet he'd had the audacity to tell her he'd negotiate his half over to her. The entitled, self-centred—

"You all right?" Mano held up his knife. "You look as if you shouldn't be in possession of one of these."

She should tell him about the change in ownership. Then again, if she and Jack negotiated a transfer, there'd be no point. "Garbage first," she said. "And then I have to prep the front. I'll deal with the fridge after the crowd."

"No one will come," Mano cheerfully predicted.

"You better hope you're wrong." Hands full, she opened the back door with her butt. The sharp November air chilled her skin, like reality itself.

Three steady-Eddie customers told her at the funeral that they didn't know if they'd keep coming because it was just too sad to see the place without Auntie Penny there. "Maybe after Christmas, when I'm feeling better," said one.

Maybe after Christmas, there'll be no Penny's to come to, Bridget had felt like telling her.

She heaved out the garbage and was cutting past the kitchen when Mano called to her again "There are no melons for the fruit cup."

"There's an unopened fruit tray from the reception in the fridge. Use that," she answered, not stopping.

"And no whipping cream."

That was more serious. Marlene only took whipping cream in her morning coffee. Whipping, not whipped. She said it every morning, as if Bridget or Penny forgot every single time in the past half-dozen years of serving her breakfast.

"Did you check the front fridge?" she said, already halfway through the door.

"Not my territory," Mano called through the serving hatch.

Bridget opened the fridge. "Please, please, please," she whispered. Nope. Only eighteen-percent cream. No store was open, and the gas stations didn't carry it.

She'd offer Marlene coffee on the house and her firstborn.

She rattled coffee beans into the grinder and pressed the button. The racket would hopefully drown out Mano's notifications of additional deficiencies.

She poured water into the coffee maker, scraped in the freshly ground beans and flipped the switch. She headed into the kitchen, drew on a fresh chef coat, scrubbed hands and took a knife to the mushrooms.

"Why are you doing this? Isn't Cathy coming in?"

"Not today." Bridget couldn't bring herself to add that she'd let her go. She wouldn't have had the money to pay Mano next week otherwise. Still, it was a cruddy thing to do this close to Christmas. Speaking of which, it was time to decorate the restaurant. Smooth Sailing already had their Christmas lights pulsing through the night. Penny's had always been the first with lights up.

Mano waggled his knife at her mushrooms. "Too big. Half the size."

Bridget launched a fresh assault on the mushrooms "By the way, Mara and Krista are staying until after Christmas."

"That long? Don't they have men?"

"We're all spinsters."

Mano sucked in his breath. "Have them chop vegetables."

No way was she letting Mara near a knife, and Krista did mornings even worse than Mano. "Sorry, I'm all you've got."

"I have lots of someones." Mano was a born family man with a wife and a house full of kids, and couldn't understand why anyone would want to live alone.

As if aloneness was always a choice. She better fess up to her other bit of news, since it would come out sooner or later. "Jack Holdstrom is also staying at the house."

"Jack? Penny's Jack? He's here?"

Bridget scraped the mushrooms into a

bowl. "He came for the funeral, but he got in late."

"He should've been there. It was a good funeral."

Mano had cried like a baby. Great, hiccuping sobs. "He's here now. He plans to stay."

"To stay? With you? In the house? You two, together?" Mano twirled his knife, a sure sign of excitement. Bridget hated when he did that. He was going to take out an eye or a finger. If not his, then one of hers.

Mano liked Jack, but then, everyone liked Jack. Bridget didn't know how much Mano knew of her history with him.

"And my sisters, don't forget. And his two girls. He adopted them. They're from Venezuela." Bridget stopped. "You could speak Spanish to them. It would cheer them up to hear their native language."

"They don't need Spanish, they need English. When I came to Canada, I had the clothes on my back, the boots on my feet, two hands and a brain. I didn't know a word—"

"Of English. Yes, Mano, I know. Life was tough. Then Auntie Penny gave you this job, and now you have a wife and five kids. But you weren't eight or five. Like these kids."

Mano lit the grill. "They're young. They'll learn English. I did."

The girls were none of her business. And Mano was right. They should learn English. And given they were in Canada, French, too. It couldn't hurt to become trilingual. "Okay. Don't help them." She unbuttoned her chef coat. "I'm opening up."

She was reaching for the lock on the front door when Mano called through the hatch, "I'll make you a deal. I talk Spanish to the girls, and you be nice to Jack."

"I'm always nice."

"Nicer."

"I don't know what Auntie Penny said about Jack but I'm not going to date him," she said over her shoulder as she pushed open the front door. There stood her first customers of the day and clear listeners to her shout to Mano: Jack with his two girls.

JACK HAD INTENDED to sleep the day away, but his circadian rhythms were on the fritz, and he'd woken to Bridge stirring across the hall. He'd laid on his side of the queen bed and listened to the creaking of floorboards, a stifled sneeze, a rush of sink water and her stealing down the stairs.

If he'd done the smart thing twelve years ago, he could've listened to this every morning from the comfort of their bed. Or joined her.

He'd expected noise from the kitchen, but instead picked up on the clumping of boots and the snap of an opening bolt lock, and then she was gone.

It only occurred to him then that she'd left for the restaurant. He'd glanced at his phone—5:20. How long had she been doing these early mornings? As long as he'd been away. He'd hit burnout first.

He'd turned, jostling the girls on the other side. They slept suctioned together, legs entwined, Isabella's arm looped over Sofia, her chin on Sofia's head. He felt as if he didn't belong. On paper he was their father with sole custody. He had invited them to call him something other than Jack, something that acknowledged that he was more than a caregiver. While Sofia had wavered on the idea, Isabella had refused. To her, he was a necessity, a source of food and shelter only.

Sofia had allowed him to carry her through the airport when her legs were too tired, but Isabella held on to her sister's ankle, boot and all, as if afraid he'd run off with her. Isabella never allowed him to touch her. She'd ignored his outstretched hand, evaded his touch on her shoulder, taken things from him without grazing his fingers. He hadn't pressed her. She'd come around, wouldn't she?

In the darkness of the room broken only by a night-light, Isabella had stirred and her eyes snapped open. She had that superpower. To be asleep, then suddenly awake.

"I'm hungry," she'd said in Spanish, at normal volume.

"When Sofia wakes up," he'd whispered, "we'll get breakfast." He'd rustle up something. Surely Bridget wouldn't begrudge them that.

Isabella had shaken Sofia's shoulder. "Hey, wake up, time for breakfast." In Spanish.

"Let her sleep," Jack had hissed, but obedient even in sleep, Sofia had yawned and stretched herself awake.

Too early to bang around the kitchen, waking Krista and Mara. He knew of only one other place within walking distance where he could get breakfast.

So it was that he and the girls ended up listening to Bridget declare that she wouldn't date him.

There was a time she had. Had agreed to

marry him. But he blew it. He wouldn't again if she opened that door even a crack. He'd wedge himself back into her life. Date her, marry her, get it right this time.

If she didn't leave him out in the cold. Quite literally.

"We came for breakfast," he said. "The girls got up early and I didn't want to disturb your sisters."

Bridget's attention glided to the girls. "Come on in." Once the girls cleared the entrance, she let go of the door, obliging him to hold it open for himself. She guided the girls to a table by the kitchen, while Jack trailed behind. Third wheel again. Or the fourth, in this case.

"I have a problem," Bridget said to the girls. "I have a fridge full of food and no one to eat it. Could you help me?"

Jack translated. Sofia nodded.

"We can't eat it all now," Isabella said.

Jack translated back with a straight face. Bridget didn't crack a smile, either, though her dark eyes flashed humor. "That's okay," she said. "Eat what you can."

"Tell her," instructed Isabella, "that we can take the rest back to the house."

Bridget listened and made a counterproposal. "We've already got tons of food there, so how about you come here for breakfast every day until it's gone?"

Isabella accepted the deal.

"What do you say?" Jack prompted the girls in Spanish.

Thank-yous came in careful, sincere English. Isabella even granted Bridget a small smile. It had taken him three months before he'd gotten the shadow of a smile from her.

"Any allergies?" she asked him. It was the first she'd spoken directly to him since they'd entered the restaurant.

"None I'm aware of."

"Coffee?"

He assumed she meant him. "Yes. Please. Thank you."

She left before he could specify black. He wondered if he was included in the fridge deal.

The girls watched Bridget pour orange juice for them and coffee for him—nothing added, no creamers on the side. She didn't hesitate, as if she'd done it every day of her life.

As she set down the drinks, he said, "You remembered that I take my coffee black."

"You betcha," she said, as if he was an ordinary customer. "I'll be right back with your food."

Right back by way of a trucker who'd come with his own double-size travel mug. Jack hoped Bridget double-sized the price, too. A woman came in and Bridget immediately offered her free coffee because they didn't have whipping cream.

"I don't want free coffee, I want coffee the way I like it," the woman said.

"I hear you, Marlene, and as soon as I finish this morning, I'll get it for you. I do have eighteen-percent."

"I've been coming here for years. It should be a staple item, like coffee or cups," she grumbled.

A middle-aged couple came in, arms wrapped around each other like newlyweds, and took a seat at a table next to Marlene.

"She's out of whipping cream," Marlene informed them.

"Good morning, Mel. Daphne. I have eighteen-percent," Bridget repeated her offer.

"Everything's off here," Marlene said.

Jack saw Bridget's grip on the coffeepot tighten, though her voice stayed cheerful. "I assure you that every last single drop of cream here is sweet and fresh."

"I don't mean the cream," Marlene said. She made a sweeping gesture. "The whole place feels different. Without Penny, how can it still be Penny's?"

Bridget smiled. The same stiff smile she'd used last night when she'd invited him and the girls into the house. "Food's still the same. You still sit in your spot. Mano's still here." She paused. "I'm still here."

"That's the problem," Marlene said. "If you're here serving me, it means that Penny isn't. And I don't come here to feel depressed before I go to my depressing job."

Bridget had the coffeepot in a death grip. "I miss her, too, Marlene. I know you coming in every day will help me get through it."

"Great," Marlene said. "Now I feel obliged to come here and be depressed."

"No, I didn't mean—" Bridget stopped. She looked around, as if the right thing to say was lying about somewhere. Her gaze collided with his, her expression filled with the pain and weariness of loss. He'd seen it on thousands of faces over the years. He'd seen it on Isabella and Sofia when he'd first met them six months ago at the Venezuelan orphanage. To see it so stark on Bridget... Well, he couldn't exactly adopt her, now could he?

But neither did he have to leave her high and dry, standing alone with only a half-filled coffeepot to hold.

"I'm the new Penny," he announced, loud enough for Marlene to hear.

Marlene, along with Mel and Daphne, and the trucker guy, turned to him in surprise. No wonder—he had surprised himself. Isabella and Sofia lifted their heads, too, more from his raised voice than his words.

"I inherited her half of the place."

Out came the cook from the back. What was his name again? He took in Jack and called over to Bridget. "Him? Why didn't you tell me he's taking over?"

At least Jack had succeeded in chasing away Bridget's sorrow. Anger was her new look. "He's not taking over," she said, glaring across the way at him, not even trying for a fake smile.

"Sounds to me as if he is," Marlene said. "Who are you, anyway?"

Mel spoke up. "Jack Holdstrom. A friend of Bridget's. And Penny's." He waved to Jack. "Mel Greene. My wife, Daphne. We're also friends of the Montgomerys."

Jack had no recollection of him. Penny had made a point of introducing Jack to everyone who happened to be in the restaurant on the half-dozen occasions he'd stopped by over the years. He'd never paid attention, wanting only to track Bridget as she'd moved among the tables.

"Hey," he said to the girls. "I'm going over there to talk. I'll be right back, okay?"

"Okay," Sofia said immediately and went back to sucking the bottom of her orange juice dry with a straw. The level on Isabella's glass had barely lowered, rationing herself as usual. He could feel her watchful gaze on him as he crossed to Mel and Marlene. And Bridget.

"I didn't see you at the service yesterday," Marlene said.

"I arrived last night. I've known Penny since I was a kid."

Recognition lifted Marlene's eyebrows. "Oh, you're that Jack." Whatever that meant, and she didn't seem to care to explain herself, peering into her cup of black coffee instead. "Well, New Penny, what are you going to do about the fact I have no whipping cream for my coffee?"

"I am going to take personal responsibility going forward for your creamery needs. In the meantime, I would recommend Bridget's generous offer."

"You don't have anything else?"

"I have ten percent," Bridget said. "But that's a worse solution."

"How about," Jack said, "we put in ten and eighteen for twenty-eight, that's almost whipping cream concentration. Or double shots of eighteen, and we'll be over the top."

His illogic pulled a near smile from Marlene. "Sounds reasonable. I'm nothing if not agreeable."

Bridget jumped to make it happen and Jack edged past the cook and retreated to his seat. Maybe it was wishful thinking, but the girls seemed to relax now that he was back. Or maybe it was Bridget coming past with a big, genuine smile for the girls. "Two plates of breakfast coming," she said pointedly to the cook.

"I make real food. I don't serve leftovers."

"I can—" Jack began.

But Bridget snapped, "I will do it." And cut back to the kitchen.

The cook turned to Jack. "The old Penny fed herself, you know."

"I don't expect her to feed me or the girls." He remembered the cook's name. "I came here for breakfast like everyone else, Mano."

"Except it turns out you're not everyone else."

He wasn't. But despite what he'd said, he wasn't Penny's replacement, either. He fully intended to approach Bridget about her buying out his half. He would have given it to her, if his finances weren't so bleak.

The doors opened and there was Bridget with two plates heaped with strawberries, melons, sausage rounds, crackers, cheese, date squares and, on side saucers, three strips of bacon each. The thank-yous came spontaneously this time in Spanish and English.

"De nada, de nada," Bridget said. Then she frowned. "Did you wash hands?"

The girls shot questioning looks at Jack. Bridget pointed. "Back along there. Stool's under the sink if you need it."

"Thanks," Jack said as the washroom door closed behind them. "I keep forgetting the little things."

She set egg-salad sandwiches and chunks of cantaloupe in front of him. No bacon. "I shouldn't have interfered. They're your kids."

Your kids. He felt a punch of pride that she accepted the girls as his, even if the girls saw him only as a primary source of their basic needs. "First met them six months ago. Final adoption papers came last month."

"That was fast."

A process expedited by his connections in Venezuela and Canada. "Not for nothing was I in the business of providing relief to the world's most needy."

"And now you appear to be in the hospitality business."

He lowered his voice. "Listen, Bridge, I said that because I wanted to… I don't know, cause a distraction, I guess. I don't mean to take over. I was hoping we could talk, come up with a plan. Are you free later?"

"Not today," she said flatly and swung away, just as Isabella and Sofia emerged from the washroom. Right. Well, considering they now lived under the same roof, she couldn't avoid him forever.

Jack had learned that the girls didn't like to talk when eating. He'd have to work on the art of mealtime conversation, but later, when they didn't eat as if the food could be yanked away at any moment. For now, he would chow down on sandwiches and once again pretend he wasn't watching Bridget.

She used every part of her body. One hand for the coffeepot, left arm for the serving tray, foot to hook the high chair and her butt to bump the bar fridge shut. Her black hair, in its ponytail, swung, too. All the while, her eyes roamed the tables so she could top up coffees, settle bills. She was kept busy not because the place was hopping, but because she was the only one there.

The girls were picking date-square crumbs up with moistened fingertips. "Manners," he said in Spanish. "Use a fork."

"He's doing it," Isabella said and pointed. Sure enough, trucker guy was finger-pressing up his hash-brown remainders.

Bridget reappeared. "Can I get you another coffee or are you finished?" Her tone suggested that the latter option was much preferred.

He would go, but not before he tried again with a different tack. "Bridge, let me help out here for a little bit in the mornings. While the girls have their breakfast. Fair exchange for the meals."

"Thanks, but I can handle it."

"I'm already duty-bound to deliver the perfect cup of coffee to Marlene."

"I've got it covered."

"Seems as if you've got enough to deal with."

She gave him a pointed look. "Tell me about it."

"Bridge—"

"Sorry, I didn't get your answer. Coffee or are you done?"

He was far from done, but he didn't know how to reach her. "We'll see you back at the house, Bridge."

CHAPTER THREE

BRIDGET WAS CROSSING the bank parking lot to keep her appointment when Mara phoned. "I've got news." She sounded both excited and worried. "You've got another guest. Mom."

Bridget halted, hand on the freezing steel handle of the bank. "Is she here to sort out Auntie Penny's affairs?"

"And to see us."

To see Krista and Mara, specifically. Deidre and Bridget had never clicked. While Bridget had loved Krista, Mara and Dad at first sight... Well, Bridget had never called Deidre "Mom." Maybe because she'd known her real mother. A drunk. A thief. A drug addict. Transferring the title of Mom seemed way back then, to be unloading the same toxic personality on Deidre, too. She started with "Deidre" and that was how it stayed. Sometimes Bridget wondered if it was the name that created the distance between them, or if the distance had always been there.

At any rate, she could strike inviting Deidre off her list. Bridget pulled open the bank door and stepped into its foyer.

"How did she get here from the airport?" For that matter, how had Jack and his girls traveled from Calgary? No one had been there to greet them.

Before Mara could answer, she heard Deidre pipe up in the background. "Friends. I met them at the Phoenix airport."

In other words, she started a conversation with people until she'd found someone driving north from Calgary and played them into giving her a ride. Bridget's parents had spent their entire life together traveling the world practically for free.

"She wants to have a reading of the will today with everyone present. When will you be home?"

Inside, Bridget leaned against the cool window front of the foyer. "She's the executor. Why isn't she asking me this?"

"She's right here. Did you want to speak to her?"

Bridget pictured Deidre waving her frantic refusal. The two got along as well as they did because they didn't speak to each other unless absolutely necessary.

"I should be home at five thirty or so. We can have supper, and then do the will. Wait, Jack will have to be present, too. Let's do it after the girls are in bed, whenever that is."

Mara relayed the information and replied. "Jack said that'll work."

Of course, it would work for Jack to get the official word that he was to take everything that had once belonged to Penny. What had her aunt been thinking?

Bridget saw Tanya, her account manager, hovering at her office door. "I got to go, 'bye."

She'd come to the bank to find out in cold dollars and cents where the restaurant stood. By the time Tanya finished with her circles and arrows and negative numbers, Bridget felt as numb as she had when Deidre had called her about Auntie Penny's death.

"Your aunt never told you the situation." Tanya spoke softly, like a doctor delivering a fatal prognosis.

"I knew things were bad. I knew she'd cashed in some of her savings to make payments, but this—"

Bridget couldn't say it, could barely think it. Two months without mortgage payments, into the third month on the house. Three months of delinquent payments could trigger foreclosure. And this wasn't a first. Her aunt had done this time and time again in the past two years. The bank had long ago flagged the account.

"If it was up to me," Tanya said in the same calm manner, "I'd let it ride. But head office in Toronto makes the decisions, and I've seen it too often these past years. They follow a formula, a pattern, and yours fits it."

"Couldn't we renegotiate? Smaller payments over a longer period. Could I take equity out of the house?" That would work. If Jack agreed.

Tanya winced. "There's no wiggle room, I'm afraid. I'd recommend making a payment this month. In full."

She might be able to do that.

"Back payments would stop the process," Tanya went on.

No way that was going to happen, unless there was a decent chunk of change in the will. There must be. There had to be. Auntie Penny had always expected the restaurant to pay for itself. That was why she'd resisted dipping into her savings. These financial problems would be solved in a matter of hours.

Moving forward, Bridget could rent out the units attached to the restaurant. Auntie

Penny hadn't bothered to get new tenants when they'd closed up. Bridget had urged her to, but she kept saying it was more trouble than it was worth.

Or had she willed them to Jack?

"I'll get a payment in this month. Back payments, too."

"That sounds great." Tanya didn't say it with much belief but Bridget let it go. Based on past performance, Bridget didn't blame her skepticism.

Onto the next order of business. "Do you have time to talk about Christmas Crates?"

For the past nine years, Bridget and Auntie Penny had headed up an annual campaign to stuff crates for needy families in Spirit Lake. This year Tanya had volunteered to help Bridget organize the event. "It might be our biggest year yet, unfortunately. People have dropped names into the crate since the day I set it up." Each year, a lidded crate was set up outside Penny's for people to slip in their names or names of other families. "It could top fifty."

Tanya plucked at the corner of a page. "Yes. I've been meaning to talk to you about that."

Her tone was the same as it had been when she'd explained the financial situation. Regretful but unmoved. Bridget said it for her. "You're dropping out."

"It's not that I want to." She was twisting the page corner now. "I don't think I should."

"Because of your job here? Because of the restaurant's finances? The two are completely separate. The campaign money is in a separate account and—"

"My mother has cancer."

Bridget sat back.

Tanya blinked hard. "I only found out a week ago. It's small, barely there. They can probably get it with a few rounds of radiation. But I want to be there for her. And the campaign, it's meaningful, but—"

"It's a lot of work. I understand."

"I feel bad."

"Don't. How are you doing?"

"I'm fine. Sleeping less than I should. This stuff makes you think about what matters in life."

"Yeah. Auntie Penny's death has thrown me for a loop. I plan to dedicate this year's campaign to her memory. Give me something positive to think about instead of how she— how it ended."

Tanya brightened. "You could totally use

that to drive your donations. Her name carried a lot of weight in the community."

"I'm not worried about donations. There's still loads of money from last year. Hey, since I have you, can I arrange to have her name taken off the account? I have the certificate." Bridget had taken to carrying the death certificate like a driver's license, she'd had to produce it so often.

"Sure." Tanya clicked her nails across the board. "Do you have your account number?"

"No, but it will be under our names, labeled Christmas Crates."

Tanya pulled up the account. "Ah, here we go—" She frowned. "How much money did you say was in there?"

"I haven't checked it since last February. A little over ten thousand."

Tanya swiveled her monitor around for Bridget to see and moved her cursor to the balance.

Fifty-two dollars and thirty-seven cents. Bridget suddenly felt light-headed. "No."

"I take it you knew nothing about this," Tanya said softly.

Bridget shook her head numbly.

Tanya examined her screen. "It was one withdrawal. Looks as if she came in to this branch back in September. Exactly ten thousand dollars."

"She never told me," Bridget said. "She never told me anything." She couldn't have used it for the mortgages. The last payment was made in August. Bridget had paid bills and wages through the restaurant account, and she would've seen the deposit of such a large amount.

"I will verify her signature is on the withdrawal slip," Tanya said.

"It'll be hers," Bridget said absently, her thoughts on overdrive.

"With your name also on the account, it's best that's confirmed," Tanya said in her banker's voice.

"You mean, I could be held responsible?"

"Nothing illegal has been done technically. You two didn't ever form a charity, per se. No receipts were given out, right?"

"No. It was just me and Auntie Penny. She was trusted as the day is long."

"Then you should be safe."

"But what about all the people who donated last year? What about all the families this year that need help? What do I say to them?"

Tanya's answer was a helpless, sympathetic shrug. In other words, "Sorry for your troubles."

BRIDGET WAS NO CLOSER to answers when she came home. Everyone was already crowded around the supper table.

"Bridget." Deidre came around the table, her wide, paisley sleeves draping from spread arms, and hugged Bridget, short gray hair tickling her cheek. "How are you?"

Maybe it was the absolutely horrible day she'd had or the unusually quiet concern in her adopted mother's voice, but Bridget cinched her arms tight around Deidre's slim waist. "I've been better."

Deidre pulled back to examine Bridget's face. "I bet."

Her mother had always been this tender to Krista and Mara, but never to her. It felt good. Almost too good: tears started to build. She plunked herself down in the single remaining chair at the crowded table. Auntie Penny's old chair.

"Lasagna," she said. "What a surprise."

Deidre took a seat at the other end of the table. Krista and Mara sat opposite Jack and his girls.

"Hola," she said to them. Sofia chirped back her "hello." Isabella mumbled hers, and immediately returned to her food.

"They don't talk much when they're eating," Jack said.

"Good idea," Bridget said and smiled her thanks as Mara slid a square of lasagna onto her plate and then passed her the salad. Bridget reached for the bowl, then halted. Who was she kidding? She doubted her energy to choke down the lasagna. "Maybe later."

"How did the meeting at the bank go?" Mara said.

"Not good." Bridget gathered a forkful but couldn't bear to lift it to her mouth. "Horrible, actually."

They must have expected her to explain because everybody stayed quiet. Where to start?

"The restaurant isn't doing well?" Jack said.

Bridget glanced at the girls.

"It's okay," Jack said. "I'm working on their English, but it's low. They won't understand."

Bridget forced down a mouthful before speaking. "This is it in a nutshell. Two months behind on the restaurant mortgage. This month will be the third. Three months behind on the house. The bank manager worries that if I miss this month on either the house or the restaurant, it could trigger a foreclosure given the pattern of missed payments that have occurred over the past two years. And, no, I didn't know about any of this until today because Auntie Penny didn't tell me and because—because I trusted her."

She could feel her voice go shaky and told herself to get a grip. The girls didn't understand English, but they did understand tears. She exhaled. "And that's not the worst part. Auntie Penny embezzled all the money from the Christmas Crates account."

Stunned looks all around.

"How much?" Krista said.

"Ten thousand dollars to the cent."

"But don't you have access to the account?" Deidre said.

"I do, but I never checked it. I only did today to take off Auntie Penny's name. That's when I discovered she cleaned it out back in September."

Jack set his elbows on the table, pressed his fingers against his temples. "Can you remember what day in September it was?"

"The seventeenth."

Jack groaned, closed his eyes. "I know where that money went."

All eyes went to him. "I'd found contacts who could get me the adoption papers but let's just say there were fees attached. I didn't have the resources myself—that's a whole other story. I texted Penny more to blow off steam than anything else. We'd kept in touch."

Bridget nodded. Auntie Penny and Jack had developed their own friendship, and Bridget had driven herself half-crazy over the years, torn between not wanting to hear about Jack and hanging on to every shred of news.

"She said not to worry. She'd transfer me the money and sure enough there it was, ready for me to accept." He blew out his breath. "That was on the seventeenth of September."

He fixed his blue eyes on her. "Bridge, I had no idea she'd taken from the charity fund. None. She said she had a little money set aside. I told her that I'd pay her back as soon as I could."

"Okay," Bridget said. "When will that be?"

Jack pushed away his plate. "Definitely not before Christmas. I've got to pay for a dentist, clothes and food for the girls. Gas. Childcare while I job-hunt. I am sorry, Bridge."

"But you sold your dad's house when he died. That was only three years ago," Bridget said, "and he had savings, didn't he?"

Jack's head sank lower. "Let's just say I trusted the wrong people."

Sofia slipped under his arm to squirm onto

his lap. Isabella surveyed the somber expressions on everyone's faces, and chewed on her lower lip.

Jack murmured to Sofia and spoke to Isabella. Bridget didn't catch a word, but it was reassuring enough for Sofia to return to her chair, and for them both to resume eating.

They were the only ones left with any kind of appetite. To top it off, as everyone pushed back their chairs, Deidre said, as if talking about a book-club meeting, "Don't forget we have the reading of the will at eight thirty."

As if the day could get any worse.

DEIDRE ADJUSTED HER eyeglasses and flipped through the will, her long legs folded up in an armchair by the fireplace "I guess I start at the top and read through. I've never done this before." The Montgomery sisters' dad had died of a stroke, without a will. When Deidre's parents passed, Penny, as next-of-kin, had handled the will.

It occurred to Bridget that Deidre's entire family was gathered right now in the living room. All three daughters lined up on the couch, and each of them only had each other.

And Jack, in the armchair twin to Deidre's, had no one except his adopted daughters, now tucked into Auntie Penny's bed. Here in Canada with him because Auntie Penny had stolen money intended for others. And Bridget was left to deal with the fallout.

The will had better rain gold coins.

"'This is the last will and testament of Penelope Ann Dixon of the town of Spirit Lake in the Province of Alberta, made the sixth day of' blah, blah, blah…"

Deidre read on silently, as if skimming a salacious article. Bridget rested her head against the back of the couch. Deidre lifted her voice. "'To Mara, my beloved niece, I bequeath full and clear title to the bay immediately above the restaurant with the legal description of' blah, blah, blah, 'subject to the condition of clause' blah, blah, blah."

All eyes turned to Mara. "How…generous," Mara said quietly.

So much for selling the unit for a quick profit.

"'To Krista, my beloved niece, I bequeath the full and clear title to the bay immediately adjacent to the restaurant with the legal description of' blah, blah, blah 'subject to the condition of clause' blah, blah, blah."

"Wait, what's the condition?" Bridget said.

Deidre flipped pages again. "Here it is.

'The properties shall only be deeded to Mara Montgomery providing she operate a legal business for the space of one year from the time of her agreement to do so, which must be given no later than thirty days from the reading of this will.'" Deidre squinted. "Oh, there's a place here for me to sign and date to confirm the reading." She read on. "'In the interim, it shall remain in the protection of the executor as named in this will. If Mara Montgomery chooses not to exercise the right to the property, or fails to fulfill the requirements, the property is granted to Bridget Montgomery.'"

Deidre silently mouthed the next part, then said, "Basically, it's the same deal for you, Krista. Also, you're both allowed to switch properties within the thirty-day time frame."

Imagine, all three of them together, in the same building. It would be like the summer days when they were kids. Not just visitors in each other's lives, but every-day family. Bridget could have them not just for Christmas, but for a movie on a weeknight, clothes shopping on a Saturday, camping on a weekend.

"I was hoping just to get her funky jewelry," Krista said faintly.

"Nope," Deidre said. "I get that. Right here.

'To Deidre, my beloved sister, I bequeath my jewelry and all other personal effects not detailed in this will.' Basically, her jewelry and underwear."

Krista opened her phone. "If it's thirty days from the reading of the will, do I count today?"

"I don't think so," Mara said. "It would have to be thirty full days."

Under her breath, Krista began counting off days.

"I can tell you right now it's December eighth," Deidre said.

"The date doesn't matter," Mara said. "At least, for my part. I'm going to decline the offer. The unit is yours, Bridget."

"Same here," Krista said. "My life is in Toronto."

"Besides," Mara said, "you could do with the money from the sale of the units. Or the rent, if you choose not to sell."

Yes, she'd have no financial worries. And no sisters close by. Bridget clamped her hands, one on each of her sisters' knees. "No. Don't. Make your decision based on what you want. Your problems are not mine."

Jack spoke for the first time since sitting down. "What do you want, Bridget?"

"What does it matter? It's not my decision."

Krista poked Bridget's arm. "We know that, but if you could choose?"

"I'd choose both."

"That's not how life works," Jack said, his voice quiet but relentless.

"I know that, what I'm trying to say is that I would choose to have my sisters with me and I'd choose to have them doing what makes them happy and oh, I'd also choose to have a way out of the money mess I'm in due, in part, to what Auntie Penny chose to do for you. Does that answer your question, Jack?"

He rubbed his thumb across his lower lip. She remembered his tell from when they dated. He was hiding a smile or some other emotion. "It does, Bridge."

"Nothing needs to be settled right this minute," Deidre said, adding to Jack, "I'm sure there are certain hasty decisions you now wish you'd taken more time to make."

He winced. "Point taken."

Deidre brought the will back in line with her vision. "Anyway, here's your part. 'To Jack Holdstrom, I bequeath my share of the residential property located at—'" Deidre rattled off a lot number. "I assume that's the house."

Bridget said, "It is."

"'To Jack Holdstrom, I also bequeath my share of the restaurant known as Penny's in joint ownership with present owner, Bridget Montgomery.'"

So. Just as Auntie Penny had said in her letters to her and Jack.

"And that's it," Deidre said. She refolded the document and tucked it back inside a large manila envelope.

So nothing for Bridget. No stash of cash. No secret account. It had been a foolish hope. If Auntie Penny had the money, she wouldn't have drained the Crates fund. Bridget had half the house, but she'd paid Auntie Penny for it out of her wages. Same thing with the restaurant. In her own will, Bridget had bequeathed the restaurant and the house to Auntie Penny. To her sisters, she had settled on contents and cash, which amounted to nothing now. Time to revise her will.

Krista waved to Jack. "Welcome to the Montgomery family."

No way. "Owning half the house and half the restaurant doesn't make him family," Bridget said.

"About that." Deidre slid out a small laminated document from the envelope. "What if he was Penny's son?"

CHAPTER FOUR

HE MUST'VE MISHEARD. Jack looked over at Bridget and her sisters, side by side on the sofa. They stared at their newfound cousin with dubious fascination, as if he'd pulled off a magical trick they couldn't figure out.

Deidre clapped her hands on her knees. "I suppose you're all dying for the details?"

"Yes," Jack gritted out.

"I left home the September after graduation. Went to university, met Tom, dropped out for a trip abroad and not long after, became a mom myself. Penny stayed behind to help our parents run the family restaurant. She'd already worked there for two years and had taken over the business to the point our parents were taking their first holidays in twenty years.

"I learned later, and I mean years later, from Penny that she was pregnant when I left in September. She stopped working for those months because she didn't want to face looks and questions from the customers, she said. Our parents were ashamed enough."

Shame. Ashamed of him.

"She had you down in Calgary with friends of our mom's. February nineteenth."

His birthday.

"She gave you up for a sort of open adoption, and came back here. And that might have been the end of it except that thirteen years later, into the restaurant walks this boy and his father."

Thirteen had not been his best year. His mother—his real mother, the one who had overcome her fear of water so she could join him in the deep end of the pool, the one who made his favorite meal of spaghetti and homemade meatballs whenever he squeaked a pass out of his science exams, the one who could take one look at him and know his heart— had died two months previously from a severe asthma attack. Jack hadn't even known that was possible.

"Your father," Deidre said to Jack, "had a huge favor to ask your mother. He wanted a kind of mother figure for you. Not a replacement, just someone out there that would care about you. Your father didn't have a lot of good options, if something should happen to him."

That, Jack believed. He'd met his father's lone sibling, a brother who drank vodka like water, and heard about cousins who lived in the States somewhere.

"Your father's biggest selling point was you, Jack. Penny saw you sitting there eating apple pie and root beer, and she couldn't refuse you or your father."

"Couldn't refuse you on September seventeenth, either," Bridget muttered.

Auntie Penny had lied to the niece she'd been the closest to. What if he and Bridget had gone through with marriage? Would she have continued to pretend that Jack was nothing more than her niece's husband?

"Your father revised his will to make Penny your guardian in the event of his death. Of course, that didn't happen, and he rewrote the will after you turned eighteen."

Jack pointed to the document in Deidre's hands. "You've got proof?"

"I've got the adoption papers, if that's what you mean. This is the original birth certificate."

"Didn't Jack need the birth certificate when

he got his passport?" Krista said. "It would've said right on there."

Jack shook his head. "No, because my parents got me my first passport." He read the certificate. No parents listed.

"So…did she mention who—who the father was?"

Deidre shook her head. "No, Jack. I'm sorry. She just said that he was someone she should never have become involved with. I got the feeling she never told him or he never owned up. At any rate, I doubt they kept in contact."

Which meant he'd never know.

No. Jack knew who his father was. He'd buried him three years ago. The man Penny had slept with had never mattered in his life.

And now Penny was gone. Dealing with tonight's revelation was going to take a long time to wrap his brain—and heart—around.

"That's what she was planning to tell us at Christmas," Bridget whispered.

"I only found out last month when she came to visit. She spilled out the whole story to me. Including how she paid to have Jack come back here with his girls."

Paid at the price of the community's trust in Bridget. There was no way that if word about the Crates fund leaked out, Bridget wouldn't face blowback.

"Jack!" Krista said. Her voice was all high and twittery. "You just got yourself a bunch of cousins."

"You three," Bridget said, indicating him and her sisters, "are related by blood. I'm not. Just to make that clear."

"We get that," Krista said. "Otherwise that whole dating thing in high school would've been beyond weird."

Was he to read anything in Bridget's quickness to place their relationship firmly outside family boundaries? Would she ever be interested in dating again? Still, Krista was right. He suddenly had cousins.

"Hardly fair," he said, trying not to smile. "You two have to share me."

Krista leaned forward to look past Bridget to Mara. "I get custody on Easter and the July Canada Day holiday and Labor Day."

"So I get him for Christmas and the August long?"

"August, yes, Christmases we alternate, and oh, I get him the May long weekend."

"And who gets me the rest of the year?" Krista shrugged. "Bridget."

"Didn't I just finish saying we're not related?"

"Yeah, but you guys share the house and the restaurant," Krista said. "You're more than cousins."

"Partners," Mara said from Bridget's other side.

"We're not—" Bridget began but Jack liked Mara's take.

"Partners is accurate," he threw out to test the waters with Bridget.

She threw him an annoyed look. "You're right. Unfortunately."

The waters were definitely frigid, but not frozen solid.

JACK QUIETLY STEPPED off the stairs into the living room. Bridget was a long roll under the quilt on the sofa bed. She was turned away, her black hair puddled across the pillow. Back when they were dating, her hair constantly caught on his buttons or tickled his nose, or he'd lean on it and she'd elbow him one.

Her hair caused no end of friction between them. Except when they were kissing, and then they both loved to have his hands in the dark, soft shininess.

"Bridget?" he whispered. With Deidre in

Bridget's room, Mara and the girls also upstairs, and Krista bunking downstairs, their talk had to be whispered.

"Yeah." She didn't sound surprised or sleepy.

"We need to discuss the house. The restaurant. The will. Everything."

She heaved the quilt up around her shoulders and kept her back to him. "Jack, I have work in six and a half hours. How about we do this tomorrow?"

"Tomorrow you'll be working and I'll be busy with the girls, and then tomorrow evening everyone is around, and then we're back to it being tomorrow night and you feeling beat."

"Nothing will change until after Christmas. We'll figure it out then."

"We don't have to do anything, but we should talk before then. Before Christmas craziness hits." The girls' first Christmas without either of their parents.

She sighed, pulled herself up from the quilt like a seal coming to land and flopped against the back of the sofa. "Talk."

He perched on the hard sofa arm. "Am I to assume from the state of the finances at the restaurant that you don't have the personal funds to clear off the money owing?"

Bridget scrubbed her face with her hands, the sleeves of her red pajamas falling to her elbows. He wished there was more light coming from the porch bulbs. She looked amazing in red.

"I had savings, but I used them to buy out half the restaurant two years ago. Auntie Penny used my money to keep the doors open, and there were lots of months where I didn't take wages. Auntie Penny's funeral expenses and the lawyers with the will have wiped out what little I had. It's really been touch and go the past while. Not just us, but the whole of Spirit Lake."

Penny had mentioned in emails how one business or another in the town of twelve thousand was closing shop, but Jack hadn't paid much attention. He'd figured that hard times in rich Alberta paled to the daily struggle to secure flour and soap in Venezuela. Now he was back in Canada, and while the struggle wasn't life-threatening, it was real. Very real. "How much are we looking at?"

He could hear her suck in her breath and she whispered the number.

No way could he cover that. "What about

Krista and Mara? They might have leads, they might loan you—"

"I'm not taking a cent from them." Her voice was hard, all sleepiness gone.

"Not exactly the time for pride right now," he challenged.

"It's not pride. Krista's looking for work, as it is. I know for a fact it would wipe Mara out to make these payments, and then where would she be? And her eyes are enough of a worry."

"Her eyes?"

"Retinitis pigmentosa. Inherited disorder. Her eyesight is already going downhill." Bridget tightened the quilt around her. "She might go blind."

Mara. Blind. His…cousin.

"What about Krista?"

"She doesn't carry the gene. And don't worry, neither do you. As soon as Mara was diagnosed, Auntie Penny got herself tested. We wondered back then why she was bothering, but she was probably thinking of you. Mother thing."

Mother thing. Penny. Bustling, generous. Beloved by all. Cheated quite a few. Lied to her family. And…dead. Gone before he could meet her as his own flesh and blood.

Bridget touched his leg, a skimming of her fingers. Their first physical contact in too long. "Tonight must've shaken your world. How are you doing?"

"Processing."

"Yeah, I get it. She has messed with who you think you are, who you think others are."

She was right. He shifted off the sofa arm to sit down by Bridget's knees on the sofa mattress. "When we were dating, I sometimes thought about how you were adopted. Turns out that we were, and Pen—she knew about it all along."

"She kept secrets from you, from me, from all of us. Left us all a huge mess. Left us all—" Bridget pressed her hand to her mouth and whispered, "Left us all."

Once, he could've pulled her into his arms and comforted her, and been comforted. He wanted that again, but it was enough tonight that they could have their first heart-to-heart talk since their breakup.

"There has to be a solution for the house, the restaurant," Bridget said, changing the topic.

"I'm hoping to get a job."

"Not much call for humanitarian-relief workers."

"Not much interest in being one."

"What are you going for?"

He had a degree in social work, so it made sense to chase down jobs in that field. But… "I'll take whatever will put food on the table for the girls."

"There's the fridge full of food at the restaurant. Freezer's full here," Bridget answered.

Charity, in other words. Not the kind of charity that had bilked him out of his entire savings. No, this was the true kind, where she was offering up what she had even when she had little and it wouldn't profit her.

But still, it rankled that he had to accept it. Even more because it came from Bridget, someone he'd hurt all those years ago. He couldn't stand being in her debt. And he was. For helping to take care of his daughters. For the ten grand taken from the Crates fund.

"I'll help at the restaurant," he said. "I already offered to, and it makes sense."

"Doing what?"

"I dunno, serving or helping Mano in the kitchen. I'm not asking you to pay me, but half the tables were empty this morning at any one time, and you were still run off your feet. Like I said, I'm the new Penny." A thought occurred to him. "In a way, I am half Penny. And half—" He swallowed. "I don't know who my biological dad is."

The quilt fell away from her as Bridget leaned forward, grazed her fingertips down his arm. "Hey. One step at a time."

The gentle pressure of her touch allowed him to breathe, to pull together a few shredded thoughts. "Right, then. Partners and all. To get through this rough patch."

"To get through Christmas," she said.

That was what the season had become. Something to grind their way through.

Bridget frowned. "If you're working, what about the girls?"

"I enrolled them in school today. Sofia goes to kindergarten Tuesdays and Thursdays and every other Friday, and Isabella will be there every day starting Monday. If they eat breakfast at the restaurant, I could take them directly there and pick them up. I'll make it work."

In the pale light filtering in from the porch, he could see her old habit of gnawing on her cheek. "If you want, and they want," Bridget said slowly, "I'm happy to help out with the girls. I—I like them," she said almost shyly.

It had been an incredible roller coaster of

a day, and it looked as if the chaotic ride would continue for the foreseeable future. But those three words from Bridget spoke— okay, whispered—of a future where they might be together for reasons other than duty.

He didn't push it. "Sure. Sounds good."

"WHAT IS SHE DOING?" Jack said as he joined Mano at the bar counter. They stared through the window at Bridget leaning a ladder against the roof, Christmas decorations on the sidewalk around her.

"You know what she's like, she won't climb it," Mano said confidently. Then he must've caught sight of the same grim set to Bridget's jaw that Jack saw. "Then again…"

"She'll get halfway, faint and fall off," Jack said and stripped off his apron. He walked straight outside into the minus double-digit Celsius temperatures, not risking the time to retrieve his jacket from the back.

As it was, her foot was already on the bottom rung, and she had lights in hand. He took hold of the ladder and said, "I can go up."

She gave her head a shake. It looked more like a shiver. "I'll do it."

"You're already scared. You'll fall off or get up there and then fall off. Or get too scared to move and we'll have to call the fire department to get you down."

"I need to deal," Bridget whispered, as if speaking too loud might bring the ladder crashing down. "I've been scared of heights since—since forever. We can't afford to hire someone else to do it."

"I said I would do it. And I will. I've only been on the job four days."

She shifted her eyes to stare at his arm. "You don't have a jacket. Or a toque. You'll freeze up there."

"I will go get my jacket and toque and gloves and scarf and boots and earmuffs and long underwear and whatever else you deem necessary, if you promise to stay off the ladder."

She gave a sharp nod and then stood there, still with a death grip on a rung. He covered her gloved fingers with his bare ones. "Bridget. Take my hand. Please."

She slowly let go and he slipped his fingers between hers, then lifted away her hand, turning her so that her foot dropped naturally from the ladder. Bridget instantly broke from her trance and wiggled her hand from his. "I'm fine. Go on."

"You got her to back off," Mano said when Jack cut through the front to the back closet.

"For now."

Mano grunted. "That's the best you can hope for."

Jack was hoping for more, a whole lot more. Starting with a reset on their breakup, something he'd never intended. All those years ago, a phone conversation had caused the cracks in their long-distance relationship to widen into craters that they'd fallen into. He longed to have a different kind of conversation with her, like the midnight one on her bed.

For now, he'd put up her Christmas lights.

And two hours later, what an operation that was turning out to be. He crouched at the edge of the roof. "I've helped stage world conferences that required less lighting."

She stood on the sidewalk with yet another box of lights for him to haul up. "Nobody made you go up there."

"Nobody's making me stay up here, either."

"True." She squinted at him. "But then you'd be backing out of a promise."

Again. Backing out again.

He gazed out over the snow-covered lake. All the miles he and Bridget had skated on its cleared-off surface. The winter before he'd left, the wind and cold had performed a once-in-a-thirty-year event. The entire lake frozen crystal clear. They'd skated then, under the light of the moon...

"Whatcha doing, coz?"

Krista and Mara were walking up the street, carrying insulated mugs. They'd both taken to the whole cousin thing, and the more they said it, the more he liked hearing it.

"Freezing vital parts so we can have a higher power bill next month."

"It'll be the best-looking business in town," Mara said. "You'll see when you're done."

Bridget gasped and set down her box. "I should show him a picture. Then he'll know how great it's supposed to look."

She gave Krista the job of climbing the few rungs up the ladder with the photo pulled up on her phone. It was beautiful, and very, very complicated. "It looks like the witch's candy house in 'Hansel and Gretel.'"

Bridget gave a squawk. "It's adorable, it's eye-catching, it's mouthwatering."

"It's a royal pain in the—"

"The girls will love it."

Jack sat back on his heels. They would. And he'd keep his promise to Bridget. "Fine.

And if either of you care to help your cousin, that would be appreciated."

"Sure, but we're here to view our—" Mara glanced at Bridget "—properties?"

Bridget pulled a key ring from her pocket. "As good a word as any."

Jack kept his mouth shut. The sale of those properties would have solved a lot of money problems, but Krista and Mara were family. He could relate to Bridget's dilemma. Check. He was related to the dilemma.

Bridget was gnawing on her cheek. She was worried for him. At least, that was what he decided to believe.

"Go," he said. "I'll be okay."

CHAPTER FIVE

BRIDGET FIRST TOOK Krista and Mara to the better of the two bays.

"It needs a new window," Bridget said of the boarded-up front.

"And a paint job," Mara observed. One wall was covered in a mural of a disproportioned metalhead musician.

"Why is he holding daisies?" Krista asked.

"There were a lot of questions about this place." Loud, wall-shaking music. Twitchy, frowning customers. Needles that may or may not have had to do with tattooing. And still Auntie Penny had given the tenants the benefit of the doubt. When Marlene had complained that the stink of pot was in Penny's signature pancakes, she finally evicted them.

"It took the police to finally get the previous tenants out. Auntie Penny put new locks on the place, and that was two years ago. We were too scared to rent it out and then too broke to fix the place up."

"Last time I was out here was summer a year ago," Krista said. "I don't remember it being boarded up."

"Windows were broken this summer," Bridget said. "Vandalism."

Krista tapped her pointed boot on a broken tile. "Needs new flooring, too."

"You could probably lay carpet right over this," Bridget said. "Commercial or Berber wouldn't be much." Was she talking them into staying? She either loved her sisters or had not an ounce of self-preservation.

"I'd go with planking," Krista said. "It'd suit my purposes better."

"What? Why? What did you have in mind?"

"I don't want to say anything yet, because I haven't got it all figured out, and I don't want you guys shooting it down."

"We won't shoot it down," Mara said and gave Bridget a firm look.

"I promise I won't," Bridget said. Even if she should.

"I was thinking of a spa."

Bridget felt her eyebrows rise and she forced them back into position. "Okay."

"Something small, of course. It would just be me. But I did take aesthetician courses, you know. And I worked in other studios. And I've been on enough modeling sets to know the gig. I can even cut hair. How's the wiring?"

"Good," Bridget said. "This unit has electricity. Wait. Don't distract me. I thought you said you had a life in Toronto. What gives?"

Krista rubbed the toe of her boot against the loose tile. "Oh, well..."

Mara crossed her arms. "Philip."

Krista opened her phone and scrolled, then showed her sisters an Instagram post. It was of a heap of clothes outside a dumpster. Bridget read the caption. "'What happens when the ex doesn't believe me.'"

Bridget felt a hot rush of outrage. "He threw out your clothes?"

"Yep. I told him that I was thinking about moving here and... I guess I wanted to see what his thoughts were. He said I had twenty-four hours to get my crap out of his place. That was Sunday. I told him to give me a few days to make arrangements, and then this morning, he posts this."

"What. A. Jerk."

"You didn't tell me," Mara said. She sounded surprised, and Bridget didn't blame her. Telling anything to one of them was like telling them both.

Krista scrolled and then held up her phone. "Here. You can be the first to see this." Mara grimaced at what she saw, and Krista switched to exhibit her phone to Bridget.

It was of Philip kissing a girl in sequins as she artfully held a wineglass. Bridget read aloud the caption underneath. "'Catching some under the mistletoe.'"

"What a self-obsessed, narcissistic, arrogant poser," Mara said with uncharacteristic viciousness.

Krista's eyes brightened with tears. "I wish I'd figured that out ten minutes after I met him, instead of ten months." She swiped at her eyes. "Anyway, now I'm looking at other options."

"Are you sure—" Bridget began.

"Washrooms are back here, aren't they?" Krista interrupted and went deeper.

"About those—" Bridget hurried after her, and nearly slammed into Krista on a fast retreat.

"Yeah, you'll need a plumber or an exterminator. Probably both."

At the front of the building, Krista breathed again. "I can't do this. Even with minimal fix-ups plus having to buy the equipment, I can't swing it."

"Perhaps I could cover costs," Mara said.

"No," Bridget and Krista said together instantly.

"You two haven't even seen the unit upstairs," Bridget said. "Take a look before making any decision."

They clambered up the back stairs that wouldn't have passed inspection, and crossed the entrance where a door should've been. She could hear Jack on the roof. Good—noise meant he hadn't fallen. Worse than being scared of heights was being scared for people she cared ab— For other people on the roof. "This has all the windows. And, as you can see, is quite spacious." Good grief, she sounded like a Realtor. Selling swampland to her sisters.

"There's no floor," Krista said the obvious. "Like none."

It had been stripped down past the underlay. "The pipes burst last winter and the place flooded." Water seeping through the ceiling had been the first sign that the tenant had done a scamper. There was a huge water stain on the ceiling of the kitchen now, but at least it'd been caught before spreading to the dining area. Small mercies.

"Carpet, pipes, paint, door," Mara listed off. "Anything else?"

"Well, the reason the pipes burst is because of the windows," Bridget said. "See?"

Bridget showed them the full quarter-inch crack where the seal had dropped away from the window frame.

"Wow," said Krista. "It's a wonder the windows haven't fallen out."

"Are you heating these places?" Mara said.

"Yeah, I run it through a separate vent."

"That must jack up your heating bill bigtime," Mara said. "Does Jack know about this?"

"Know about what?" Jack entered through the doorless frame. His voice was mild but Bridget heard the edge.

"Mara wanted to know if you'd seen the place," Bridget said quickly.

"I haven't." He gave it a once-over. "It's unfit for occupancy."

"At least you can breathe in this one," Krista said.

"So I take it neither of you are going to take Penny up on her offer?" His tone was casual.

"They don't need to decide right now," Bridget said. "There's a lot to think about."

"Most of which involves money no one has," Krista said, disappointment clear in her voice.

"Look," Bridget said, "if money wasn't an issue, if say, tomorrow you won the lottery, would you go ahead and do it?"

"Duh," Krista said.

Mara expressed the same sentiment with more kindness.

"But," Jack said, "that's not going to happen."

Bridget set her hands on her hips. "Did you come here just to tell us what we'd already figured out ourselves?"

"I came to say that I have to pick up the girls from school."

"Where are you with the lights?"

"An hour or two more, but by the time I get through at the school and get them settled at the house, it'll be too dark to be up on the roof."

Snow was forecast for tomorrow, and who knows when he could do them after that. "How about I go get them?"

"I don't know," Jack said. "I told them I'd be there. And it's only Sofia's second day."

"How about I pick them up and bring them straight back here for them to check in with you? Serve them up cinnamon buns."

"Meanwhile," Krista said, "I'll help Jack with the lights."

"No. You'll fall and break your neck," Bridget said.

"There's still the window trim to do," Mara said, sliding between them, somehow managing to shoot both of them quelling looks.

Jack sighed with a faint smile. "Is this what it'll be like under the management of cousins?"

"Welcome to an organized, considerate and meaningful existence," Bridget said. "Back soon."

She made it two steps before he said, "Park along the side street, the one where Mano lives. And Sofia's through the west entrance. Her class gets out ten minutes before the other grades. Wait there for Isabella."

"Yeah, okay." She took another step.

"Isabella has an agenda and a home reading book. Ask her if she has them. She'll know what you mean."

"Yeah, yeah."

"Oh, and check to see Sofia has both mittens. She only has the one pair and it's supposed to snow tomorrow."

"I know." She managed three steps.

"And make sure Isabella sits in the booster seat. She's still seven pounds short of the required weight."

"Can I go now, Mrs. Dad?"

"Huh. I'll see you three in a bit."

You three. A common phrase, like he said it all the time. It was just a little scary how the man she'd seen only seven times in the past dozen years was fitting so easily back into her life.

BRIDGET JOINED THE parents hanging outside the kindergarten door like relatives at an airport gate. The door to the classroom was closed, though she could make out the teacher giving last call for folders, backpacks and "whose mitten is this?"

Jack was right to worry about missing mittens.

Bridget looked around. Moms her age chatting quietly or corralling toddlers. A couple of dads, one holding a baby under his arm like a football. She didn't know any of them. Kidless, she was out of touch with a whole sector of the Spirit Lake population. If she and Jack had married, she might have been one of them.

One mom holding a baby and a toddler wrapped around her leg smiled. "You're the new girl's mom. My name's Jolene. I saw her this morning when I dropped off Grace. Sofia, right?" She laughed and her baby giggled, too. "Grace loves to meet new people."

Bridget picked through the blast of facts. "Uh, I'm not the mom."

"Oh, you're not? I'm sorry. You two look alike."

True. Same brown-black hair. Same brown eyes and brown skin.

Bridget shook her head. "No, I'm—" Not Jack's friend. Not Sofia's stepmom. She caught the flash of the big diamond wedding ring on Jolene's finger. Definitely not that.

"I'm Sofia's dad's business partner." That was a mouthful. "Jack and I co-own Penny's, the restaurant. He's there now."

"I love that place. I mean, I've heard so much about it. I'd go there in a heartbeat but… this little guy—" they rubbed noses "—is an absolute terror in public."

A customer too scared to come in case her child got out of hand? If she was worried about that, it meant others were, too. "We love kids. They eat for free on the weekends."

They didn't. Jack was going to kill her.

"From seven to eight. In the morning. From now until Christmas." There. "To go with our Christmas menu." Dead again, this time by Mano.

"That's sounds great. We'll be by."

And since she was well and truly dead, Bridget added for everyone to hear, "This weekend, ten percent off to all families with kids five and under."

The kindergarten door opened. Parents and kids were reunited and Bridget watched the easy pairing of kid to parent. The joy on the young faces, the affection on the parents', the chatter about wet socks and snacks and what they would do now. When Sofia appeared, she looked around for Jack, not noticing Bridget. Her eyes widened in panic.

Bridget crouched. "Hey, Sofia. Here I am. Jack couldn't come today, so he asked me to pick you up. You and Isabella."

Sofia, in her oversize pack and sock feet, stood there. Then she stepped back, closer to the teacher. The teacher rested her hand on Sofia's shoulder. And squared her shoulders. "Hello. I'm Ella Simmons. And you are?"

"Bridget. Bridget Montgomery. I work with Jack. At Penny's. He's tied up, so I offered to get Sofia. And her sister."

"Does their dad have you down as an alternate?"

"A what?"

"He would have had to sign a form, giving you permission to pick up the kids."

Of course. It had never occurred to her, not having picked up kids before. Probably Jack had forgotten, too, given this was his first week dealing with the Canadian school system.

Sofia kept staring. Bridget knew Sofia knew her. Sofia had started to smile at her lots, even asked for milk this morning. In English. Last night Bridget had told them a bedtime story.

The buzzer sounded for the dismissal of the other grades. Isabella would soon be here and clear up matters.

"I'll call Jack, and he can talk to Sofia. Tell her it's okay."

The teacher nodded, tight-lipped. "Sure. You do that." She kept her hand on Sofia's shoulder. "But we'll need to sort this out at the office."

The call went to Jack's voice mail and

Bridget left a message, just as Isabella wandered up, carrying her jacket and boots. She looked beat—her eyebrows were upward slashes, and her mouth was drawn down. Uh-oh. Everyone in the Montgomery household had discovered that Isabella got hangry if kept from her postschool snack. Bridget fought the urge to hustle them away. "Hi, Isabella. I'm here for you and Sofia. Take you to the restaurant, where Jack is. Get a cinnamon bun into you."

Isabella looked at her with glazed eyes. How much had she understood? "Isabella, are you—"

The teacher took Isabella and Sofia down the hallway and into the office of the principal, Ms. Melanie Lever, leaving Bridget to look at them through the office window. Isabella slumped onto the office couch. Not good.

Bridget rapped on the door and then let herself in. "Look, I know we need to sort this misunderstanding out, but could we give Isabella a snack, please?"

She didn't wait for an answer and reached for Sofia's backpack. "Sofia, do you have any snacks left over? Anything to share with your sister?" Nothing but wrappers and a dirty thermos and soup spoon.

"I've noticed she likes her food," Melanie Lever said. Whatever that meant. "We keep snacks on hand. Just a moment." She stepped out and Bridget took the opportunity to dial Jack's number again. Voice mail. She called Krista. Maybe she was still there and could shout to Jack. No answer. Of course. Both of them up on the roof putting up her freaking decorations. She called Mara.

"Yes?"

"Mara! Are you still at Penny's?"

"No. I'm walking back to the house."

"Listen, can you go back there and get Jack to call me? I'm at the school but I can't take the kids because my name isn't on the form. He needs to come here after all."

Melanie Lever returned with two small plastic sandwich bags of cereal. "Two kinds. Which would you like, Isabella?"

Isabella shook her head. Why were both kids pulling away from people trying to help them?

The principal laid the bags on the couch within Isabella's reach. "I'll leave them here in case you change your mind. So." She turned to Bridget. "I understand you work for their father?"

Before Bridget could answer, Isabella stood and grabbed Sofia's wrist and dragged her from the office. "Where are you going?" Bridget called, following them out, the principal right behind.

Isabella didn't answer, but continued out of the reception area and to the front doors, Sofia being towed along. At least they had their boots and jackets.

Bridget caught up to Isabella outside at the street crossing. The crossing guards from the older grades raised their stop signs to signal traffic. Isabella did a quick left-right check and stepped onto the crosswalk without the go-ahead form the guards.

"Wait!" Bridget called.

Kids began to spill across and the student guards waved their signs to bring order back to the situation. Bridget caught up to the girls and trotted behind them. "Okay, you're away from the school, Isabella, but where are you going? I can take you there."

Sofia looked over her shoulder at Bridget, her lower lip wobbling.

Bridget began to talk to keep a connection going. *Jack, where are you?* "I don't blame you for running away from school. You stayed longer than I usually did. I'd go to Auntie Penny's for lunch and half the time never went back." Bridget didn't know how much Isabella was getting of this, but she thought her steps slowed, enough so that Sofia wasn't running to keep up anymore.

"I know what it's like to be lonely, Isabella. I was lonely today, too. I didn't know anybody at the school except for you and Sofia, and I've lived in this town for a lot of my life. And I run a restaurant. You'd think I'd know everybody. I don't blame you for feeling weirded-out."

Isabella stopped. "I am hungry. I want Jack."

That she could help with. Bridget pointed to the large pinkish building straight ahead. "See that place? We need to go about five more blocks from there.

"Or—" she pointed in the opposite direction "—we go back to school. We get in my car, and then drive." She mimicked driving. "To Jack."

Sofia squealed suddenly and charged down the street. What now? Jack. Running to them.

He'd made them the happiest three people in all of Spirit Lake.

THIS, JACK THOUGHT, was why he'd brought the girls to Spirit Lake. Not for the death of a woman he was supposed to think of as his mother, not for the contents of her will, but for this moment. The four of them—the girls, Bridget, him—gathered at a booth in the restaurant, eating cinnamon buns. The late-afternoon light on the lake outside. Them together inside, pulling apart their treats and licking sticky fingers. And every now and then, his foot or his leg happening to bump against Bridget's.

He smoothed his hand over Sofia's static-shocked hair and asked in Spanish, "Did Bridget put enough icing on the bun?"

It was Isabella sitting across from Sofia who answered. "Yes. Every one is perfect. Better than the last."

Jack was about to translate the compliment to Bridget when he came up with a better idea. "Isabella, you tell her. I'll give you the words."

It wouldn't be the first time today he'd asked Isabella to speak directly to Bridget. Before meeting the three of them outside the school, he'd already been filled in by Mara and then the principal. His run over—he was getting a vehicle as soon as he could rub two nickels together—had ended with Sofia slamming into him. He could still feel the jolt of her body as she crashed into his arm, the tightness of her arms around his neck. His first real hug from her.

"Look," she had said in Spanish, and bared her teeth at him. What she had of them.

"You lost your tooth," he said.

"On a carrot. I wanted to show you first, but Bridgie came, and I couldn't talk to her or get up close because then she would see, and then the teacher thought…" Around the lisping of her gap, Sofia spilled her version of events, so by the time he reached Bridget and Isabella, he'd pretty much known where things stood.

He'd filled in Bridget on Sofia's dental status, and Bridget dutifully inspected the gap and the tooth preserved in a plastic bag.

Meanwhile, he'd kneeled before Isabella. "I'm sorry. But I let Bridget come because I trust her completely. If you're with her, it's like you're with me."

He'd said it to reassure Isabella, but he knew it for the truth. He'd always trusted her and still did. He was the one who'd disappointed everyone. "I'd like you to apologize to her. In English, so she understands."

And when she'd muttered her apology to Bridget's stomach, Bridget had melted and wrapped her arm around Isabella's shoulders. "I accept. Now let's go see the surprise your fa— Jack has made for you two. Tell them," she said to Jack, "that you've made them a gingerbread house."

She'd turned it all around and made him into a hero when nothing could be further from the truth. They'd driven back to the restaurant with Bridget teaching the girls to sing "All I Want for Christmas Is My Two Front Teeth" with him providing translation.

The least he could do now was make sure Bridget received a compliment straight from the source.

Bridget immediately rewarded Isabella's accented English with a huge smile that he knew would make Isabella feel as if she'd scored the winning goal. It was how he always felt.

She turned to him and her smile retracted like an elastic. "I said a few things at school. Don't worry, nothing to do with the kids. About the restaurant." She explained that somehow in the quarter hour there she'd promised a discount to every new customer.

"You told me the other day that the best

Penny's has ever done was a nine percent profit margin. What's the point of keeping the doors open?"

"Don't be so dramatic."

"Why didn't you tell me? I thought we were partners." He could hear his sarcasm.

"How was I supposed to tell you beforehand? It just came out."

"So your first thought when someone said that they haven't come to the restaurant is to pay them to come?"

"It's not paying, it's promoting."

"We're here to make money, not friends."

Sofia touched his arm. She and Isabella were staring at him, their brown eyes wide. So much for a happy memory. He'd blown it by attacking Bridget for at least doing something to get customers in the door.

Mano suddenly stepped out from the back where he'd been testing a new omelette. "Is there something about this business I should know?"

"No," Bridget said. She shot a warning look at Jack. He understood. If Mano knew how bad things were, he'd pack up his wife and five kids, and bang pots at the next fine casual eatery. Without a chef, Penny's would have to close its doors.

Mano waved his meaty paw. "Which means 'yes.' How bad is it? Tell me straight up."

Bridget looked as if Mano was asking her to give up the secret recipe of her cinnamon buns. Jack would say it for her. "We need to make the payment this month or the bank will move on us."

"I didn't want you to know how bad it is," Bridget said, head down.

Mano pointed at her. "You think I didn't know? You think I don't count the meals served? You think I'm some kid you have to hide bad news from?" He turned his finger on Jack. "It is good you told me."

He swiped off his hat, pulled the string on his apron. Bridget gasped. "No, Mano, look. I'll make sure you get paid. Please don't leave."

Mano stopped in the middle of removing his apron. "You think after all these years I will walk off not a month after your aunt leaves this world? No, I am taking off my apron to sit with you two and we will think. We will think about how to make money for our families."

He settled his girth beside Bridget, which meant Isabella was pressed to the wall. She slipped underneath the table and emerged on the other side beside Sofia, then pulled her cinnamon bun across the table and resumed eating.

"How much does it cost to make one of these buns?" Jack asked Bridget.

"Nothing, really. The ingredients are simple, the power to bake is nothing. They are honestly the highest margin item on the menu. Problem is I don't sell enough to keep a candle lit." She paused. "I was thinking we'd go ahead with our traditional Christmas breakfast menu all December instead of just the week before. I put red and green sprinkles on my cinnamon buns. And crushed gingersnap chunks. I also have small ones. Minicinnis. Set them out in a display case. We make Santa pancakes for the kids, specialty coffees, things like that. And prices are a little more. It is always our best week."

"The best week," Mano said, "because it was only one week. Every day, and people will get sick of it."

But Jack saw where Bridget was going with this. "We might as well capitalize on the Christmas lights outside, make them a draw for at least the first hour in the morning when it's still dark. People still have the option of the regular menu. It's more how the plate is dressed, right?"

Bridget nodded, then chewed on her cheek. "It won't be enough, is the thing."

Jack had been tumbling an idea around all this week. "How about we run a dinner service? Not every day. Just Friday and Saturday, say. For Christmas."

"I thought about it," Bridget said. "We did it last year as a windup to our Christmas week. We were full for two entire sittings. But this year we don't have the staff. And I can't afford to pay."

Mano slapped his hands on the table. "Didn't I just say I'd help my family? You help us by letting us help you. My wife can cook. Better than me, but she doesn't like to show me up. And the two oldest? Seventeen and sixteen. One can do expo—" he turned to Jack "—dress the plate, garnish, do a few sides. The other, she can, I don't know, do as she's told."

Bridget's face lit up, then dimmed. "But will we make money?"

Today was Thursday. "Could we run with a modified menu this Saturday?" Jack proposed.

"Yes. Definitely." Mano stood and reached for his apron. "I'll call the wife."

Isabella had finished her cinnamon bun and was eyeing Jack's. "Don't even think of it," he warned her in Spanish. "It will spoil your supper." He didn't think it would, but she needed to know that meals came regularly. "How about you and Sofia come by every Tuesday and Thursday, and we'll all have cinnamon buns together?" Time with the girls from here on in would be calculated in hours and minutes. He needed to arrange for as many as he could.

Isabella looked across the table at Bridget. "Will she be here, too?"

"Is it all right if she is?"

Isabella nodded. "She's your partner."

Bridget was miming to Sofia how to eat the bun with her back molars to avoid the tender front area. It involved extravagant, slow-motion chewing that had Sofia in wide-mouthed, gap-toothed giggles.

Partners, yes. And this Saturday he'd prove that he was a worthy one.

CHAPTER SIX

"WOULD YOU LIKE to do the honors?"

Lemons in hand, Jack looked over the counter at Bridget. She tilted her head to the front door. "Is it that time already?" he asked.

She held up her phone. "One minute to four."

"How did that happen?" For the past two days, Jack had ridden a learning curve so sharp his brain had contracted altitude sickness. Either that, or the combo of sleep deprivation and skipped meals accounted for the pounding in his head.

"Be glad it has," Bridget said. She flashed her glossy-lipped smile, part of the package with her sleeveless cocktail dress and the updo Krista had given her. Even if tonight was a complete bomb, at least the sight of Bridget would stand out in his memory.

He raised the lemons. "My hands are full. You open." He watched her clip away on short heels, tiny gold bells jingling around her ankle. Krista's idea. His cousin had lots of good ideas when it came to Bridget.

He popped the lemons into the fridge and went to do…what? There was nothing left to take care of. The interior had been re-staged for the dinner service with a candle centerpiece, the lights dimmed, Christmas instrumental music flipped on and the dinner menus stacked under the register. And in the kitchen, the fridge was stocked, the sides prepped, the grill hot. He'd even switched into a white dress shirt and black slacks to play the part.

All that was missing were the customers. Bridget puttered about, scrolled through her phone and looked as if an empty house was perfectly fine. But after she'd rearranged the same table for the third time, Jack's nerves jangled like Bridget's bells.

In his decade working in relief agencies worldwide, he'd pulled together high-profile meetings as naturally as snow fell. This was different. People he loved depended on him to provide for their basic needs. Isabella. Sofia.

Bridget.

Outside there was a slap and thud. The sandwich board with the evening specials had tipped over. "I'll get that."

Outside he nearly collided with a group of four women bubbling with giggles and chatter. Dressed for a night out. Time for him to get to work.

"Ladies." He righted the board. "It must be a sign, don't you think?" He let them groan at his pun, let them soften up. He held open the restaurant door and gestured inside. "Our fine establishment awaits you."

"Are you open?"

Jack turned to the speaker, a pretty woman in glasses. "Yes, we are open for dinner every Friday and Saturday during the season. You are in luck."

She moved to follow up on her luck, but another held back. "I'm paleo. Do you cater to that?"

Was that a disease? "Our kitchen will customize your meal, not to worry."

The other two were reading the steak special on the board. "I suppose I could go for that," said one.

And with three down, the last trailed after the others inside.

"Nice work," Bridget said, after seating them.

He wiped his hands, ready to become their

server. "If you can get it. Which apparently I can."

She waggled her phone. "Hockey tournament. Kelsie finished putting flyers in the parking lot windshields an hour ago."

"They'll go to the sports lounge."

"It's not giving away apple cider and mini-cinnis."

He sighed. "I take it we are."

"One of each only. And a chance to buy them by the half dozen from the display case."

"That might work. I'm going to pitch it to the ladies."

"The one in glasses? She's Tanya, our bank manager. Give her an extra one. Or whatever you're willing to offer up."

Was there a tinge of competitiveness in Bridget's voice? She had no reason to be, but it meant she had feelings for him she couldn't hide. He hoped the sandwich board fell at the feet of every passing female tonight.

AT A QUARTER to midnight, Jack sat at the bar, the first his feet had been off the floor since they'd hit it at five that morning. "Please tell me we made so much money we can retire to a Maui beach."

Bridget didn't break in her counting of

cash. She wrapped bills in an elastic, wrote a number on the top one. She started in on a pile of loonies and toonies. "Forget the one and two dollars," Jack said. "Give me a ballpark figure before I die here."

Bridget reverted to counting aloud. There was no stopping her. There'd been no stopping all night. At one point, the restaurant had a wait time of ten minutes to be seated. Mano and his family had worked with the speed and precision of marines on a sinking ship. Hopefully, one that could be bailed out.

Bridget tapped on her phone and then looked up and smiled. The gloss had gone from her lips, but this smile was the biggest he'd seen yet. "We'll make payments this month. I'll take it in Monday. Two weeks after the first-of-month due date but it's done."

Jack spoke to the ceiling. "Thank you, hockey families everywhere. Anything extra?"

She named an amount. He gave a low whistle. "That's good, real good. We can put it toward back payments. Or aside for next month's. Whichever."

"Or—" She tilted her head.

"What? What else is there?"

Instead of answering, she crossed to the

front door. No. Was she actually— She lifted out the Christmas Crates box from its stand and brought it in.

"You still plan to do the campaign? There's no money."

Bridget set the crate on the bar counter and lifted the lid. She peered inside, grimaced. "Just as I feared. There are more than ever."

"All the more reason to cancel it. At least for this year."

"All the more reason I need to do it. In memory of my aunt. In memory of your mother."

Mother. A week had passed since he'd learned that Penny was his mother and he was no closer to dealing with it, other than to bury it under the crush of other worries. "Emotional blackmail doesn't work on me."

"I'm not asking for your help. I can do it myself."

"Do you have anyone to help you?"

"Tanya had volunteered to take over from Auntie Penny. Now she can't. Her mother has cancer and she needs to be there for her."

"We need you to be here for us." He could use emotional blackmail, too.

Bridget's shoulders sagged. He was getting through to her.

"The girls shouldn't have to fear for a roof over their heads or food in their bellies. You, more than any of us, know what that's like." She'd never spoken much about the reasons she was taken into foster care, but she once said that she taught herself how to cook an egg when she was three.

"I do, Jack, but…"

"But what?"

She turned pleading eyes to him. "Not doing it endangers Christmas for dozens of families. Life hasn't been easy these past few years around here."

Poverty in Canada looked a whole lot different than poverty in Venezuela. The poor here weren't dining on rats. Thousands of abandoned children weren't walking to other countries. He was thankful to be back in a community where there were people like Bridget who treated individual family struggles like a humanitarian crisis.

She rested her arm on the crate. "This event is more than a charity. It brings people together. Businesses up and down this street, and over in the downtown, and even big places like Walmart and Canadian Tire chip in by way of products or services or even cash so we can package everything up. Volunteers prepare them and then on December twenty-third, Auntie Penny, myself and other volunteers who aren't busy with family deliver them. People talk to each other, people who don't see each other any other time of the year. Yes, it benefits those in need, but it also benefits those who want to give."

"You make it sound too good to be true."

He couldn't keep the bitterness from his voice. He braced for her to bite back, to tell him what a selfish jerk he was and how he'd no business running her life. Instead she sat on a bar stool, pillowed her cheek on her hand and contemplated him. All the lights off except the overhead one above them, dimmed to what a bedside lamp might give off.

"Jack. What happened?"

He hadn't told anyone the real story—not Penny, not the stream of officials, not the blank lines on the forms. But this was Bridge. And if he wanted back in her life, then he was going to have to let her into his.

"I had a desk at an orphanage in Caracas. I wasn't working at the place but the agency assigned me there because that's where there was an internet connection, and my job was to coordinate emergency supplies from around the world and bring them into Venezuela."

He grabbed a towel and wiped at a stain on the counter. It had soaked right in and wouldn't come out, but he kept forgetting. He tossed the towel back down. "The biggest problem among good agencies is finding a sure and safe way to get things to where they need to be. Past the corruption and to the people who need it. I learned about a charity that coordinated the money and supplies. I did due diligence on them, and they seemed aboveboard. I ran a couple of operations with them. They were small, only four employees, but they had a long reach. That should've been my first clue. Anyway, they came to me with this idea of expanding their scope, and I thought I could make a real difference. Make a mark, leave a legacy, whatever. So I put the proceeds from the sale of Dad's house into the organization."

It burned how much of an egotistical fool he'd been. "Turns out I was the mark for their long con."

Bridget didn't say anything, just curled herself closer to him.

"I found out when I logged into my bank account. All of it was gone."

She gasped. "They hacked into your account?"

He gave short nod. "Probably happened when I transferred the first amount over. They hacked into my other accounts, as well. Took my savings. Luckily, the account for my wages was at a different bank."

"Can't you go after them?"

"I called my contact and he told me the name of his criminal boss. It was basically a courtesy, a sign of goodwill, that they wouldn't kill me—if I shut up and left the country. The sooner, the better."

Bridget's face twisted into deep sympathy and shock. The way she was prepared to take care of Spirit Lake's needy, she would naturally feel for him.

"But my story has a happy ending. While I was at the orphanage, I got to know two little girls."

"Sofia and Isabella," Bridget said softly.

"Yeah." He still remembered the first time he'd met them. They'd been found on the streets, starving and in rags. Isabella refused to let Sofia out of her sight, and Sofia screamed if they tried to separate them even a little ways.

"I wasn't at the orphanage a whole lot. Just to use the computer. I came in one day, opened a drawer and there was a bunch of food. Beans, dried noodles, a packet of peanut butter. I looked up and there they were. All eyes and silent, like scared animals, arms wrapped around each other. Isabella had crackers in her hand."

Bridget smiled. "Ah, Isabella. Clever of her to hide it in your desk, where no one goes."

"She probably knew I had no idea what to do with dried beans."

Bridget laughed. Yes. Just for a bit he'd made her happy. "I told Isabella to come and add to her stash. But she just stayed there. I pushed away on my chair and asked her again. She and Sofia crept over. She dropped it into the drawer, closed it up and left. Not a single word. My work with the bogus charity brought me into the orphanage more often, so I was there when Isabella and Sofia would come in.

"Over time, I could sit at my desk, and Isabella would drop in the food. I found crayons and paper for them, and they'd sit and talk with me. Well, mostly Sofia. I started to look forward to their visits. I'd drop a chocolate bar into their stash now and then.

"When things went south, I told them I had to leave. Sofia broke into tears and begged me to take them. Isabella, she asked if I could leave them a chocolate bar. That's when I decided to bring them with me."

"And that's when Auntie Penny drained the Christmas Crates fund to help you."

"Yep."

Bridget pushed off the stool. "That's a great story, Jack. It proves that you always do the right thing."

Her airiness made Jack feel a flicker of unease. "Oh?"

"Yes. Since you borrowed the money from the fund, it's only right you pay it back."

"But I can't—"

"And since you can't, isn't it fair that you earn it back through honest labor?"

"I would, but the girls and this restaurant are taking up all my focus. I barely have time to sleep. You barely have time."

She yawned. "Sleep is for Boxing Day. So you in?"

Another opportunity to partner up with her. Guess he would cave to emotional blackmail. "I'm in."

"THIRTY-NINE, FORTY, FORTY-ONE—" Bridget stacked each counted crate against a garage wall, an upright square pattern emerging from the heap of crates on the cement floor.

She should've been out here a month ago to sort through the mess but…well, a whole lot of life had happened.

She needed a minimum of fifty-two based on the names in the crate, but experience had taught her to add another two. Make it an even fifty-five. She'd have to repair a few, and get replacements. That was nothing new; every year some weren't returned. Maybe she'd send Jack out after they'd finished putting the girls to bed. Sofia had talked her into telling stories, inspired by her singing of "All I Want for Christmas Is My Two Front Teeth." She made up stories and Jack translated.

But for now, where was the hammer—

The garage side door opened to Deidre, wearing the red plaid couch throw over her light Arizona clothing. "There you are!"

Bridget could've said the same. In the short two weeks since arriving, Deidre wandered in and out of the house at all hours, only appearing regularly for supper. She was as nomadic as when Bridget and her sisters had been kids. Bridget fully expected to come home to find Deidre had gone back to Arizona, and was a little surprised that it hadn't happened already.

Deidre tightened the throw around her

shoulders. A jacket would have been far more suitable, but that was Deidre all over. She toed a broken crate. "What's all this, then?"

"Christmas Crates. Auntie Penny and I did it every year for the past decade. We package crates for the families who are struggling."

"Oh, right. Penny talked about that when she— When she visited."

An awkward silence fell between them. "She was in charge of repairing the crates," Bridget said quickly. "Looks as if I'll be handling it this year. Unless Jack steps up."

"He's helping you?"

"I guilt-tripped him into it. As payback for Auntie Penny giving him the Christmas Crates money."

"Oh, I don't know." Deidre picked up a hammer on the bench. There it was! "Jack doesn't strike me as one to feel guilty about much."

Bridget picked up a crate with only one missing slat. Another was less a crate than a few slats hanging together. She could cannibalize it to fix the first. She held out her hand for the hammer. "I'll take that."

Deidre handed it over. "I don't know how much he'll help between the restaurant and the girls. You don't have much more time.

You hardly have time to visit with your sisters, much less me."

Bridget yanked a nail loose. "You're hardly one to lecture me about being a good family member."

Deidre's eyes widened. They were the same blue as Jack's. "Mistakes," she said softly, "make phenomenal teachers."

This was new. "You admit you made them."

"Of course, I made mistakes. I should've— I should've asked you to call me 'Mom' instead of Deidre when we took you in. Or given you the choice." Deidre flapped the corners of the plaid throw like a giant, agitated bird.

"Just to set the record straight, I would never have called you 'Mom.' I already called one woman that. I wouldn't ever disrespect you by calling you by her name." She didn't need to say anything more. Deidre would have read the background file at the time of adoption.

"Thank you for saying that. I've always… wondered." She gave herself a shake. "Still. I should've been here more. I just…didn't see the point. Penny was always a better mother than I was. And you preferred her, anyway."

"I preferred her because I could count on

her being around." Bridget pried out another nail. This would take her all night at this rate. Frustrated, she tossed down the hammer. "Why did you even adopt me if you didn't want me around?"

Deidre gave Bridget a long look. "Truth?"

Bridget bit down on her cheek. "Truth."

"Your father and I became foster parents when Krista and Mara were young. And you were our first. You instantly loved Krista and Mara, and they loved you. When you three were together, I couldn't break into your tight circle. And that was when you were just tiny kids. You didn't seem to even want my love. From what you've just said, I expect you didn't trust mothers."

Bridget picked up a nail, rolled it between her fingers. "I think… I think you're right."

"Isabella with those big eyes and quiet walk reminds me of you, back then," Deidre said. "At any rate, Tom more or less told me to deal with it, because long after we were dead and gone, you three would still have each other." Deidre flapped her throw again. "And he was right. Just because I couldn't connect with you didn't mean you didn't deserve a place in the Montgomery family."

Oh. "And here I always felt like the odd one out," Bridget said softly.

Deidre pulled the plaid tight around her shoulders. "You were in one respect. You were the only one who didn't like traveling. Happy-go-lucky until the wheels started turning."

There was that. Bridget had dreaded vacations when Tom and Deidre would haul their kids off somewhere. In the end, it was easier on everybody if she stayed with Auntie Penny. "I just—couldn't."

"And you still can't," Deidre said softly.

She was right, but what did it matter? Up to her eyeballs in debt, and no place to go. Bridget got busy with the hammer again. "Move, you flipping nail!"

Deidre held out her hand. "Here. Let me have a go at it."

It was on the tip of Bridget's tongue to refuse, but hey, there were plenty more crates to fix. Throw slouched over her arms, Deidre grabbed a screwdriver and applied it to the crate. "So what's between you and Jack? I know you dated in high school, but you two together sucks the air from the room."

"Suck the air...? Hardly." Bridget shook a crate free from the jumble on the garage floor. If her mother could confess a painful truth, then so could she. "We were engaged."

Deidre stared. "You never told me. Nobody told me."

She looked so stricken Bridget quickly added, "No one knew except Auntie Penny. She was the first we told and she persuaded Jack and me to keep it absolutely secret until he returned from his overseas mission. He didn't, and that was that. Auntie Penny was right about keeping it quiet. Saved me a lot of embarrassment."

"Let me get this straight. Jack broke it off with you?"

"Yes. He called me from Nigeria."

"He broke up with you on the phone?"

"Yes. I mean, how else was he to do it?"

Deidre hissed through her teeth. "Not even Krista and Mara knew?"

"No. They were still in high school. What could they have done?"

"You never told them later?"

"No. What was the point?"

"The point? So they could ream him out for having made the biggest mistake of his life." She slammed down the screwdriver. "Maybe he needs to hear it from his aunt."

She snapped the throw into place and made to exit stage left.

"No!" Bridget wedged herself and the crate in her hands between Deidre and the door. "Think of the girls. They don't need to get even an inkling of how the man they depend on left someone. They wouldn't understand the difference, and shouldn't have to be scared that he'd desert them. Because he won't. Ever."

Deidre slowly dropped her avenging-angel pose. "Only for the sake of the girls. But I will not promise what I'll do if I ever catch him alone."

"Fair enough." She should warn Jack that Deidre knew of their old engagement. Then again, it felt unbelievably good to have someone in her corner. "Thanks, Deidre. There's— there's a chance I might miss you when you leave."

Deidre crossed her arms, the red plaid drawing tight around her thin shoulders. "I've been meaning to talk to you about that. You and Jack, I guess." She lowered her eyes, the fire in them gone. "The thing is, I was wondering if I could stay on after Christmas. I'd like to move here. To a different place, of course. But if I could stay on until I sort things out, I'd really...appreciate that." She raised her eyes to meet Bridget's. "Please."

Well, weren't they both just one exploding secret after another? "Why? You and Dad loved Arizona."

"We did. But he's been gone for seven years now, and there's nothing left for me there. I want my family. My daughters, my nephew, you. And those girls, if they'll have me. And if the truth be told, my dollars will go further here than in the States."

How could she refuse Deidre? To refuse her was to refuse Krista and Mara their mother and Jack his aunt. "My house is your house. And Jack's."

"Thank you," Deidre said, and they stood awkwardly together. Their unusually honest conversation had left Bridget, and probably Deidre, a little unnerved,

Her phone pinged. Girls want you.

Yes. "Story time," Bridget said. "Coming?"

Deidre hefted up the hammer. "You go be with those gorgeous girls. I'm in the mood to rip and bang."

CHAPTER SEVEN

BRIDGET ENTERED Auntie Penny's bedroom to the scent of vanilla and strawberries.

"Auntie Krista gave me bath bubblics," Sofia said from the bed. Krista and Mara and Deidre were all aunties. Jack and Bridget were called by their names only. Bridget wondered at that, but hadn't gotten around to discussing it with Jack. He glanced up from where he sat on his cot and then dropped his focus back to his phone.

Bridget flopped down on the bed, tossing aside a penguin stuffie and a Spanish-English picture dictionary to do so. Not two weeks in and they'd already laid claim to the bed with books, hair scrunchies, stuffies, paper, markers and puzzle pieces. Bridget tugged one of Sofia's wet braids. "Did Krista braid your hair, too?"

"Yes, but Isabella said, 'No.'"

Isabella scowled at Sofia. Her dark hair spread like a shawl over her back in a damp mass and had likely soaked through her pajama top. "I detest braids."

Sofia snuggled against Bridget. "Tell us a snow story."

"I'd love to once Isabella lets me braid her hair and she puts on a dry jammie top." She mimed the actions well enough for Isabella to understand.

She turned her scowl on Bridget. "No."

"Is-a-bel-la," Jack said, looking up. "Either you do as you're told or Sofia misses out on her story."

Sofia instantly played her part with a lip tremble.

"Okay, okay. One braid."

"One braid," Bridget agreed. "And one dry jammie top."

"I only have one."

Jack dug out one of his T-shirts from a dresser drawer and tossed it to Isabella. All of Auntie Penny's clothes had disappeared somewhere. She ought to thank Deidre for taking care of it; she would've cried buckets before the first drawer was emptied.

Bridget helped Isabella keep her end of the bargain, making a mental note that sometime soon she must undertake her traditional Christmas trip to Cozy Comforts, a boutique that specialized in Christmas pajamas for the whole family. She should go while selection was good, if she could find two hours together.

Bridget latched her arm around Sofia and started in. "Once upon a time there was a princess who decided to find her sister."

"You're not telling her the *Frozen* story, are you?" Jack said.

"Sofia loves *Frozen*, and it's her turn."

"My head will explode if I have to retell that story. It's bad enough I actually know the lyrics to the songs in English and Spanish."

"You tell a story, then."

"Sofia wants you, not me."

"I can't think of one."

A sly smile spread across his face. "Tell her," Jack said and set his phone facedown, "about the time you and I skated across the lake. When we were in high school."

No. Not that one. "I don't remember that."

"Sure you do, Bridge. It was about this time thirteen years ago."

"Sofia wants a snow story. There was no snow."

"But that was the miracle of it all. There was no snow when there should've been." He spoke softly to the girls in Spanish. Bridget picked out her name and the word *lago*. Lake. He was laying out the story.

Sofia sucked in her breath as if she'd seen a pretty picture, and twisted to look up at Bridget. "Tell me, tell me."

Bridget shot daggers—no, icicles—at Jack. "Or I could tell it," he said.

And what parts would he tell? "I will tell it, if you promise to translate it word for word."

His sly smile widened. "I promise."

As if she had a choice. She threw him a final icicle. "One afternoon, Jack and I went skating on the lake."

"The one with a Christmas tree?"

Sofia and Isabella—when she let herself— were in excited knots to see the official lighting of the traditional Christmas tree erected in the middle of the family skating area next Saturday. Deidre had promised to take them down while Bridget and Jack served steak dinners to the lakeside crowd.

"Same lake but the tree wasn't up yet. The lake was frozen as deep as you are tall, yet it hadn't snowed. The lake was like glass. A huge sheet of clear whitish blue." She paused for Jack to translate.

"He and I decided to start skating across the lake."

Sofia listened to Jack, then asked Bridget, "Just you two?"

"Yes."

Just the two of them, hands joined, the scrape of blades in unison, the sway of their bodies side by side. "You could see straight down into the ice. There were all these incredible patterns and sometimes you could pick out a fish moving beneath." Heads touching, cheeks grazing, breaths held at the sight of a fish, gazes linked in shared excitement. Jack's Spanish trailed off and he looked across the girls at her. The sly smile had given way to a soft, remembering one.

Sofia jiggled under Bridget's arm. "Then what happened?"

The rest was not a children's bedtime story. "Then it got dark and we skated back."

Jack made a grumbling noise. "Tell them about the moon."

"There was a moon that night."

"A big, bright, white moon." Jack said the simple description in English.

"It meant we could see where we were going."

"We could see each other."

"Of course, we could." Why was he bringing up all this old, painful history in front of his kids? Turning this excruciating, embarrassing episode in her life into a bedtime story?

Jack crossed from the cot to the bed and sat on Sofia's side. His hand almost touched Bridget's, and she straightened. "Bridget was wearing a pink toque and pink mitts, soft and fuzzy, and the moonlight lit them up. And when she smiled…"

"You see her teeth!" Sofia peeled back her upper lip to display her missing ones.

"You could see a lot of her teeth, because she was smiling so big. And…she spun in circles on her skates."

Sofia gasped, jiggled Isabella's arm and spoke in excited Spanish. Then she queried Jack, who nodded gravely.

"Yes," Jack said, "she spun like a music-box dancer."

Honest to Pete! "Who's supposed to be telling the story here?"

"You," Jack said. "Anything you want to add?"

He was daring her to tell the full story. "You were smiling, too."

"I was."

"Why smiling?" Isabella asked suspiciously. "What was so funny?"

"Because it was so beautiful," Bridget said.

"So beautiful," Jack agreed quietly. Her murderous glare drew up against his soft smile. He didn't back down.

"And when we got back to shore," Bridget said in a rush, "it was so cold. We had a key to the restaurant and went inside and had hot chocolate with a cinnamon bun."

Jack translated. At least, she could only hope he was sticking to his promise. "That," he added, "was beautiful, too."

What did he want from her? "So after that, we were very tired from our long skate and we both had school the next day, just like you two, and so we went home and went to bed, just like you two are about to do. The end."

Jack translated and then added, "Except we slept in separate beds in separate homes. Not just like you two."

Bridget felt her face grow hotter than Mano's grill. The girls burrowed underneath the quilts. Neither Jack nor Bridget kissed them goodnight yet. They had agreed that they would let the girls make the first move.

Bridget slipped to the door while Jack did the final bedtime rituals with the dimming of the lamp and arrangement of stuffies.

"Bridgie?" Sofia called.

"Yeah?"

"Will you tell that story next time?"

Not a chance. "Maybe a different one."

"Good. This one had a—a boring ending."

Bridget couldn't see Jack's expression in the darkened room, but he'd likely agree. "Yeah," she said, "it sure did."

JACK WOKE WITH a start. His girls were calling out to him from...the backyard? What? He sat up in the cot, his phone sliding from his chest, and forced his brain to get oriented. Bridget had picked up the girls from school and took them for their minicinni, so he could price out suppliers and vacuum the girls' room. He remembered lying back on the cot as he typed an email and then— He checked his phone. The half-written email didn't even make sense. And it was forty minutes later.

He flicked open the window blinds. Sun and snow brightened the backyard into a flat whiteness where he could see Bridget and the girls rolling a ball. The makings of a snowman. Sofia's dream was coming true. She'd been disappointed to discover that Alberta snow was typically too powdery to form balls. But a clash of weather systems had created snow and warm temperatures, perfect for sticky snow.

A perfect picture of the three people he wanted for his family. If Bridget would have him. He didn't know how to convince her that he would never let her down again.

Last night he'd brought up the story of their skate on the lake to see if she'd remembered. She had, though she had dragged her heels down that particular memory lane and had veered right into the ditch at the end.

As they'd skated across the clear expanse, hand in hand, blades scraping the ice, he'd acted on a force that had been building within him all that evening, maybe for weeks, maybe since he'd first met her at the restaurant as a stringy thirteen year-old. "Let's do this together for the rest of our lives," he had said.

"Yes," she'd replied. And they'd skated on.

Only when they were in the heated darkness of Penny's with mugs of warm chocolate did Bridget lick whipped cream from her lip and whisper "Just to be clear...you asked me to marry you, right?"

"Yes," he said, "and just to be clear, you accepted, right?"

"Yes."

They had kissed, long and deep. When he

had pulled back, he said, "I don't have a ring. It doesn't seem real without a ring."

Now, watching Bridget mess about with the girls, he wished he had produced a ring, even if it was made out of a paper clip. Slipped it on and raised her hand for all the world to see. But Penny—his mother—had convinced them of the wisdom of keeping it a secret until after his overseas internship. He'd thrown himself into the work, eager to prove his value to the agency, to himself, to Bridget. Then he was offered a permanent position. He'd called Bridget to ask her to join him, but she'd talked about the quirky restaurant customers, a summer concert she was organizing, her sisters visiting, Auntie Penny's garden, the cold lake, anything but how much she loved and missed him. When he broke in and told her about the offer, she'd gone quiet.

"I don't know how this'll work between us going forward," he'd said. "You have your life and now I have mine."

"Yes." A simple confirmation.

"I was thinking that—that you could come and join me."

"Oh. But—but what would I do there?"

Do? He hadn't given it much thought. She could sit in their apartment until he came home. Shop on strange streets. Barter in unfamiliar languages. Follow him into poor, unsafe territories. Or he could give her the opportunity to stay where she already had a good life living out her dreams, not his. "Nothing you'd like, I guess," he'd said.

"That's what I was thinking." Thinking. As if she'd expected his invitation. Which meant that she'd already put thought to their relationship and their future, and seen how hopeless it was.

He'd been sitting at a desk in a tiny office he shared with three others who didn't know English. One looked pointedly up at the clock because he had an important call to make to the agency contact in Bangladesh. "So we should probably let—let our plans to be...to have a future together...go."

"Yes." Quiet but solid. "I get it."

Did she also get how much her answer had hurt? Still, there was nothing for it but to replace bad memories with good ones. Starting with one about the time they'd made a snowman with Isabella and Sofia. Work could wait until later.

The spiced scent of apple cider hit him upon reaching the kitchen. Deidre was ladling it into a mug from a stock pot on the stove. "Want one?" she said as he cut to the back closet.

"Not right now, thanks. I thought I'd help Bridget and the girls."

"They're doing fine on their own."

He stopped zipping his jacket. Her tone suggested that he should leave them alone. "They look like they're having fun."

"So why do you want to go out there and spoil it?"

She held the steaming mug with such a look of ferocity, she might well toss the contents at him as drink it. He wanted to leave, but Deidre was family—his and, more important, Bridget's.

"Bridget told me last night that you broke off your engagement with her."

Is that the way she saw it? "It was mutual."

"Not the way she told it. She said you chose your work over her."

His heart thudded like a boot falling down stairs. "I didn't. We talked on the phone. She wanted to be here more than she wanted to be with me."

"Is that what she said?"

"She didn't have to. She made it pretty clear she had a full life here without me." Had he been wrong? Bridget was always giving—

discounts, minicinnis, money, time, energy. Had she given him not up, but away?

"Why did you make her choose between you and her life here? Weren't you the one who was supposed to come back to her?"

She was right. "I believed that I could make more of a difference in the world than I could being part of her world."

Her fierceness eased. "And now?"

"And now," he said, shoving on his boots, "I am going out there so just this once she can remember that I chose her above everyone and everything else."

The back door slammed and Jack appeared at the top of the deck stairs. When Deidre texted Bridget to say that Jack was snoring louder than a diesel engine, she'd directed the girls straight to the backyard to give him a bit of quiet. She'd made a good call. He looked… energized.

"Want help with your snowman?" he called.

"Snow angel," Sofia corrected. "We're making a snow angel. Gabriel."

He continued to stand there, his boots on but not laced, his jacket on but not zipped, one glove on, the other sticking from his jacket pocket. Was he seriously waiting for an answer to his question?

"Hurry," she said, "we're into the heavy lifting."

Bridget figured she and Jack could handle the middle section together, but he swung it into place himself. Right. "Your muscles are for more than show, I see."

She meant it as a joke but he held her gaze as he answered, "They are for show, too. If you want."

There he was again with his innuendoes. The girls hadn't picked up on a thing—they were quarreling over a lump of snow, cracked and dotted in red mitten lint. The angel's head.

"Jack," she muttered. "Not now."

His gaze continued to bind to hers. "Not never, either. Agreed?"

"Agreed," she said, not quite sure what she was agreeing to. Viewing his muscles or talking about what she wanted. Supposing the two were different.

Sofia let loose with a loud shriek. Isabella was stomping the angel's head to bits. "Stop it," Isabella said. "We need to make a new one." At least, that's what Bridget assumed she'd said from what she could pick out from the Spanish.

"Here," Jack said, plunging into fresh snow. "Let's start again."

Sofia had grown attached to the present monstrosity, so it took all the delicate diplomacy of nuclear-disarmament negotiations to bring the peace of the season to bear on the creation of Gabriel.

"Good job," Bridget said to Jack when the girls had dashed inside to grab carrots and raisins for the final decorative touches. "Left to me and the girls, spring would've melted Gabriel away before he was done."

Jack gave the snow angel an appraising look. "Honestly? If I was the Virgin Mary and this appeared before me with glad tidings, I'd be worried. For my sanity or God's."

Bridget laughed and Jack gave her one of his later-not-never looks. What did he want?

He pointed to the garage. "You need help there?"

"Deidre is working on the crates. She wants to feel useful."

"Then what do you want me to do?"

"There's still the problem of finding money for the event."

"Do you have a list of sponsors? I can call around."

"Auntie Penny announced last year when thanking sponsors that there were enough funds to cover this year. I don't think they'd take kindly to either of us hitting them up for more money."

Jack kicked a chunk of snow apart. "You know, I can't decide whether or not to be annoyed or grateful about what my *mother* did." The word came out bitterly.

"If it's anything like how I feel about my mother, it's both."

The door opened to the girls and, surprise, Deidre. They were weighted down with all kinds of clothing and accessories, and as they descended the deck stairs, Bridget recognized exactly whose.

"You can't use Auntie Penny's things."

"They're mine now," Deidre said, "and I'd like the girls to enjoy them."

Deidre and Bridget locked gazes. Jack shifted beside her, and Bridget picked up on his tension. She had no business creating a scene in front of his girls.

She plucked off a gaudy orange shawl that Auntie Penny had worn to book-club meetings. Sofia gasped. "Jewels!" Bridget understood that Spanish.

Sofia tried to drape the shawl around the wide triangular bottom of the snow angel as a skirt. It twisted and rolled and looked more like something the wind had blown onto it.

"Here," Jack said. "How about we put it around her neck instead?"

He arranged the material tenderly, as if putting it on a real person.

"Next, how about we use the coat —the red one, yes?" He arranged it on Gabriel's shoulders with all the care of a valet and brushed and smoothed the weft of the wool.

Piece by piece, Jack, with fashion advice from the four females, dressed Gabriel until he looked like not quite an angel, not quite a snowman and not quite Auntie Penny. Deidre said quietly, "Isn't that something else entirely?"

"Yeah," Bridget admitted. "It's…good."

The sun was banking off now, light giving way to the sunset blaze of oranges and pinks.

"What's for supper?" Isabella asked Deidre, who had designated herself as the cook for suppers. An easy enough job, considering they'd barely skimmed the surface of the meals from the funeral service.

Guiding the girls inside with a hand on each shoulder, Deidre said, "I do believe it's lasagna."

Alone again with Jack, Bridget said what she could no longer not say. "Thank you. For taking care of Auntie Penny's clothes." She whisked stray snow from a jacket shoulder.

"I remember that jacket. It was worn-out years ago," Jack said. "I see here she's sewn up holes under the arms and restitched the lining. She couldn't give up on things. You're like that, too, Bridget."

Her hand still on the jacket shoulder, he laid his hand over hers, lightly, like when he helped her from the ladder. Touching, not holding. "But I gave up on us. That phone call I made. From Nigeria."

Bridget gave an involuntary flinch, and her hand twitched underneath his. "The last thing I wanted was to upset you," he said softly. "I didn't think— You sounded so calm on the phone. It was easy to convince myself that we'd grown apart, that you wanted it, too."

"I guess I was in shock."

"You cried." A flat statement of regret.

"Yes."

"I am sorry. You don't know how sorry."

"That," she whispered, "was a long time ago. Apologies aren't necessary."

His fingers curled around her hand and squeezed. Definitely holding hands now. "Apologies are absolutely necessary," he whispered, "for our future."

He powered up another of his we-must-talk looks, and she stood inches away from kissing the only man she'd given her heart to.

Truth was she had forgiven him. Or rather, she'd never blamed him. It was as Auntie Penny had said when she told her they'd broken up. "It's sad to hear but, my dear, you weren't meant to be together."

She'd believed her aunt for twelve years, but now... Had they all been wrong?

"Yeah," she said, "I get it."

He released her hand slowly, gently, like it was the last thing on earth he wanted to do.

CHAPTER EIGHT

BRIDGET WAS WRAPPING silverware for tomorrow's breakfast service at the bar counter when Jack set his open laptop in her line of vision.

He singsonged a line from the Christmas tune "Do You Hear What I Hear?" and pointed to the bottom row of a spreadsheet.

Bridget stared at the number. It wasn't a negative. Very much a positive. And plump. And to the side, the confirmation: profit.

"A way, a way, to pay for our mortgage," she answered, keeping up the Christmas carol.

"With a little more for our fund," he ad-libbed.

"With a little more for—" she began, stopped, then said in a flat voice, "Wait, what fund?"

Jack held up a finger and disappeared into the back. Bridget glanced at the girls playing by the chairs and table. They had a talent for playing with anything. Utensils were children put to bed under a napkin. Ladle and spatula were Mr. and Mrs. Santa Claus. The sleigh was a breadbasket.

Jack returned with a tin box and set it on the counter. It was the one Auntie Penny had kept in her office filled with buttons and loyalty cards and gift cards with little or no balances. Jack flipped open the lid and Bridget saw he'd chucked the lot and replaced it with a wad of cash. "Tips. From last week's service."

"All that? I add mine into the deposits. How did you separate it out?"

"I didn't," he said. "This is all mine. After Mano's cut."

"Yours? Wow. I'm not the only one who thought you looked sensational in that shirt this weekend." He'd worn a soft cotton shirt that had set off his tan and made his blue eyes pop.

Those eyes gleamed. "I didn't know you thought that."

Bridget got busy placing a fork and knife just so on the white napkin. "I said you looked good."

"Yeah, but not sen-sa-tional. And I don't wear that shirt in the morning, when I pick tips up like crumbs off toast. Sofia and Isabella rake in a lot for me. Customers see me as this hardworking single dad, just trying to get by in a woman's world."

Bridget snorted. "It's Marlene, isn't it? You run over like a happy dog with her coffee and cinnamon bun."

"Yeah. Mel, too."

"Mel and Daphne, both. They've got their own nieces and nephews to spoil."

"Hey, are we really going to complain that they willingly give us their money?"

Bridget waggled a freshly wrapped fork and knife at him. "Sounds like charity to me."

"It's not charity," he said. "It's payment for a service."

"It's charity disguised as payment for a service."

"What it is," he said, "is a tiny rainy-day fund for us to build on to cover payments in January when business tapers off."

"Um, I don't know that your tips—as great as they are—will take us over the top," Bridget said.

"No, but I figure it'll be enough for us to get by until we sell the units."

Bridget's heart struck a few downward

beats. "Have Mara and Krista decided not to take them?"

"They haven't said one way or another, probably because they know how upset you'll be when they decline."

Bridget would be sad. But it would also be a relief not to worry every second about how to make ends meet. Jack gave a small, secretive smile. "Until then, you've no idea what a table full of tipsy ladies will pay for my charms."

"I thought you were laying it on a bit thick the other night."

Jack leaned on the counter. "Not jealous were you, Bridget?"

"No," she said quickly. Too quickly. At his knowing grin, she added, "Okay, a little. Of your tips."

"Don't be," he said. "Your talents probably lie in other areas."

She feinted a poke at him with a fork. "Are you implying that I can't bring in the tips?"

He shrugged as if to imply just that.

"You are on, Jack Holdstrom. You are so on. Starting tomorrow with Monday's breakfast and ending next Saturday closing."

"What does the winner get?" Jack said. Oh. He was getting that *later* glint in his eye.

"A cinnamon bun."

"Boring. I could get those any day of the week."

"What then?"

"If I win, you have to come skating with me."

That was a no-brainer. She loved to skate and she'd not been out all year. "Fine. I've been meaning to take the girls to the lake, anyway."

"No, Bridget," he said and leaned on the counter, his lips inches from hers. "Just you and me."

And a whole bunch of other people in a public area. "Okay," she said, and tried to move on quickly. "And if I win, you have to serve me dinner. Tablecloth, napkins, wine— the whole shebang. Like we're at a fancy restaurant."

His lips remained close to hers. "Will you dress up for it?"

Bridget's heart rattled like a lid on a boiling pot. "Yeah, sure, why not? Can I bring a date?"

The glint flickered into a heated glow. "That won't work. I'm only serving you."

"Maybe I should adjust the bet."

Jack straightened. "Too late. If I win, you and me go dating... I mean, skating together.

Sorry for the slip of the tongue," he said un-apologetically. "And if I lose, I serve you dinner after hours, the two of us alone, you and me all spiffy, as if we're on—"

"Don't even say it," Bridget said.

"I don't think I need to," Jack said and whistled a short *gotcha* tune. "Win or lose, I'm going on a date with you."

He took up the tin box. "I'll drop this back in the safe," he said. "Girls, we're leaving now. Time for supper. Clean up and make sure the chairs are exactly back where they were."

Bridget hopped off her chair, and her phone chimed a text. Hello. Albert here. Before Penny left, she placed a minimum order of forty turkeys. Let me know if you need to increase the order. I take it you're in charge. I will need payment by the end of tomorrow to confirm your order. Bridget sucked in her breath at the cost of forty turkeys.

She didn't have the money. And neither had Penny. Why did she place an order that she didn't have the money to fill? She seemed to have played free and easy with money for years. And there was no putting off Albert. Payment in full or no turkeys, and the frozen bird formed the centerpiece in the Christmas Crates. If she didn't make payment, she would be letting Auntie Penny down. And fifty-five families.

Jack strode from the back, stuffing himself into his jacket. "Isabella, put the chair back. Sofia, there's a fork under the table. Otherwise, good job. Get your boots and coats on, and let's blow this Popsicle stand."

The girls stared quizzically. "I'll explain on the way home," Jack said and turned to Bridget. His half smile slipped away. "What's wrong?"

She couldn't unload on Jack, not with him so upbeat. Sofia tugged on Jack's hand. There, Bridget's perfect reason to evade an answer. "The girls have been patient long enough. Let's call it a day."

Jack looked at each of the girls and, as if cued, they gave him pleading looks. "Fine. We'll talk after the girls have gone to bed."

Not another of their sofa-bed talks. Those were getting way too…cozy. "Out in the garage," she said.

He gave her a fleeting smile, as if knowing exactly why she wanted the change in venue.

But his smile wasn't in evidence later that evening when she revealed her quandary. "Forty turkeys? With probably another fifteen needed? There's no way we can swing it, Bridge. Tell him you're sorry, but it's not happening this year."

"But that's the thing, Jack. He'll wonder why. He knew that we had the money. Everybody knows. If we cancel—"

"Right. You could be accused of embezzling."

"Not technically. I would look bad, but I'm more concerned about what they'd think of Auntie Penny. She robbed them, yes, but for a good cause."

Jack rubbed his face, leaned against the bench in the garage and glared at the crates. Fifty-five in all, scrubbed, repaired or built fresh, stacked into a rough pyramid that rose above their heads. Deidre was all kinds of surprises.

"I honestly don't know of a way around this," Jack said. "I am willing to go to last year's donors and explain the situation. Let them know that I promise to reimburse the Christmas Crates fund just as soon as I can. At least that way, no one will blame you."

"I appreciate that, Jack. But it's also the families that were counting on a crate to get through Christmas."

"I would prefer to disappoint fifty families

than further endanger the restaurant. A sorry-looking Christmas for them doesn't outweigh us losing the means to any kind of living. Even they'd understand that."

"Yes, but in the end, it was their money Auntie Penny took."

"Money she gave me," he said. "Look, if you're up-front with Albert, would he accept part payment now, and you pay him back with interest?"

"Auntie Penny asked him that last year before we struck it rich with the fundraising. He expects full payment because Christmas is when he makes his profits for the year. He would sell them to someone else."

"Would another supplier cut us a deal?"

"Not for meat."

"How about Krista and Mara? Or Auntie Deedee?"

Bridget widened her eyes. "Auntie Deedee?"

"Sofia's choices. I think it'll stick."

"I need their help to prepare the crates. I can't expect them to fork out money, as well. I have five hundred dollars I'd set aside for Christmas gifts. I will put that in."

"I can't give up my Christmas money," Jack said. "The girls deserve a present or two, especially after what they've endured. But I'll hand over my tip money."

Bridget groaned. "But then the little fund is gone."

Jack shrugged. "Do we have a choice?"

Bridget sighed. "No. I am sorry, Jack."

"Don't be. Penny took the money. And she did it for the girls, because I didn't have the means otherwise. So if there's anyone to blame for this mess, it's me."

"If anyone met Sofia and Isabella, they wouldn't blame you," Bridget said with absolute certainty.

"This might resolve itself," Jack said. "If either Krista or Mara give up a unit, you could do a fire sale and our restaurant problems are solved. I could funnel more of my earnings into replenishing the Christmas fund."

That would also mean her sisters would be gone. Why did getting always mean giving up?

"IT'S A DISASTER, a complete disaster," Mano moaned, his head stuck in the fridge.

Auntie Penny said Mano did melodrama better than a soap opera. Bridget looked up at Jack from where they were preparing fresh cinnamon buns for the display case. A disaster! He mimed and Bridget squelched a smile. Auntie Penny's son could do daytime television, too.

"We're half a kilo short of cream cheese," Bridget said, sprinkling crushed candy canes on a tray of minicinnis. "I'll go to the store and get more."

"That stuff is glue mixed with sawdust mixed with chalk mixed with chicken feed mixed with—"

Jack trailed behind Bridget's sprinkles, popping in Santa toothpicks. "How about we go with a different dessert?"

"A different dessert?" Mano closed the fridge and slumped against it. "You tell me what else I should make with mandarins, chocolate and half the amount of cream cheese we need?"

"Don't give me that look, Mano," Jack said. "That's why I leave you in charge of ordering ingredients, so we don't have this problem."

"How was I to know that Bridget would steal my cream cheese?"

"How was I to know that units sold— that's Jack talk—doubled from a week ago? I needed the cream cheese today. You don't need the dessert until Friday. That's two full days for you to restock."

Mano pointed an accusing finger at her. "For you to restock."

"Fine, I'll run over to the dairy tomorrow."

"You are lucky I'm so well-organized," Mano said. "If it wasn't for me—"

Rapid knocking on the front door interrupted them. Bridget peeked through the serving window. Krista and Mara. This was an unexpected but welcome reprieve from Mano.

Krista and Mara came in on a cloud of frosty air and laughter. Not unusual for Krista, whose blond curls were bouncing in time with her bouncing feet, but even Mara radiated excitement.

"We won't be long," she said.

"But we—" Krista waved her hand between her and Mara "—just wanted to say, and before we say anything, just so you know, Bridget, we talked about it a lot, but in the end—"

Krista's stops and starts gave Bridget enough time to know exactly what they'd been thinking about. She held her breath…

"—we've decided to keep the units."

Bridget shrieked with joy and hugged Krista, then Mara. And then did them both again. *This*, she thought. *This is what I want.*

Jack shot out from the back. "What's going on?"

"Krista and Mara are staying. They're taking the units!"

Jack reverted to a carefully neutral expression. A short-term solution to the restaurant woes had just dried up. "There'll be a lot of up-front costs with renovations," he said.

"We know," Mara said. "We'll take it slow."

"What will you do about getting a client base?"

"I'm working on that," Krista said. "I'm building a social platform already."

"There'll also be—"

"Jack!" Bridget cut in. "They've made up their minds. Leave it alone."

Jack stripped off his apron. "I'm trying to look out for everyone's interests, but fine. Congratulations," he said to Krista and Mara with a total lack of enthusiasm. And to Bridget he said, "I will go get the girls today."

"You do that," she said to his retreating back, before remembering. She raised her voice. "Sofia lost her mitten. If you could look after that interest, it would be—" the back door slammed shut "—appreciated."

Bridget turned to catch Krista and Mara exchanging their patented secretive looks. "He wanted us to give them to you, didn't he? To get the money?"

"It would've still been my money to spend how I see fit. We're partners in the restaurant only," Bridget said. Never mind that she would've most definitely plunked the money into the business. "Coffee?"

By way of saying yes, Krista perched on a stool. Mara chose to lean on the counter. "I think," she said, "you two have become partners in pretty significant ways."

Krista began ticking off. "The restaurant."

Mara continued. "The house."

"The girls."

"The girls? Hardly. We're all partners in those two."

Another exchange of knowing looks. "We don't read them bedtime stories with Jack," Mara said.

"Or share picking them up from school."

"Or them coming here after school."

"Let's face it," Krista said, "you two are their parents."

"Jack is, I'm not," Bridget said.

"To-may-to, to-mah-to," Krista said. She poured a dollop of Marlene's whipping cream into all three coffees without asking. "What do you think, Mara? Do you think that they're partners in romance, too?"

Mara studied Bridget. "Could be."

No way was Bridget telling them that she'd agreed to a possible date with Jack. But her face must've betrayed guilt—or, heaven help her, excitement—because Krista crowed, and raised her hand to high-five her sister. "We knew it."

"Nothing is going on," Bridget said.

Mano appeared at the window. "Things are so hot between them, flames leap up from the grill when they walk in."

"Is that right?" Krista said.

"That coffee you're drinking?" Mano continued. "Stays hot because of the way he looks at her when she tops up his cup."

"He doesn't even look—"

Mara nodded. "I've seen those looks."

"So hot that the eggs go from over easy to scrambled when he passes her the plate."

Bridget groaned. "Carry on, Mano. No one believes you."

"Oh, really?" Krista smiled at Mano. "Try sitting at the supper table with them. Even with the girls between them, it's e-lec-tric."

"I worry about using metal utensils around them," Mara said in a choked voice paired with a perfectly timed hitch in her breath.

"Honest to Pete," Bridget said, trying to bring a shred of rationality to the conversation, "we dated a dozen years ago and then we both moved on."

Krista said flatly, "You stayed in the same place. And no serious boyfriends."

"And he's moved back."

"So hot," Mano said softly, "the years melt away."

Bridget looked in disbelief at all three of their dreamy expressions. They could all star in a melodrama.

BRIDGET THOUGHT IT could have been a scene from Sofia's *Frozen* for all the so-called e-lec-tri-ci-ty between Bridget and Jack at the supper table that night. Krista and Mara had told Deidre about their decision, which delighted her to no end. She plied them with questions and tossed out extravagant suggestions that, thankfully, her sisters nullified or modified. Isabella and Sofia got in on the act, too. Sofia identified several colors of nail polish Krista should carry and Isabella wanted to know if Mara would serve her clients food while they talked. Jack shoveled food into his mouth and made clipped replies to anything directed at him.

He did have one question. "Where are you planning to stay?"

"Right here," Bridget said.

"I believe I have half a say in that."

Mara leaned sideways to catch her cousin's eye. "And I believe Krista and I have complete say about where we live. We signed a lease on a two-bedroom duplex rental this afternoon. We move in January first. If that's soon enough for you."

Bridget gave Jack her best hope-you're-happy glare. He seemed unfazed. "Probably a good idea."

He must've also thought it a good idea to clear out himself. As soon as he'd tucked in the girls, he drove to the restaurant, citing paperwork.

He hadn't returned by the time she pulled out the sofa bed and burrowed under the covers. Her body now still, her mind got busier than a mall at Christmas. Krista and Mara, renovations, cream cheese, Sofia's mittens, dry cleaners, Christmas tree, Christmas pajamas, Christmas stockings, Jack alone at the restaurant, holding hands, skating on a moonlit lake. With all her tossing and turning, it would be another messy bed for Mara to make in the morning.

She still hadn't fallen asleep when she heard his steps on the porch and the snap of the bolt lock opening. She listened to him shed his coat and boots. Then, silence.

"Bridge?"

She could pretend sleep, but they might as well hash out whatever was on his mind.

"Yeah?"

"Sorry for waking you. I lost track of time."

"Doesn't matter. I wasn't asleep."

She felt more than saw him slip over and sit on the sofa arm.

"The thing is," Jack whispered, as if they were in the middle of discussion, "with Krista and Mara staying, it'll be one hard, slow grind for us to get out of this hole."

"You could get a job. I mean, one somewhere else."

"That will take time we don't have. Meanwhile, what will you do? Right now, the only reason the place is turning a profit is that neither of us draws wages, and Mano's family works for free outside of tips. I suppose we could ask Aunt Deidre if—"

"I will kill her if we have to work together."

"Then it's back to us."

Us. Partners. Bridget suddenly felt hot. She kicked away the covers to cool off her feet.

"Stop it," he said. "Making this bed is already a royal pain."

"You make my bed?"

"When I come back to pick up the girls. First morning they were jumping around on it as if it was a gym mat. Easier to keep them on track if I do it first thing."

"Oh," she mumbled. "I mean, I would do it, except thumping around at five in the morning would wake Mara and Krista. I always thought Mara did it. She's the neat freak. Thanks."

"Once more with enthusiasm." His teeth shone from his sudden grin. "Anyway, it's small. I've never thanked you for the stories you tell the girls."

"My pleasure. Really."

"We could spend all night thanking each other for the things we do for each other."

Bridget swallowed. "Yeah, but who needs that?"

"When we've got bigger problems," Jack concluded. "Look, the bottom line is that I'm not ruling out getting a job elsewhere, but it also makes sense to invest time into stabilizing Penny's. I studied the books tonight, laid it out on a spreadsheet, did some projections and we just might squeak through this."

Classic Jack. "So Penny's is your personal humanitarian relief project?"

He gave a short, hard huff. "Hardly. There's

a chance this plan will succeed. I'm thinking of what's good for the girls. I have the flexibility to fit their schedule, they can come to my workplace and feel safe and warm and fed. Get a little older, they can walk back and forth between here and the restaurant."

"A little older? Wait." She raised herself onto her elbow. "Are you saying you're not interested in selling your share of the house? You want to live here forever?"

"That's what I mean. There's room for the girls to grow, a backyard. I won't get a better deal."

"Then I'll have to move."

He shifted from the arm down to the bed. When he sat beside her like that last time, she'd touched him voluntarily for the first time since their breakup. She wiggled away. "You can stay, Bridge," he said softly. "It's your house, too."

He was making plans and they included her. Like he had wrapped a huge Christmas gift for her that she wasn't sure she wanted to open.

"All I'm asking for now," he said, "is that you trust me."

Thanks to Auntie Penny, she didn't have a choice. Still, she couldn't deny the thread of eager hope in Jack's voice. He wanted her to believe in him.

"But what will we do about Christmas Crates?"

"As much as I hate that Penny stole the money, she did it for me, so it's my responsibility."

"It's not just your responsibility."

"Yes, it is. I took the money. From a charity. There is no one on earth who can better understand what it's like to be taken advantage of, so I will see to it that the money is replaced."

"How?"

"Trust me."

She had no reason to. Then again, if she agreed to forgive him, then she couldn't sabotage it by not giving him a chance.

"Okay. I trust you because I'm too tired to come up with a reason not to."

She felt the quilt loosen as he rose. "Good enough for me," he said. "Good night, Bridge."

Jack wanting to make things right for her and for their future? Yeah, plenty good enough for her, too.

CHAPTER NINE

SATURDAY NIGHT AND Penny's was full again. Good news for the restaurant, not so great for Jack's chance to win his bet. Bridget was on fire tonight, and the clientele seemed to bask in her glow. It had started on Friday, when workers had come in for happy hour, and Bridget had worked the bar—and every guy. Tonight was no different. When he saw one customer, whose idea of cleaning up was to wet-comb his hair, slide Bridget a fifty for a seventeen-dollar tab, Jack decided that if he couldn't win fair and square, he could at least try to cut her off. Forget the good fortunes of Penny's. He had a date to win.

He shouldered her aside. "Cover tables for me. I got this."

She opened her mouth to protest, then they both clocked who walked in. Four, all men, all sounding as if they'd already washed down a few drinks.

Bridget swept by him so fast he could feel

the wake of her vanilla-scented wind. "Good evening, gentlemen," she said, "Thank you for coming to my home away from home." She clicked on her high-beam smile, the one that had propelled him to ask her out on their first date.

"I'm so going to lose the bet," he said when she came to the bar with their drink orders.

"Oh, I don't know. Remember, it's over the week. You were leading going into tonight." A fact he found hard to believe. She settled the serving tray onto her arm and made for her table of men, shooting him a grin over her other shoulder.

Her smile foretold his doom.

Three hours later, the two of them sat alone at the bar counter, Jack's laptop open to a spreadsheet. The debit numbers put Bridget in a slight lead, but he knew that the cash count would blow him out of the water. Bridget finished with hers, while Jack was still counting. It meant nothing—she could've had larger bills.

"Okay," he said. "How much?"

She named the figure.

"No way," he said. "No way could it have been that low. You made that much tonight."

"I made most of this tonight. My week

wasn't as brilliant as you seem to think it was." She pushed the pile toward him. "Count it yourself if you don't believe me."

Like he'd look a gift horse in the mouth. "Looks as if we're going skating."

"Do you even have skates?"

"I will by our date."

"It's not a— Forget it, I'm not arguing. When?"

"Wednesday night."

"Make it Tuesday. Cold front coming in Wednesday. Temperatures go down to minus twenty-five." She fussed with the money, head down. "I might have tried to guilt-trip you into giving your money to Christmas Crates." She looked downright guilty herself.

"Are you saying you deliberately under-reported your earnings in order to give me a pity date because you feel guilty?"

She snapped an elastic around their bills, still not meeting his eye. "I might have."

The honorable thing to do was to let her off the hook, but then he'd miss out on their date. "Double or nothing."

That challenge lifted her brown eyes to his. "What do you have in mind?"

"I win, we go on two dates. You win and no dates."

She thumbed the bills thoughtfully. "Agreed."

"And no holding back because you secretly want to date me."

She gave him a full eye roll. "Agreed."

That was quick. "And second dates usually end in a kiss, so it would have to be a full-fledged date, no holding back."

"If that's all it takes to clear up my guilt," Bridget said, "I could throw one your way."

To demonstrate, she blew him a kiss before departing to the back with the money.

He was so cleaning up on tips next week.

"BRIDGIE! LOOK, we're in the paper!" Sofia waved the local newspaper and dashed head-long to where Bridget was set up in the living room, ironing.

"Careful of the cord," Bridget said, holding the iron just in case. Sofia had no sense of danger whatsoever. It drove Isabella and Bridget crazy. She reached for the paper.

There on page three of the twenty-four-page newspaper was a full-color picture of Jack with Sofia and Isabella. It was taken at one of the viewing points of the snow-covered lake. The girls, bundled up, were tucked close to Jack. The headline read, Son of Deceased Philanthropist Appeals to Lakers.

What? She skimmed the article, reading in black-and-white, as everyone in Spirit Lake could, about how Jack discovered that his biological mother was the founder of Penny's, and how she'd drained the Christmas Crates fund to expedite his return to Canada from the tumult in Venezuela.

"No, no, no. What have you done, Jack?"

She didn't realize she'd spoken aloud until Deidre called from the kitchen island. "What? What's going on?"

"This," Bridget said, thrusting the paper at Deidre. She couldn't read any more.

But Deidre could. "'There's no excuse for what she did, but if she hadn't, then I don't know where the three of us would be right now,'" she read. "'I owe people and businesses a total of ten thousand dollars that I'm in no position to pay. But if people find it in their hearts to give again this year, I'd be most grateful.'

"'Needless to say, my New Year's resolution is to repay the money in time for next year's Christmas Crates program.'"

If Jack had been home and not out with Isabella at the dentist, Bridget would've killed him in cold blood.

"How dare he tell the town that Auntie

Penny was a thief?" Bridget blurted out. "That's all people will believe about her now."

"It couldn't have been easy for Jack to admit to the world that his own mother wasn't all that everyone thought her cracked up to be."

"He told me he was going to fix this. Told me not to worry. Told me to trust him. And here he goes again. Off with another cause, and not caring how it'll affect me."

Deidre's face softened. "Is that the real problem?"

Bridget looked away. Sofia stared at her with a shocked expression. How much had she understood?

There was a thump of boots on the steps outside, and in came Jack and Isabella with shopping bags.

"Look!" Isabella said. "Napkins. Christmas napkins." She produced a thick package of them. White with red trim. "For now and for Canada Day."

Canada Day? Optimistic of Jack to think Penny's would still be around on the first of July. Sofia tugged on Jack's coat and chatted to him in Spanish. Jack spotted Deidre holding the newspaper and then glanced Bridget's way. Her expression must've clued him in to her raging feelings because he took his time shaking off his outdoor gear.

She could barely contain her temper. It rose inside her like nausea. She yanked out the cord for the iron—she was not having the girls physically injured— and headed to the back closet. "I'm going to Gord's next door. I said I'd help him put up his tree lights." She was throwing on her gear like a firefighter on a three-alarm call.

"But you haven't had supper," Deidre said.

"I'll eat later." Bridget flipped back the lock.

For someone who seemed to spend her entire day sipping drinks and composing haikus, Deidre moved like a bullet. She snapped shut the lock before Bridget could open the door.

"Listen." She had a mother's edge to her voice that had Bridget doing what she was told. "My sister has left us with a problem to solve. Not for you alone, or Jack alone, to deal with. For all of us. Understood?"

"Christmas Crates is my project," Bridget said.

"There was no mention of it in her will."

"Why would there be?"

"Exactly. It wasn't hers to give, so I guess

it belongs to whoever claims it, which in this case is Jack and the rest of us Montgomerys."

Deidre's logic had loose wiring.

"Krista! Mara! Get up here right now," Deidre called past Bridget. "You sit down. We'll sort this out over supper."

Bridget didn't think she could swallow a mouthful in Jack's presence, but neither could she stand to have the brainchild of her and her aunt snatched from her care.

She sat there, picking away at her casserole while the others bandied about ideas to somehow conjure up ten thousand dollars. Jack stayed quiet and avoided eye contact with her. *Wise move, Jack Holdstrom.*

With berry crumble set to be served and still no solution in sight, Bridget pushed away from the table. "Let me know how this turns out. I'm off to Gord's."

"Why does he need help?" Deidre asked. "He looks capable enough to me."

"He has a tremor. He can't steady his hands enough to snap the lights on the tree, and he won't give up on the tree because his wife bought it their last Christmas together."

"That's very kind of you, Bridge," Mara said.

"Kind, very kind," Deidre said absently.

Her expression turned faraway. "You know, that just might work."

Boots on, one sleeve in her jacket, Bridget listened.

"Everybody's putting up their Christmas decorations or their lights, or trying to get their house cleaned for guests or get a bit of shopping done."

"And we could do it for them," Mara said, understanding.

"For a small donation," Krista added.

"With one hundred percent of the proceeds going to the Christmas Crates program," Deidre finished.

For the first time since discovering Auntie Penny's theft, Bridget felt she'd been handed a solid break. "This way people will feel they're getting something for giving. We earn the money back."

Krista beelined for the living room to her laptop on the sofa. "I'll start a Facebook page and get something on Instagram, okay, Bridget?"

"Link it to a GoFundMe page," Mara called after her.

"Can I join, too?" Isabella said.

"Me, too," Sofia said.

Krista was typing on her laptop one-handed as she carried it back to the table. "So what do we call ourselves?"

"Christmas Crates... Craters... Crates 'R' Us?" Mara improvised.

Krista tapped her lower lips. "Hmm... something to do with Bridget, maybe, too. We could capitalize on her name. I dunno... Bridget and her sisters... The Three Sisters... Three Wise Sisters."

Jack waved his hand. "The lone male here requests recognition."

"I'm part of it, too," Deidre said. "I helped repair the crates."

"And I bet a couple of my coworkers would help out," Krista said. "I could definitely promote it at the Christmas store. It would help sell stuff there if people knew that we did installations by donation."

Bridget had gone from being alone to part of a committee of five. A very vocal five. Bridget's Christmas Brigade was born. A social-media campaign was hatched, a target launched, goals shared.

All because Jack had gone ahead and told the town that his mother—her aunt—had stolen from them. That was the silver lining to the dark, humiliating cloud of how donors like Mel and Marlene and Penny's customers would look at her tomorrow morning. They'd see the niece of a thief, maybe even a cocon-spirator.

If they bothered to come.

JACK WAS CLIMBING the stairs to the school doors when his phone sounded. The princi-pal, Melanie Lever.

"I wanted to catch you before you went to Isabella's classroom. She's here in my office. With Sofia."

What now?

Isabella wasn't adjusting as well as Sofia. Nobody adjusted like Sofia. Isabella resisted speaking English and her perpetual frowns weren't winning her friends.

The principal was frowning, too, when Jack walked in. He closed the door and itched to close the blinds on the windows facing the administration side. This didn't look good. Isabella had the same vacant, stony expres-sion as she'd had at the orphanage.

Bridget would take one look at Isabella and know how to smooth out matters. She could get Isabella to do anything.

As if to emphasize the point, Isabella looked out the glass partition into the larger school office, her mouth twisting when she didn't see Bridget.

"There was an incident," Melanie Lever began.

Another girl in the class had asked Isabella for a piece of her cinnamon bun. Jack knew the bun very well. A dental appointment immediately after school yesterday meant she'd missed out on her cinnamon-bun routine. Instead, Isabella's share was added to her lunch today.

Not surprisingly, Isabella had refused the girl. "Which was her right," Ms. Lever added.

But the girl didn't listen and made a grab for it. Isabella had shoved her to the floor. The girl was shaken, but unharmed.

All over a cinnamon bun. This part of Isabella he understood. How to explain that for Isabella it was more than a sugary baked good? It was everything good about being here. It was security. It was packaged love. It was…Bridget.

"The other student apologized for her part, and has gone home," Ms. Lever said. "Our counselor worked with Isabella this afternoon about how to handle anger, but with the language barrier, she wasn't sure how much Isabella understood."

From her fixed stare at the door, Isabella understood she was in trouble. Jack stepped in front and crossed his arms for good measure. The last thing he needed was a repeat of two weeks ago.

"Seven, eight is socially a difficult age. Girls especially start forming best friends, hierarchies of friends, and it shifts from day to day. Isabella as the new girl in a new school in a new land with a new language faces special challenges but—"

"But that's no excuse," Jack said. "I will speak to her about the matter tonight."

Ms. Lever leveled him a look that Jack felt sure would make sociopaths apologize. "The other girl apologized for her part, but Isabella has so far refused to."

Jack began to feel for Isabella. He wanted to peel out of the office, too. Find a quiet place to regroup. Find Bridget.

He should have put aside his hope for the girls to start fresh, unburdened by others being privy to their painful and damaged past, and advised the school, asked for their cooperation. He might have plenty to prove to Bridget and the people of Spirit Lake. His girls had proved their worth simply by being there.

"You should know, Ms. Lever, that my daughter comes from a place that was once one of the wealthiest in the world and now where kids fight over a loaf of bread. I personally know someone—very dear to me—in this town who has never forgotten her hunger pains from when she was a kid. I'm not sure that the pains will ever go away for Isabella. But you should also know that she will only return to the school when she's prepared to believe that she doesn't have to defend her right to her food while at your school. Fair enough?"

Ms. Lever's severity eased into a more thoughtful expression, and Jack hustled Isabella and Sofia to Penny's, not wanting to disrupt their routine. Isabella walked in first, straight past the kitchen to the front and to her table. Bridget had already set it with glasses of milk and minicinnis. The girls went to the bathroom to wash her hands.

The door had barely closed before Jack filled Bridget in about the incident.

Bridget polished glasses, as if nothing was wrong. Isabella and Sofia emerged and slid into their places. Isabella began to eat her treat as if she'd not knocked a girl down over one. After carefully taking in Jack and

Bridget, Sofia set to work on hers, unusually quiet.

"Isabella," Bridget called. "Good thing that I made up an extra batch of bun dough today. From what I hear, we'll be busy tonight making up a pan for your class tomorrow. Jack, could you tell her so there's no misunderstanding?"

"Let me get this straight first. Everyone will get one? How many are there?"

"Twenty-four, twenty-five…and the teacher."

"Don't forget the principal. And the janitor."

She ignored his sarcasm. "Perfect. We'll do two pans, to be sure. And we'll make an extra big one for the girl from today so she won't need to feel jealous anymore."

Isabella listened to Jack's translation and frowned. "She was…jealous?"

"Of course," Bridge explained. "People drive from miles around to buy these buns."

"Except for the ones who came today," Jack interjected, still shaking his head over Bridge's decision to give every single one of their breakfast customers a free minicinni as an unspoken apology for her aunt's crime. He hadn't been able to persuade her that everyone would understand it wasn't her fault and that they might not even blame Penny—hadn't she herself said that anyone who met the girls would understand?—that if they didn't, a couple mouthfuls of sugary bread wasn't going to cut it. Not a single customer mentioned the newspaper article, as he'd predicted.

Bridge had credited the minicinnis. And here she was falling back on them again to get Isabella out of trouble. "The principal only asked for an apology from Isabella to the girl involved," he said.

"Which she'll also get."

"You are already stretched to the breaking point between the restaurant and the Crates campaign. You are not responsible for Isabella. I am."

"Then why did you tell me?"

Because he'd come to see Bridge as a parent-partner. He wasn't prepared to have that conversation with her yet, so he said, "People tell other people their problems so that they can find a good way to solve them. Not to pawn them off."

Bridge looked over at the girls licking the last bit of gooey icing off their fingers. "I can't," she whispered. "Not when it comes to those two. My head knows they're yours, but my heart— I think I fell in love with them the minute I saw them."

Music to his ears. Stadium-filled, sold-out, wild music, but…she didn't get how worn out she was becoming. If she was dead set on taking care of his girls, then the least he could do was treat her right.

He'd win the bet this weekend, one way or another. Two dates where he could treat her with the same attention she gave to his kids, a classroom, the town's poor.

No minicinnis involved.

"COOKIE OR CARROT?" Jack said to the girls that night as they slipped and slid like seals in their bubble bath. Said in English, he found it a fun way to build their vocabulary and to learn more about them.

"Cookie," said Sofia and Isabella together.

"Milk or juice?"

"Juice," Sofia said.

Isabella hesitated, then said, "Milk."

"Hamburger or hot dog?"

"Hot dog!" said Sofia. Hot lunch at her school had been hot dogs and they were now number one on her list of favorite foods.

"Hamburger," Isabella said with a shake of her head at Sofia.

Her definitiveness caught Jack's interest. "Why?"

"Hot dogs come with ketchup and mustard. Hamburgers are meat and cheese and tomato and—" she gave him the word in Spanish for which he translated "—and lettuce. Hamburgers are more food."

"But hot dogs taste better," Sofia argued.

"Taste doesn't fill you up," Isabella said.

Sofia seemed crushed by her sister's logic.

"Chocolate ice cream or chocolate cake?" There. At least Isabella would have to choose something totally fun.

Sofia waffled back and forth but Isabella's answer came quick. "Chocolate cake. Because," she said in anticipation of Jack's question, "I can save it for later, if I'm full."

Sofia swished water at her sister. "You are never full."

That was the truth. Despite the stuffed freezers at the house and the extra food at the restaurant, Isabella still cleaned off her plate like a starving dog.

"Hey, smells like peaches and cream in here," Bridget said from the bathroom doorway. She looked like peaches and cream in a faded orange sweatshirt. "Book story or Bridgie story?"

Jack and Bridget had figured out that if she didn't come along, the girls would stay in the tub until, as he'd warned them, the water turned to ice and they'd be stuck there until spring thaw. After a sisterly debate that ended with Jack putting them on a countdown, book story won out. Next there was the issue of which Christmas book of the two Bridge held up.

"The girl and the singing insect," Sofia said, shooting from the tub, water droplets flying. She hopped from the tub and Jack caught her up in a towel.

"The mouse sister and the big bed with the small blanket," Isabella said. "It's longer."

A huge advantage that Sofia agreed to.

"I'd choose the same, girls," Jack said, rubbing down Sofia. "Anything to spend a minute longer with Bridge."

"More like anything to put off lights-out," Bridget said. "I'll meet you in the bedroom, girls."

That cue was like a starting gun for them, as they raced through teeth brushing and getting into pajamas to cuddle down with their new favorite person. And his long-time favorite.

Since they were reading a book tonight, they all had to squeeze close together to see the pictures amid the heap of toys, books, clothes and girl-related detritus. He really ought to sort through it all, which became too apparent when Bridge finished reading and returned the hardcover to the stack of library books on the bedside table and they all cascaded to the floor.

"Here," Bridget said, "I can move a bunch of Auntie Penny's stuff—" she picked up three ceramic figurines of cats, a flashlight and a bottle of lotion "—and put it in the drawer."

She opened it and froze. She turned around to look at Jack and then Isabella.

"What?" He flipped himself over the bed to see. Inside the drawer were a sandwich bag of sunflower seeds, another of unshelled peanuts, two juice boxes, two granola bars, a sandwich bag of raisins and a jar of green olives.

"Is this yours, Isabella?" Jack said.

She looked equal parts guilty and resolved. She gave a single nod.

Bridget gently closed the drawer and Jack followed her lead. "Okay," he said. "Just so we know and don't take it. Okay?"

She nodded again.

"I'll take the knickknacks to my— Deidre's

room," Bridget said, as if Isabella's hoarding was as normal as pie. "Good night, girls."

"Good night, Bridgie," Sofia said. Isabella's quiet reply came a couple of beats later.

"Is Bridgie angry at me?" Isabella whispered as Jack kissed her good-night.

"No, no."

"She'll still give me cinnamon buns?"

"Yes," Jack said. "For as long as you want." He had an idea. "Me or Bridgie's cinnamon buns?"

"You," Sofia said. "I guess."

"You," Isabella said. Jack's ego swelled. "Because if you brought us to Bridgie's cinnamon buns, then you can bring us more food." And deflated.

CHAPTER TEN

BRIDGET HAD FORGOTTEN how much mind space a date with Jack occupied. Having lost the bet by a lousy twelve bucks on Saturday night, she set the skating date with him for Tuesday. Since then, she'd checked the weather half a dozen times a day to make sure the expected temperature didn't dip beyond the already chilly minus seventeen degrees Celsius. She sneaked two portions of the specialty hot chocolate from the house to the restaurant. She got her skates sharpened. She'd debated if she should wear her snow pants or go with leggings underneath her jeans. She splurged on a pink toque with fleece lining and matching gloves, justifying it as a Christmas present to herself.

At least she was keeping her excitement to herself. Jack blabbed to everyone.

"Mel," he said, pouring him his dark roast on Monday, "you're the guy to talk to about getting a good deal. How might I go about getting a pair of used skates by Tuesday at eight thirty in the evening?"

Loud enough for the whole restaurant to hear. Marlene, at the next table, perked right up. "That's awfully specific," she said. "What happens then?"

"Funny you should ask. Bridget and I are going skating on the lake," he said, topping her cup without her prompting.

"You mean doing laps as a kind of sponsored thing for the Brigade?" News about the Brigade had spread through the town like spring cracks on the lake ice.

"Nope. Just me and Bridget." At the counter packaging up a dozen holiday buns for Daphne, Bridget felt all eyes turn to her.

"Say, Jack," she said, "should we have the town run an announcement on their highway road-alert signs?"

"I think that's a lovely idea," Daphne said hurriedly. "The skating, not the signs. Mel and I were out there yesterday with all the nieces and nephews. It was just lovely."

"Lovely? Wobbling around on blades in the frozen dark?" Marlene shrank under Daphne's quelling stare. "All right, all right. Lovely, it is."

And if the restaurant crowd wasn't bad

enough, home life was even more excruciating.

"Just so you know," Jack had announced during Sunday supper, when they were trying to figure out who would decorate the Sandersons' tree outside and who would bake Elsie McPherson her family recipe for molasses cookies, "that Bridget is unavailable Tuesday evening."

"Uh, okay," Krista said, with a questioning lift to her voice.

"Good. I just wanted to get that out there." He grinned at Bridget, leaving her to explain or, worse, suffer through his shameless telling.

"Yeah, okay," she said. "We're going out skating Tuesday night. Down at the lake, after you girls are in bed. For an hour."

"Or two," Jack amended. "We might go out for hot chocolate afterward."

"Hot chocolate," Sofia said dreamily. "Can I come?"

"No," Isabella said. "We're going to be in bed."

"That's right," Jack said, his grin still in place. "Just me and Bridget." His voice dropped as if they were the only ones there at the table, without her whole entire family staring, their forks suspended.

Bridget said, "We won't be skating alone. Other people will be there. Tons."

"Well," Deidre said, "then we need to schedule for someone to be here while they're out."

"I can stay here," Mara said, "and wrap presents for the Giffords."

"Oh," said Krista, "that reminds me to bring back ribbon from the shop. Rebekah said I can have ten yards of whatever I want. What kind should I get?"

Answering that question took the rest of supper, during which Jack thankfully made no further comment.

That didn't stop Krista and Mara. They crept upstairs the second the house fell quiet and burrowed under the covers on either side of Bridget. "So it's a date, then," Krista said into her ear.

"Shush. He can hear."

"I'm whispering."

"He can hear what customers are thinking, he can hear you."

That didn't stop Mara. "Are you and Jack getting back together?" she whispered into Bridget's other ear.

"No," Bridget said. "We're going skating because I lost a bet with him at work. He earned more tips than me."

Krista said, "I don't believe that."

Mara looked skeptical, too.

"I think you purposely blew it," Krista said, "because you wanted to go on a date with him but didn't want to admit it."

Exactly what Jack claimed, which didn't surprise her. That Krista thought so suggested there might be truth behind it. Or at least, a willingness on her part to lose. She hadn't thrown the bet, but neither could she bring herself to care that she had lost. Quite the opposite. "Think what you want."

Krista never had a problem doing that. "You two should get back together. It's been twelve years, you guys have clearly been holding out for one another and, let's face it, you're not getting any younger."

"I'm thirty-one, not fifty-one. Just because I am the oldest of us, doesn't mean that I'm old, period."

"It would be nice," Mara mused. "You're the missing piece for Jack and his girls. You'd turn them into a family."

And that was the problem. Her sisters and Deidre all seemed to think it highly convenient for her and Jack to become romantic partners because, hey, they were partners in everything else. Once upon a time only their love joined them together. Now it was something that happened on a weekday evening for an hour or two.

Somehow they'd become the stereotypical married-with-kids couple without the courtship, proposal, wedding or honeymoon years.

And, yes, love was more than moonlight and roses, but well, a little romance helped.

As Jack tied a skate, the lace broke.

"Didn't Mel say the laces needed replacing?" Bridget was already making figure eights in front of where he was sitting. Raring to join her, he'd hauled on the laces too hard.

"I thought they'd last one time," Jack said. "Maybe I can tie a knot and relace them. You go and skate while I do this." He'd already seen her look longingly at the soaring Christmas tree, with its multicolored lights, in the center of the skating area.

Instead, she sat beside him on the bench and examined his skate under the beam of one of the floodlights staged around the skating area. "Jack, it's totally shot. It'll break again if you retie it."

"I'll go out on my boots," he said. No way was he giving up on his date with Bridget. She was wearing the cutest pink toque and matching gloves, and underneath her coat a pink sweater peeked out. He'd see the rest later when they had hot chocolate. She knew he liked her best in pink. Though really he'd take her in any color, but in high school she'd nagged him into picking a color, and so he'd settled on the one she happened to be wearing at the time.

"You tell everyone about going out with me, and then you don't have proper equipment," she scolded, untying her skates.

"Go do your thing. I can watch."

"I fully intend to. And, no, you're not going to walk and watch. That's creepy."

She brought out a Swiss Army knife. Jack experienced a happy shock. "Is that the one I gave you back in high school?"

"Could be," she said and cut off part of her lace. She handed it to him. "Use this."

"But now we've got two broken laces," he said. "What are you going to do?"

"I wrapped lace around my ankle three times it was so long. I'll rethread and be good to go."

He sat with her lace. She'd wrecked her

own lace to fix his, to make it so they could still have this time together.

Bent over relacing, she glanced at him. "What's the matter? Hurry up."

He evened the laces, his and hers together, tied a knot and started to do up his skate. He saw they were at roughly the same spot. "Race you."

In answer she worked faster. He bit back a grin and leaned in to give her a run for her money. Her blades hit the ice while he still fumbled with his final knot.

"I let you win," he said. "Like you let me win double or nothing, so you could go skating with me."

"And why would you let me win now?"

"Because I'm a gentleman."

She snorted. "Because all your years away have turned your fingers into little, fragile, tropic-loving stumps of their former polar greatness."

Thirteen years in hot, dry or wet countries had definitely done a number on his skating skills. "This is not," he said, his legs wobbling and splaying like a newborn giraffe's, "like riding a bike."

Bridget did a neat crossover in front of him, her blade slicing the ice.

"Show-off," he grumbled, not caring if she broke into an Olympic routine of spins and sowcows, or whatever that word was. All the more reason to watch her.

"Ah, you poor thing." She stretched out her hands to him. "C'mon. Hang on and we'll do this together."

He grabbed hold of her hands. He'd baby-step all night long if it meant keeping her close. At the Christmas tree, she tipped back her head, the floodlights and the thousand pinpoints of colored light casting her face in a warm glow. "Guess how many lights there are."

"I dunno. Do you?"

"Yes, but I want you to guess."

"I hate to jump to conclusions. Let's count."

"Yeah, because we've nothing better to do."

"We don't." His words came out scratchy and low, because suddenly he couldn't manage to speak in a normal voice.

"Jack—" she said warningly. But she didn't pull away from his hand.

"One, two—"

"Six thousand, two hundred," she blurted. "I read it in the paper. Apparently, there's a really bored public-works employee who calculated by the number of strands how many there are."

"I was just counting off the seconds it would take before you said something."

She growled in annoyance and snatched away her hand. Thinking quickly, he slipped and slid, then clutched at her coat sleeve, pulling them back together.

"Seriously?" she said, and took his hand again.

He hid his smile below his zipped-up coat collar. This time when they skated around the tree, he threw in a wobble or two. They saw a single guy lapping the perimeter so fast that his blades cut a harsh, static noise, and a teenage couple. The girl shrieked and squealed at every bump in the ice, and her boyfriend swept to the rescue every time.

Bridget sighed. "She's doing that to get his attention."

"Pathetic," Jack said and stumbled.

They'd skated a little way from the tree, but he could still make out the flash in her eyes. "Are you telling me you purposely—"

His expression must've told the story because she tried to pull back. Not this again. He held on, squeezing her hands in their pink mittens. "Yes. I'm telling you. If my public-service announcements these past two days haven't convinced you, then let me tell you here and now that I want you. I want for us to be more than business partners. I said that from the start and nothing has changed. We haven't had the time or the energy since I've come back to act on it, but it's there. It's always been there."

"If it's always been there," she said, "why did it take you twelve years to act on it?"

"I'd already decided three years ago," he said. "When I came back for Dad's funeral. You were there with Penny at the service, and afterward serving lunch. I caught glimpses of you all afternoon. And, Bridge, all I wanted was this, like we are now, you at my side, holding me up, getting me through that painful day. But I couldn't. I'd given up my right."

"If you'd asked, I would have."

"I know. But I wanted more than your sympathy."

"I would've given it," she whispered.

By *it*, what did she mean? "Losing someone you love can make you rethink your life. I saw you across the room and I made up my mind that I would wrap up my dealings with the agency and get back to you. But—"

"But you changed your mind." She spoke lightly enough, but he could hear the bitterness.

"I didn't change my mind. That was the thing. I went there originally to make a difference, and after nearly a decade, I still felt I hadn't. I didn't want to come back having nothing to show for it. It seemed like a waste of our years apart. Like I'd let you down all over again. So this opportunity to create a charity came up, and a few more months became a year, a year and a half and then more money, more promises. In the end—" He broke off. "In the end, I screwed up big-time."

"But you came back with the girls," Bridge prompted. "You made a world of difference for them."

"With Penny's—my mother's— help," he said. "And yours, though you didn't know it."

"True, but I'm glad Auntie Penny did it." Bridget chipped the ice with her blade tip. "I wish she hadn't snuck behind my back. I wouldn't have stopped her."

"But for me to have the girls, you've had to sacrifice. The restaurant is at risk, and that's your livelihood. I don't want to cause you more pain."

She shook her head, the pom-pom on her toque bobbing madly. "Believe me, you're not causing me pain. Other than—" she stretched her fingers in his grasp "—a bit here."

He relaxed his hold but didn't release her. "You know that I don't have much. That doesn't make me proud, believe me. I know that for the next few months we're threading the needle to get through this mess, but I know we can —" he tugged on her hands and she glided close, toe-to-toe "—together."

He hesitated, giving her the chance to push away. But she didn't, and he touched his mouth to hers. Their lips were cool at first, but as he held still and she deepened the contact, coolness shifted to the heat of a long, dreamy kiss. Thirteen years, but their lips had not forgotten.

When their kiss ended, he drew her into a hug, not wanting their contact to end. "I'm not going to screw it up this time, Bridge," he whispered. "I promise you."

WEDNESDAY FLEW BY for Bridget with hardly a second to herself, much less with Jack. The night's event of tree decorating at the house was the closest they'd come to being together all day. Bridget fastened the lights on the tree, while he fed her the strand.

"I could've done this yesterday on my day

off," Krista said from her station with Mara setting up the Christmas village on the mantel. "You made it out that there was this big secret to putting up lights. Once I had to put lights on twelve Christmas trees for this store display. They were huge. And I had to do them by myself. I didn't have an assistant, like you do."

"If I'd known what an exhausting experience this is," Jack said, "I would've been there for you, Krista."

His experience was to hold coils of light while Bridget fixed them to the branches. She paused to face him. "Flown halfway around the world to put up Christmas lights?"

"Seeing how absolutely riveting it is to circle this tree a hundred times, of course I would've dropped everything." Definite sarcasm, but there was warmth behind it that made her own cheeks heat up.

She glanced away to catch Deidre studying them with open speculation. Deidre was in charge of setting out the Christmas books Auntie Penny had saved from when she was a girl.

Deidre made a soft exclamation. "I'd forgotten all about this one!"

She held up a Little Golden book with its

classic golden embossed spine. *Walt Disney's Santa's Toy Workshop.* "Our mother read this to us, and then when we could read, Penny and I read it to each other. Penny always fussed about why Santa and his wife had to rely on elves instead of their kids helping."

"That's easy," Krista said. "The kids grew up and moved away and never came back."

"Like sisters," Bridget couldn't help mumbling.

"We're back now, aren't we?"

They were. To stay.

"I'll read it to the girls tomorrow night," Bridget said. Jack had pushed up the girls' bedtime tonight by a half hour by eliminating storytime, with the promise that tomorrow they'd wake to a Christmas miracle in the living room.

On the sofa, Deidre flipped through the pages. "I cared more that Santa got to travel the entire world in a single night. Penny spun stories about how Santa discovered his long-lost parents. Something to do with how the cookies laid out for him tasted exactly like those when he was a little boy."

Krista was setting down a church with a rickety steeple as she observed, "That's ironic, considering how she sort of turned Jack into the same kind of Santa."

Bridget felt Jack tense. Rejection sucked, whether it hit you at six years of age, or as an adult. She unlooped a coil of lights, her fingers skimming his, and he visibly relaxed.

"Honestly, I can't even wrap my head around the fact that Penny is my mother. That you two are my cousins."

Krista pointed playfully at Bridget. "You three."

"No kissing cousins here," Deidre said. She raised her hands at Bridget's glare. "What? It's true. You two are dating, aren't you?"

Krista and Mara looked on as if Bridget was about to declare the last number on their near-to-winning lottery ticket. "We had a date yesterday, yes. You all know that."

"After twelve years, the first of many more," Jack agreed. "And we're having another soon."

"We are?" Bridget said.

"We are," he confirmed. "A romantic dinner for two at the restaurant," he informed the rest of the room.

"Then you *are* dating again!" Krista said.

"Let's hope it turns out better than last time," Deidre said.

"Mom!" Krista said. "That's not the kindest thing to say."

"I'm not saying it to them." She fixed Jack with a pointed look. "I'm saying it to him. He knows exactly what I mean."

The engagement.

"What? What?" Krista said.

"They might as well know," Jack said quietly to Bridget. "I don't think we can exactly keep this a family secret."

He was right. Might as well pop it open like a Christmas cracker. "Back when Jack and I broke up, we were more than dating. We were…engaged."

Krista turned to Mara. "Didn't I tell you that there was more to it?"

"You did," Mara said, using a wet wipe to clean the doors of a miniature school. "And didn't I say that it was none of our business?"

"Of course, it's our business. What happened?"

Deidre, Bridget noticed, was back to reading children's books, knees crossed, as if she had nothing to do with setting off her daughters.

"Jack went overseas and then a year in, he called and—"

"We agreed that it wasn't working out,"

Jack said quickly. He was trying to save face for her.

Bridget worked the lights on the tree, Jack silent as he fed them to her. The whole room was silent. Nothing seemed to segue nicely from the fact that two people who'd once been engaged were decorating a tree together.

But leave it to Krista to find a connection. "I understand about long-distance relationships having a low rate of success."

Right, her social-media breakup with Prince Philip wasn't much more than twelve days ago, much less twelve years. Bridget left the tree and hugged Krista hard. "I'm so sorry." And then because she didn't want Krista to feel alone, she said, "If truth be told, Jack was trying to soften the fact that he was the one who dumped me. And, hey, I'm okay."

Krista pushed free of Bridget, her hurt expression hardening into anger. She whirled on Jack. "You dumped Bridget? Were you out of your mind?"

This was unexpected—and loud. "Krista," Bridget said, "don't wake the girls."

Jack stood with lights coiled around his arms and shrugged. "Looking back on it, I think I was. I mean, I'd have to be, right?"

His admission took the wind out of Krista's

sails, so she tacked back to Bridget. "Why didn't you tell us? Mara, did she tell you?"

Mara shook her head. "No, but we were teenagers ourselves. And I'm sorry, Krista, but you were a full-blown teenager. I don't think we would've been much support."

Krista didn't sound convinced. "I would have so kicked your butt, Jack Holdstrom."

"Need I remind you," Mara said wearily. "that he was on the other side of the world?"

Krista gripped Bridget's arm. "He broke off your engagement...over the phone?"

"Yes, but how else could he have done it?" Jack answered, his eyes on Bridget. "I could've flown home and said it to your face. I could've seen how you looked when you said 'I get it.'"

Bridget didn't want him to be like this. Him against a room of females, against his own flesh and blood because of something that he'd already apologized for and she'd already forgiven.

She slipped another length of lights from his arm. "Sure. Now, how about we all get back to creating a Christmas miracle here?"

Krista took Bridget's lead, but not before rounding on Jack one last time. "You are officially on cousin probation. One more incident and I swear—" Krista clamped her mouth shut, then frowned. No doubt conjuring up suitably heinous retribution.

"But there won't be another incident, will there?" Deidre said to Jack.

"No, Auntie Deidre," Jack said, his eyes on Bridget, "there won't be."

Bridget ducked his relentless gaze. She couldn't escape how much her family wanted them together. Or how much she wanted to be his one and only. His kiss last night had torn apart all the careful stitching over her heart. And she'd woken to him still here, in the same house as her, living and working with her. Exactly as she'd once planned, and as he seemed to want again.

There was nothing on earth to hold her back from taking what Jack seemed so eager to give her. And yet…she was.

What was the matter with her?

CHAPTER ELEVEN

"ARE YOU WAITING UP for me?"

She was. Bridget had left all the Christmas lights ablaze, the tree in full glitter. Colored lights trailed through the fireplace garland, up and around the front windows, through the bookcase, across the entrance and then descending back into the tree boughs. It was cozy, glittery...and romantic.

She shut the cooking magazine she was flipping through. "I might have been."

Jack stretched out on top of her quilt and she tossed him one of her pillows, which he propped his head on. She wondered if he remembered when—

"You remember us doing this when you were in high school? We'd pull out this sofa bed, heap it with pillows and eat popcorn and watch bad movies until your aunt would come down halfway through the night and tell me to get on home."

Bridget experienced a stab of sorrow. "She won't tell you that anymore."

Jack covered her hand with his and squeezed. "True," he said softly, "but I think that if I stay down here for too long tonight, *my* aunt will send me back to bed."

"Deidre? She's a free spirit."

"Free." Jack flipped to his side, raised himself up on his elbow. He let go of her hand and she instantly missed the contact. "She's a mother bear around you girls."

Bridget was about to tell him that mother bears didn't leave their cubs for months on end to be raised by their aunt. But Deidre had changed. She was there for them all now. She had taken over much of the organizing of the Brigade and the household. In the past two weeks, she'd become a fixed part of their lives. "Good to hear," Bridget conceded.

"And after tonight, I have my cousins on my case. Krista will kill me if I break up with you. Not—" he reclaimed her hand "—that I intend to."

"You did once," she murmured.

"I did but this time there's no one to interfere. In fact, everyone in your family is now very pro-Jack."

"What do you mean *now*? My family always liked you."

She wore pajamas patterned with reindeer—right, she still needed to get this year's Christmas pajamas from Cozy Comforts—and he began to walk his fingers from one reindeer to the other up her sleeve in a slow, meditative stroll. "Between dealing with spreadsheets and lost mittens, I've been thinking about how I didn't realize back then how… upset you were." He jumped to a reindeer at her elbow and rubbed its nose, which lined up with a muscle in her arm. A tense muscle that began to soften under his touch.

"That was my fault," Bridget said. "I wish I'd come up to you the first time you came back for your fundraiser, walked onto the stage, grabbed the mic and told everyone out there what a jerk you were. Dumping me over the phone after I'd waited for a year to marry you. A year secretly flipping through magazines and checking out engagement rings at the jewelers and drawing up an invitation list. Told them you weren't a good cause at all."

His fingers stopped moving on her muscle. His eyes sparked. "I wish you had. Because that's my point. Did you tell Penny how you felt?"

"I didn't have to. I was a mess for weeks after your call. I bawled in front of a customer. Auntie Penny ordered me into the kitchen and told me to shape up or I wasn't coming back. That scared me." Bridget suddenly remembered what else she'd said. "She said I should be glad that you hadn't left me pregnant." She met his gaze. "I see now why she said that."

Jack gave a soft grunt in agreement. "Explains, too, why she kept us apart."

"You mean…?" Bridget gave a wave at their present positioning on the bed.

"No, I mean our engagement." Jack pulled himself up into a full sitting position. "Bridge, after we broke up, I called Penny. It was a month to the day. I wasn't doing so well, either, and I was kind of hoping that—that we could have another go at it. I asked her how you were. She said you moped a little the first week or two, but you were fine now. I remember her exact words. 'You could talk to her yourself, but she's out with Quinn Jenkins.'"

"Quinn? We never dated. He was into short blondes. He married one and has three kids."

"I know. I assumed it didn't work out between you two, proving once again that you could move on from any relationship."

"No. I—I never really moved on from us. She never told me that you'd called."

Bridget tracked the lights around the room. She and Auntie Penny had sat in the same living room last year, cozied up watching Christmas movies, love stories about family and holidays. Cheesy and irresistible. Every year, Bridget had thought of Jack while snuggling with the woman who had connived to break them up. No, no, it didn't make sense. "And you think it's because she was afraid you would get me pregnant and leave me? Ever since finding out you were her son, I thought she kept us apart because we were kinda related."

"I figure she didn't trust me," Jack said. "A few times I'd call for you when we were still together and you weren't in. She'd talk about all the things you were involved in. I think she was testing to see how loyal I was, how much I'd stick by you. And in the end, I proved her right. I let you down. I let her down. I was no better than my blood father."

Bridget raised herself up to look him in the eye. "Listen to me. She loved you." Then it hit Bridget, swelled in her stomach like she'd swallowed an entire warm, sticky blob of dough. She fell back. "Oh, I see. I was the one who wasn't good enough for you."

"What? No. The exact opposite. I wasn't good enough for her darling Bridget."

But Bridget couldn't deny that unbaked lump in her gut. "You were her son. She always talked about the good things you did. I ran the restaurant by myself while she organized those fundraisers for you. She saw you as the real savior of the world. Me, I was just someone who needed saving."

He lifted a strand of her hair, spiraled it around his finger. "Bridge, we all need saving. Why else did I come back to you?"

"But she left everything of hers to you. That proves how much she loved you. I wasn't even mentioned in her will." She couldn't hide her hurt.

"She'd already given you half."

"Are you kidding me? I bought out her half. Yes, it was on easy terms, but I earned my title. I considered it fair, but she used my money to help you. That's a fact. I see that now. She loved you. Loved you way more than my blood mother ever loved me."

Jack wrapped his arm around her shoulders and pulled her close. "Tell me," he said.

Bridget felt her memories, already shaken

loose by his revelations about Auntie Penny, begin to tumble out.

There was a scuffle on the stairs and Deidre, ghostlike in a long white dressing gown, appeared on the stair landing. "I don't care if this house belongs to the two of you. Both of you, to bed. To your *own* beds."

Jack and Bridget exchanged squelched smiles. He sneaked in a kiss on her cheek before leaping from her bed. Deidre let him pass before launching a look of reproof at Bridget. "And you. Get to sleep. You're already running on fumes."

Bridget did as she was told. It felt delicious to have Deidre go all mother bear on her.

INTO BRIDGET'S MIXED-UP DREAM of burnt cinnamon buns and oven mitts for Christmas stockings crept a tickling across her cheek. A small voice penetrated her sleep. "Bridgie? Bridgie, you awake?"

Sofia. Bridget pried open her sleep-gummed eyelids. She fumbled for her phone. Fifteen minutes before her alarm was set to go off. "I am now." She turned from her side onto her back, and Sofia snuggled right in, her head on Bridget's shoulder.

"The Christmas miracle is beautiful," Sofia whispered in perfect English.

After Jack had gone upstairs, Bridget meant to turn off the lights but had fallen asleep. Now she was glad, if it meant waking up to Sofia cuddled tight against her.

Sofia turned her head. "Isabella. Come on."

Bridget hadn't noticed Isabella sitting on the stair. "There's plenty of room," she said and flipped back the quilt invitingly.

Isabella left the stairs but not to get into bed. Instead, under the low shine of the lights, she prowled about the living room, examining the tree ornaments, the little figurines in the Christmas village, the Christmas books. She touched each thing with a kind of hesitancy, as if she might disturb its peace and it would crumble or fly away. Bridget wished that she could get inside Isabella's mind, if only for a bit, to see what made her tick, to find a way to let her know that she didn't need to fear for her life or her sister's ever again.

The release from that base fear was the greatest gift a damaged child could receive. Bridget knew that for a fact.

There was a heavy tread on the stairs and Jack appeared. "There you two are," he said in English.

"It's okay," Sofia said. "Don't worry."

"Be happy," Isabella said in a dead serious tone.

Jack sat on a stair. "Kinda hard when you two aren't in your beds when I wake up."

Isabella squeezed beside him on the stair and he scooted over for her. "Thank you, Jack. For the Christmas miracle. It is very interesting."

Jack looked over at Bridget, a smile playing at the edge of his mouth. The exchange between parents when their kids say something cute or memorable. Bridget could get used to this, for sure.

Sofia stretched up and kissed Bridget on the cheek. "Thank you, Bridgie."

Her first kiss from Sofia. Bridget looked over to see if Jack had noticed. His small smile had broken into a very large one.

Isabella had also noticed, but she wasn't scowling. In fact, her gaze drifted to the open spot in the bed.

But then Bridget's alarm went off, and the moment, like so many others in her life, was gone.

"READY FOR CHRISTMAS?"

Jolene's question startled Bridget from her

discreet bit of shut-eye outside of Sofia's kindergarten class.

"I'm sorry, were you napping while standing up?" Jolene said. She studied Bridget. "You do look tired."

She was. Decorating the living room and then her late-night conversation with Jack followed by her early, though welcome wake-up call by the girls had left Bridget an exhausted combo of wired and wiped, like having an adrenaline rush and crash at the same time. Jolene's makeup was perfect—she had that deliberately casual look going—and her kids, one on the hip and another bright-eyed in the infant car seat, were dressed as if ready for a fashion shoot. "I admit my days are full. Busy getting other people ready for the holidays."

"Right, the restaurant and Bridget's Brigade. It's working out?"

"For another couple of weeks. I think you're scheduled for early next week. Music system in garage, right?"

"Yes. Quinn's home next Wednesday and I would love to have it there when he rolls in. I'd do it myself but I'm writing the test for my bookkeeping course next week."

"How do you manage?"

Jolene's mascara-enhanced eyes widened even more. "I could ask you the same thing."

Melanie Lever rounded the hallway corner. "Ah, there you are," she said to Bridget. "I was hoping to catch you before you left."

Was Isabella in trouble again? Had a kid gotten sick from the buns? Had it started an entire classroom fight? Ms. Lever must've interpreted her expression. "All's good. Just a word about a separate matter."

The kindergarten door swung open, and the class began to spill out. "Do you have time to meet in my office after you've gathered the girls?" Ms. Lever said.

No easy matter to agree to. Isabella had to be cautioned that she'd have to wait for her treat. She'd glowered, but had trailed behind Bridget cooperatively enough. On the way into the principal's office, Isabella stopped at the main office counter.

"Excuse me. I would like two bags of cereal, please."

The front staff didn't waste time fulfilling her request. Part of Bridget wanted to refuse this small act of charity. The other part told her to shut up and let Isabella experience what a generous, abundant place she now lived in.

Once Isabella and Sofia were settled on the

principal's sofa with their snacks, Bridget sat across from Ms. Lever who said, "Everybody loves, loves, loves your buns."

That was from left field. "It's hard to go wrong with sugar and cinnamon on bread."

"That's what we were thinking," the principal said. "In the past, teachers have decided what they'd like to do to spread the festive season into the community. We have our traditional holiday concert, of course, but each classroom usually does their own thing, too.

"Our staff meeting yesterday was to bring it all together, but teachers are struggling this year. The sing-along at the seniors' center was canceled, the shoeboxes for the annual campaign weren't shipped for whatever reason and on it goes. Your Christmas Crates campaign came up and we thought we'd partner as a school with you."

Way, way out in left field. "What did you have in mind?"

"We were thinking of a straightforward sales campaign. The kids take order forms home and sell your cinnamon buns. As the orders come in, you fill them with all proceeds going to the campaign."

"That," Bridget said, "would be wonderful." Absolutely, mind-blowingly wonderful. "How many do you anticipate selling?"

"We don't have much more than a week to sell, but that added urgency might work for us, and among a student population of four hundred and fifty... You sell them by the half dozen?"

"Individual, in fours and a baker's dozen, thirteen."

Ms. Lever scrunched her eyes in mental calculation. "I'd say...one or two thousand."

"Two...thousand?"

"It's Christmas. And even with the economy, everyone wants to eat treats. And your buns are yummy. It's for a local cause. I don't think I'm being overly optimistic."

Bridget did her own mental calculations. Her Christmas minicinnis, iced and decorated, were priced at four dollars. Subtract out the costs—not including the labor—and the profit was three-fifty. Two thousand at an average of three-fifty a bun would bring in seven grand, which could easily finance Christmas Crates.

Bridget refrained from jumping up and down. "Let's get started, then."

"We'll have to work out some kind of financial tracking system," Ms. Lever said.

"I have a separate account already in place," Bridget said. "Parents can write checks out to Christmas Crates. And the school will have copies of the orders to make sure the cash balances out."

"School policy requires another person to make deposits generated here at the school straight into the account. Signing authority isn't even required because it's solely for deposits. We just need anyone, really. I'll see if there's a volunteer."

Someone already committed to the cause... like Jolene.

Bridget smiled. "I happen to know of a parent perfectly qualified to help."

Wow. She actually knew people at the school now, thanks to the girls. She'd hoped to show the girls her world, and here they'd stretched hers.

"Two thousand!" Krista squealed so loud Jack swore his eardrum nearly burst. Beside her, Deidre dropped her fork to the plate. "That's about, let's see—"

"Seven thousand dollars," Bridget said. "As much as eight, depending on the size of the orders."

Everybody around the dinner table, even

the girls, jabbered about all that could be done with the money. He seemed to be the only one who noticed the big picture. He caught Deidre's eye. Maybe the only two.

"Who's going to make these?"

"Me," Bridget said instantly.

"On top of all the work you do at the restaurant, on top of our evening service, on top of keeping up the display case, which, by the way, will take a hit in sales, because of the school kids making sales for the Christmas Crusade."

"Brigade," Krista corrected.

"Feels more like a crusade to drive everyone in this house into the ground. We'll be so wiped we'll sleep through Christmas Day."

Sofia waved frantically. "If we sleep through the day, when will we open presents?"

"We won't," Deidre said, deadpan. "We'll put them all away until next year."

"How about I help Bridgie?" countered Sofia.

"Thanks, Sofia," Bridget said. "I'll need help to put labels on the packages. Also, you and Isabella need to remind me to pick up the orders daily from the principal when I come to get you at school."

Bridget would fill those orders or die in the attempt. Since there was no talking her out of it, he'd have to see her through to the exhausting end. "Fine. I'll pick up the girls. I'll pick up the orders."

She paused. "If it's no trouble."

She didn't want to trouble him about picking up an envelope when he was there, anyway, but had no trouble wearing herself out to make sure an entire town got her cinnamon buns so she could turn around and give away the profits. But he couldn't deny that between these sales and proceeds from the Brigade, he might put to rest his debt to the Spirit Lake donors.

"Bridge, I'll help."

"You're already—"

"Busy. We all are. Just accept help. Okay?"

Bridget nodded reluctantly, as if agreeing to painful, unavoidable surgery. Was it all help, or just his that she couldn't accept?

"So then," Deidre said, "that leaves you and me, Jack."

"And me," Sofia reminded her.

Deidre tugged Sofia's braid. "And you. How about you and Auntie Dee take care of the labeling, and packaging, while Jack and Bridgie make the buns?"

"Deal," Jack said before Bridget could interrupt.

"And I'll help when I can, wherever I can," Mara said.

"Ditto," Krista said. "Providing I don't eat the buns first."

"There are two thousand," Isabella cautioned.

Krista shoveled in another forkful of lasagna. "It'll take a while, for sure."

"Jack's help is all I need," Bridget said and then looked cross.

He got distinct pleasure from seeing her annoyed at needing him. "Only I have mastered the correct insertion of toothpicks into cinnamon buns. Without me," he mock-boasted to Isabella and Sofia, "the whole production line would grind to a halt."

"Honest to Pete, Sofia could do your job."

"Promote me."

"Fine, can you count by twos, fours, sixes and twelves?"

"If I can't, my calculator can."

"Tomorrow, then, you are in charge of making the order form and getting it to the school by noon so it can go home with the kids."

"How much are we charging?"

The question launched a debate between them. At one point, Bridget's attention switched to Krista, who was mouthing something to Mara. Jack didn't catch it all but he thought the last bit was *tri-ckle*. Bridget looked ready to pop a vein. Krista's message clearly involved Bridget and likely him, too. Only what was going on between them was far more than a trickle.

FRIDAY AFTERNOON BRIDGET stopped at the house to drop off Isabella and to change for the dinner service.

Mara was at the kitchen island alone, frowning at paint chip samples. Isabella dropped her puck and shed her outerwear and headed downstairs, off to get Sofia for their minicinnis.

"Where's Deidre and Krista?"

"Picking up a donation and at work. I'm trying to make a decision about neutrals." Mara held up three samples. "Okay, what do you think?"

Bridget wondered if Mara couldn't distinguish between the shades, and that's why she was asking. Mara had been here for a month now, and Bridget hadn't found the time to have a serious talk about her eyes. She hoped Krista was being a better sister than her.

But she could find the time to choose a color. "This one. You really should take them to the unit and see what the light does to them there."

Isabella surfaced from the downstairs and ran upstairs.

"I know but I wanted to narrow it down a bit. Who knew there were so many?"

"I remember going through the same pain when renovating the restaurant. What have you decided about flooring?"

"Krista's pushing for planking, and I can't decide. It's easier to maintain but carpeting might make clients feel more comfortable."

Isabella appeared beside Bridget. "Where's Sofia?"

"She's not downstairs?"

"No."

Bridget pointed up. "Upstairs?"

"No."

Bridget looked at Mara who frowned. "I don't know."

Panic rippled through Bridget. "What do you mean you don't know?"

"I—"

"Sofia!" Bridget yelled. "Tell us where you are."

Nothing.

"Did she go outside?"

"I didn't see—"

"Of course, you didn't see."

Guilt spread across Mara's face.

Bridget turned away. "I'll check the backyard."

It was empty. Bridget flung open the garage door. The inside was filled to bursting with Christmas Crate stuff. No Sofia. In snow boots and a thin shirt, Bridget tore around to the front, calling out Sofia's name.

"Hi!"

"Sofia! Where—"

"I'm up here."

Bridget looked up to see Sofia, all smiles, peering over the edge of the roof. How had she— Of course. The ladder was still there from when Jack had strung up outdoor lights. Bridget was going to kill him, though likely he'd beat himself up, anyway.

"I'm making snow angels," Sofia said. "Angels on high. Come see them."

Later, Bridget amazed herself by how she climbed the ladder without giving a second thought to her fears.

"See?"

Snow angels covered every available white space of the roof. "Wow. You've been busy."

"I made some on the other side, too. Want to see?" Sofia scrambled up the side as easily as if she mounted a grassy slope. Bridget crawled after her, desperate to keep within arm's length.

"Wow," Bridget repeated at the angel-patterned snow.

"Is everything okay?" Mara called from below.

"Yes," Bridget said. "We're just looking at Sofia's snow angels and then we'll be right down."

"Sofia!" Isabella's angry voice tore upward like a launched rocket. She yelled something in Spanish and it wasn't good, because Sofia shouted back.

Sofia sighed. "She's so bossy."

"She's worried," Bridget said. "She came home looking for you and couldn't find you. You scared her. You scared all of us."

Fear, not the breeze off the lake, chilled Bridget. The mere mention of the word *scared* made it so. They'd better get off this roof fast. "How about we go down now?"

"Take a picture of it, so we can show everyone."

"I don't have my phone with me."

"Okay, I'll get Jack to do it. Let's go."

Terror immobilized her arms. "You go first, Sofia. Carefully. Tummy against the roof. Okay?"

Sofia shimmied to the top of the ladder.

"Mara?" Bridget called. "She's coming down now."

"Okay, Sofia," Mara said. "Isabella and I are holding the ladder. One step at a time."

From the rattle of the ladder, it sounded as if she was skipping down.

"Your turn," Sofia called.

"I'm holding the ladder," Mara called up. "Take your time."

All the time in the world, and she wasn't going anywhere. She'd die on this roof, frozen into place. Then topple off like a chunk of ice. It was the only way she'd see ground again.

Even moving her mouth was an effort. "Mara," she said, her voice a whisper. She tried again.

Mara probably sensed more than heard her. "Yes?"

Bridget gathered up all her strength to request her last-ditch hope. "Call Jack."

CHAPTER TWELVE

JACK COULD SEE Bridget straddling the highest peak, gripping the roof, hunched over, as if riding a runaway horse. He forcibly slowed his steps from a jog to a walk and didn't call out, not wanting to startle her. She'd probably already seen him.

Mara, Sofia and Isabella were at the bottom of the ladder.

"I hear," Jack said to Sofia in Spanish, "that you climbed this ladder without permission."

"I didn't know I wasn't supposed to," she said, her logic sound.

"True," he said. "I forgot to put away the ladder and that was my fault. I'm sorry."

"You need to apologize to Bridgie. She climbed up there and can't get down."

Another truth. Bridge wouldn't be up there if Sofia hadn't climbed the ladder he'd left there. Jack switched to English for Mara's sake. "I'll help her down. Meanwhile, how about you go inside with Mara?"

He looked questioningly at Mara who bundled the girls inside with promises of hot chocolate and cupcakes. Isabella shot Jack a worried look over her shoulder.

"Everything will be fine," he said. For the second time this month, he'd fielded a distress call from Mara about his girls. Or, in this case, his girl.

Bridge hadn't moved. She didn't even turn her head, as he climbed the roof through Sofia's snow angels. The wing of one angel was inches— *inches*—from the edge of the roof. The second he and Bridge touched down, that ladder was going into the farthest corner of the garage.

She stayed rigid as he slipped behind her, both of them now astride the peak. "Bridge? I'm going to put my arm around you, okay?"

She gave a quick jerk of her head, which he took for acceptance. He settled his arm around her, and holding her had never felt so good. Never before had it been a case of life or broken bones, at the very least. She wouldn't fall now.

She must've thought the same thing because she relaxed against him. "I was fine," she whispered, "but then I…wasn't."

"I'm here now," he said.

"You're mad at me."

"More resigned," he said. "Like when Sofia lost a mitten somewhere between the house and the car. Unbelievable but treatable."

"Like I'm a disease."

"I'm definitely terminal about you."

"That's really tacky," she said. Still, she snuggled against him.

He wrapped both arms around her.

"Ready to go down?"

She drew breath and moved to lift her leg. It stayed put. "I can't," she said. "I can't move."

Jack had no idea how to get her down. He could do something about her shivering, though. He unzipped his jacket and folded it around her as far as it would go. "Here," he said. "Don't worry. You will move. We will get down the ladder. Everything will be fine."

She kept right on shivering.

"Hey, Bridge," he said by way of distraction, "I was thinking that we needed to do Christmas shopping for the girls."

She groaned. "I still need to go to Cozy Comforts and buy my usual Christmas Eve pajamas. Did you want me to pick up something for the girls then?"

"No, I want us to do it together because I

trust your taste." He paused. "I want to put our names on the presents."

If possible, she stiffened even more. "Jack, we hardly know what we're doing."

"I know exactly what I'm doing. Starting with getting you off this roof."

"I know I need to get off. I'm making us late for the dinner service. I just can't make myself *move*."

"Don't worry. Mano and his family can hold down the fort until we get there." He pulled himself as tightly as he could against her. "You must be freezing."

"Yeah. With—" he could actually hear her teeth chatter "—fear."

He believed that. "How did you manage to get yourself up here? You're terrified of heights."

"I already told you I love your girls."

"That must be some kind of love."

She leaned her head against his shoulder. "A higher love."

Jack laughed at her pop-music reference. If she could make a joke, then he was making progress. He wondered to what heights her love for him might take her. Probably to the top of the bathroom step stool Sofia used to brush her teeth.

"You know, being scared of heights is pretty normal. It's our survival instincts kicking in."

"Survival. Right. Sort of the reverse for me."

"Oh?"

"My mother. My biological mother. I'm mostly over the bad things she did, except for this."

"She made you afraid of heights?"

Bridget covered her face with her bare hands. "She made me feel certain I'd never get down."

"Ah." He tried to sound as if he understood, or at least as if he wanted to understand.

"She was always in and out of jail, which meant that I was always in and out of foster care. I don't remember much from those years. Not much from the foster care, anyway, except for the food. There was food every few hours. And I remember a fruit bowl in one house. The rule was you could eat from it anytime, and that bowl was never empty."

"Isabella would've loved that place," Jack said.

"When I was with my mother, I seriously didn't know when I was going to eat next. Once we lived in this old, old house out in the country. Out back was a tree house. A platform, really. But there was a ladder up to it. I liked going there because it felt safe. I could see anyone coming.

"One time, there was food on the counter and I could eat whenever because my mother was in bed. But then she gets up and comes into the kitchen. I'm there about to take a banana. She gets angry, asks me what I'm doing. I panic. I grab up a bunch of food and run. Run straight to the tree house, climb up there one-handed with all the food. I look back, and she's following. Not so fast. She must've still been drunk or high or whatever she was.

"She gets to the ladder and starts to climb it, but can't get herself up it. She falls back and brings down the ladder. She says, 'I'm your mother. Your mother. I'm your mother. You listen. I'm your mother.' Over and over. And then she gets up and leaves. Leaves in a car. Leaves me up there, the ladder flat on the ground. And all I can think is that I'm okay, because I have food."

Jack didn't know what to say, except to wrap himself tighter around her.

"Deidre—Deidre said that when help arrived, I had probably been up there for three days. It took hours and hours to figure out how to get me safely down. I guess it looked as if I'd bolt over the edge whenever they sent someone up.

"She said they finally got the fruit-bowl foster-care dad to come up with an apple. I don't even remember him now. They couldn't take me in because their place was full. But there was a new family I could go to. One with two girls."

"Krista and Mara."

"They were the first people I ever loved."

Jack fought through his quiet rage against Bridget's unknown mother to speak in a light, even voice. "I'm pretty fond of my cousins, too."

"Deidre said they never left me alone. Offered me their clothes, gave me food, let me play with all their toys, brushed my hair. And then I started doing the same for them. She said we were our own self-contained unit. Dad said all he and Deidre needed to do was parachute in supplies."

Jack would hate to have that kind of relationship with Isabella and Sofia. It already grated that his time with them was pushed into the corners of the day.

"There is a ladder here today," he whispered into her ear.

"Yeah."

"Do you feel ready to give it a try?"

"You going to be my fruit-bowl man?"

He kissed the side of her head. "Your hot-chocolate man."

She giggled. A sweet, sweet sound. "Let's do this, then."

And they did. Inch by inch, rung by rung, he coached her down the ladder until both her feet hit the ground. His reward was a hug, as Bridget plastered herself against him. It was hard to pull away, but he had something more important to do.

"I'll meet you inside," he told her and reached for the ladder, "after I get this out of harm's way."

ALONE IN THE restaurant kitchen, Bridget slid two large pans of minicinnis into the fridge for Mano to bake for the breakfast service. She shut off her playlist, and in the ensuing silence she detected faint footsteps above her head from Mara's unit. What would Mara be doing there at quarter to eleven at night?

Every bone in Bridget's body ached for a few hours of sleep. But if it wasn't Mara, then it was an intruder, and she couldn't very well let that carry on. And if it was Mara, well, she had meant to speak with her ever since the incident with Sofia two days ago.

In the unlikely event of the first scenario, Bridget took along a heavy wood cutting board, not risking the chance that something more deadly, like a chef's knife, might be taken from her grasp and used on her. The stairs were pitch-black except for the flickering from a single candle. Good, no intruder dealt in candles. Only…Mara with her poor eyesight might knock it over.

"Mara?"

Bridget entered the room. As her eyes adjusted to the dimness, she made out the familiar shape of Mara with her fair hair next to the candle that, as Bridget realized as she moved carefully across the floor toward her, was battery-powered. And lavender-scented.

"What is that you're sitting in?" Bridget said.

"An armchair."

"Really? It's the size of a couch."

"I got it for clients. It actually reclines, so they could lie back, if they wanted."

"Ah. Like in a real psychiatrist's office."

"Psychologist, Bridget."

"Same diff. You deal with head issues."

"And heart. Come, it's big enough for both of us."

Bridget patted with her hands and shuffled her feet to the outline of the armchair and sank in, her left side fitting against Mara's right. "Now I know how blind people feel."

Bridget sucked in her breath, wishing she could do the same with her stupid, thoughtless words. She quickly said, "Do you get many of those coming in? With issues of the heart?"

"I've been in the field for not even a year," Mara said, shaking half her throw over Bridget. "But, yes. The two are pretty inseparable."

"What's your advice?"

The leather squeaked as Mara shifted around. "Each case is unique. And I try to let the client come to their own reasonable conclusion. I don't want them doing anything they don't believe to be true."

Mara sighed and added, "I guess I'm trying to figure that out for myself."

"Alone, in the cold and dark, at eleven at night?"

"Given what I'm trying to figure out, it makes sense."

Bridget didn't like where this was going. "Are you reconsidering taking this place?"

Mara's second sigh confirmed Bridget's

fear. "Was this about my comment when Sofia went missing? I meant to talk to you about that. It was straight up cruel and wrong, Mara. Every caregiver has had a near-death experience with a kid. Or so I've heard."

In the dark, Bridget made out Mara shaking her head, her fair hair shimmering in the artificial candlelight. "No, really. Jolene was saying last week about how her baby nearly froze her ears off because she didn't see how her toque had scrunched up. It happens. Anyway, Jack's the one who left the ladder there."

Mara's hand touched hers. Cold. "Bridget. I know you're trying to make me feel better, but I lost Sofia because I couldn't see that she'd gone. I spoke with the specialist today, and I know the truth."

Bridget inhaled and exhaled, prepping herself for Mara's news.

"You know that I don't have any night vision but I'm losing my peripheral vision, too. And not so gradually, despite the fact that I'm taking enough supplements to curdle my liver. I Skyped with my specialist and she let me know it—it has gone macular."

Bridget had no clear idea what that meant, but there was no missing the tremble in Mara's voice.

"This—this is where the real vision loss sets in. There is a very real likelihood that in five years I will be legally blind."

Bridget wrapped Mara in a tight hug, and Mara set her head against Bridget's shoulder, pulling Bridget to her as if her older sister was a body pillow.

"My world is disappearing," Mara whispered, her voice thick with unshed tears. "Before my eyes, because of my eyes."

Bridget felt choked, helpless. "I wish this wasn't happening to you. I wish there was some kind of Christmas miracle of new vision I could give you."

Tears leaked down her face.

"It's not just the loss of my vision. It's the loss of everything I thought I could have. Like a family."

"Don't say that, Mar. Blind people can raise kids just as well as sighted people."

"I lost Sofia! I didn't see her leave. If you hadn't showed up… How could I take care of a baby? How could I pass on this disease to a child?" Mara broke into loud sobs, and Bridget wondered how she could find the tissues while not leaving Mara.

She pressed a corner of her apron into Mara's hands. "Here."

Mara blew, folded over the corner, blew, folded, blew. "Hey," Bridget said, "leave some for me."

Mara's stuttering laugh was quickly drowned in more sobs, and both of them converted the apron into a giant soft tissue.

"I don't know what I'm going to do," Mara said.

Bridget sorted through various options. None seemed good. "What did Krista say?"

"I haven't told her. I haven't told anyone except you. I think that's why I came here tonight. I could hear you in the kitchen. And I stayed up here, trying to get the courage to come down and tell you."

"I had no idea," Bridget said. "I had the music on. I didn't even hear you come in."

"I know," Mara said. "I snuck in because I didn't want to disturb you. At least that's what I told myself. But it was lack of courage."

"It's a hard thing to have to say."

"You're the only one I could say it to."

"I'm your psychologist," Bridget joked.

"You're the family who thankfully has never had to worry about sharing my poor genetics."

"Just so you know," Bridget said, "that wasn't my first thought when I heard the news." She'd felt sadness and helplessness. Krista had felt guilty because she didn't have it, and Deidre had felt guilty because she'd passed it along.

"Jack doesn't carry the gene, Mom said. Because of the way it's inherited. So you'll be safe."

"Mara, we're barely dating, much less married or thinking about kids."

"Everyone knows that it's a matter of time. I wouldn't be surprised if Jack produces a ring on Christmas Day."

He wouldn't. He was too practical to buy her a ring when they were scrimping to meet mortgage payments. Mara didn't know what desperate straits the restaurant was in.

"What? No, no. He can't afford one."

Mara lifted her head from Bridget's shoulder to look her in the eye. "If I have to face the truth about my future, then you can face the fact that your future is Jack."

Bridget pressed Mara's head back down. "I face my future every day, let me tell you. How about we just focus on you for now?"

"Believe me, I have focused on myself until my head spins, Bridge. Quite a bit about whether I should even start this business."

"What do you mean? Of course you should.

There's nothing about your condition to stop you. Your job is all about listening."

"But there are so many visual cues that a client gives and expects you to catch. Who will come to a blind psychologist when there are perfectly healthy ones on the next line in the directory?"

"Too late. You've already agreed."

"Unlike Krista, I never signed the forms. This is day thirty, you know. I still can reverse my decision."

For an awful, awful moment, Bridget wondered if it might be a good thing. The money from the sale of the unit would solve so many problems. Then, the moment passed. "Not an option, Mara. What would you do with yourself? This is a godsend."

Her words seemed to have a settling effect on Mara. "I was wondering that myself. I have to do something with my life. If I can't be a wife or a mother, I can still be a psychologist."

Mara could be a wife and a mother, but right now better she knew the importance of who she already was. "Don't forget you're a sister and a daughter and a cousin."

"I think my cousin is keener on his adopted

cousin—" Mara gave Bridget's ribs a quick tickle "—turning into his wife."

"Ugh. You make it sound so inbred."

"Don't worry. Everyone can see that you're not blood-related."

"I always used to hate that I looked so different from you and Krista. Nobody ever believed I was your sister. I hated that they were right."

"They never were right in all the important ways." Mara said quietly.

Beautiful, beautiful Mara who could make others feel whole, even when she was falling apart. Bridget tucked the throw tighter around them. "How about we talk about your plans for this place? And how you will help all of us who need our heads and hearts put back together."

"You are tired," Mara said. "We should just go back to the house."

"We will," Bridget said, "but for a bit, let me be your sister."

Mara relaxed down against her. "That I can do."

CHAPTER THIRTEEN

JACK SAGGED IN RELIEF against the door frame at the sight of Mara and Bridget asleep in an oversize, red leather armchair in the upstairs unit. He'd come down the stairs at the house in the dark, chilly morning to an absent Bridget and a sofa bed that hadn't been used. Mara had left the previous evening to measure floor space at her unit and said she'd catch a ride home with Bridget. Except the SUV was missing, and after a stealth check in the upstairs bedroom, so was Mara.

Cold pricked his face as he'd run to the restaurant—would he always be running after her?—but his tension eased at the sight of the SUV. But she wasn't in the kitchen and Mano had no idea where she was. A light over the back stairs had been his only clue.

Yes, he'd felt anxious about the whereabouts of his cousin, but nothing compared to the piercing fear for Bridget. Eyes closed, Bridget looked so tired. For once her hands were still—she was holding Mara. Her hair was loose and soft along the angles of her cheek and jaw. He gently swept back dark strands. She stirred, and stirred again when he unzipped his jacket and laid it over her.

He thought she might waken but she brushed her cheek against the fleece of his collar and snuggled in.

That settled it. He would run the breakfast shift himself. If she could do it on her own, so could he. Starting in the New Year, he'd cover more of the morning shifts, so she could sleep in. He kicked himself for not insisting he handle today when he knew she was pulling extra hours last night.

"Where's Bridget?" Marlene asked as he poured her coffee.

"Good to see you, too," Jack said. "Bridget's having a well-deserved sleep-in."

"Have you thought about taking her on a vacation?" Mel asked from the table over. "We're leaving right after the holidays, but you can take our RV when we're back mid-February."

"Not everyone thinks RV travel constitutes a holiday," Daphne said. As proof, Marlene, parked with coffee and a heaping plate, raised her hand.

Mel shook his head at Marlene. "Not everyone knows how to have a good time."

Jack was not about to let any opportunity to sneak away with Bridge slip by. "I think if we could get any distance out of Spirit Lake that would be a good time."

"We're not leaving until after New Year's. Take it to the mountains. It's all winterized. You'd just need to pay for the gas. Take the girls, too. Sleeps six."

That might actually work. The four of them, like a regular family, on a getaway of no schedules and feeding only themselves. To give Bridget what she gave her customers, and the town's needy. "Might mean shutting the restaurant for a day or two," Jack mused.

"We'll manage," Daphne said. "We could do breakfast in bed." She gave Mel a knowing smile.

He brightened. "We could do that tomorrow."

Jack left them to make eyes at each other. Something he wished he could do with Bridget more often. Half his brain went on autopilot as he worked the tables, while he ran mental computations and logistics.

It was past eight thirty when Bridget and

Mara dragged themselves downstairs, groggy and apologetic.

"No worries," Jack said. "Deidre's got the girls. Go home, shower, change." He snagged Bridget's arm as she was about to exit through the back door. "And I have an idea."

She opened her mouth and he laid a finger on it. "When you get back. I haven't worked out the budget yet."

Her dark eyes rounded. "Jack, we can't—"

He gave her a gentle push. "Later."

When the only customers were the mid-morning coffee crowd, Bridget returned. His laptop open on the bar counter, Jack could smell the coconut and vanilla from her shower soaps. "You smell good enough to eat."

"Please refrain." She scanned the customers. "Did you do the rounds?"

Jack wasn't one to cater to this lot. Mostly seniors, they sat on their single cup of coffee spread over long conversations about farm equipment, golf, the government in Ottawa, the oil field and the grandkids. "They're good."

Bridget picked up the coffeepot. "These are Penny's people. Be glad they still come," she quietly reminded him and set out to re-fill cups.

His mother's people. No, he still had trouble picturing Penny as that. Here, Bridget couldn't stand to call her adopted mother "Mom" as a sign of respect, while he couldn't stand to think of Penny as "Mom"—that was reserved for the woman he'd lost when he was thirteen.

Penny was like a long-lost distant relative who'd unexpectedly bequeathed him her wealth. And her debt.

And in a way, Bridget.

She came back behind the counter. "What's this big idea of yours?"

"How about we go on a cheap holiday?"

She shoved the coffeepot back onto the stand. "Are you out of your mind?"

"If I am, it's because we're stressed to the gills. Penny, the restaurant, the girls, Christmas, the crates, bills—we deserve a break. Mel offered his RV to us. We could go on a one- or two-day trip to the mountains after Christmas. You, me, the girls. It would mostly be the cost of gas, which okay, given his behemoth, might be a mortgage payment. But let's see if we can make it happen. Make some good memories."

"You can't, we can't." She looked all wild-eyed again. "Who will cover the restaurant?"

"We'll close it down."

"We can't afford to close it down."

"Maybe we can with a little luck and planning. That was what I was doing when you came in. Figuring things out."

"There's nothing to figure out. Even if we had extra money, we can't waste it on a vacation, even to the mountains. Every cent matters."

She sounded panicked, out of proportion to what he was suggesting. "I'm not spending it. I'm checking to see if we can."

"Now's not a good time. Not with—" She clamped her mouth shut.

"What?"

"Nothing." She went to the back.

Nothing was ever nothing. He left the customers to fend for themselves. This crowd wouldn't give a cent more, but neither would they leave a cent less.

He caught up with her prepping her counter for rolling out minicinnis. Mano had already gone home from his early morning shift.

"Out with it."

"If I tell you, will you leave off about the vacation?"

"No, but I will promise to take it into consideration."

Bridget cinched her apron around her waist so hard, he could feel the pinch on his own waist. "It's Mara." Her breath hitched. "She's going blind faster than we thought."

He gathered her into a hug. He expected her to resist, but instead she sank against him and clamped her arms around his waist.

"She spoke to her specialist and it's accelerating fast." Her words were muffled against his shoulder.

"How fast?"

"She thinks she might be legally blind in five years."

He hadn't realized how advanced Mara's condition was. Even Sofia's roof stunt he'd chalked up to his own stupidity, despite Mara's profuse apologies. "That's…tough."

"She told me last night, and we got to talking and then we fell asleep."

"It's a good thing she's staying here, then. We'll be here to help her."

Bridget pulled back in his arms and touched his cheek. "That's what I told her."

Her soft voice, the glide of her fingers… He couldn't resist a quick kiss. The feel of her warm lips made him even more determined. "A few days away—you, me, the girls—won't change anything and will probably give us more energy to deal with problems when we get back."

She pulled his hands from her waist. "If just the four of us go somewhere, it'll look to everyone… It'll look to the girls as if we're a family."

"But you said you loved them."

She switched on the sink taps and began washing her hands. "I do, but that doesn't mean that I want to be their mom."

"Because it would mean marrying me."

"Jack, we've gone on one date."

"One, recently. Countless, over the course of our entire relationship."

"My point being is that outside of that one very nice outing, it's like we're married. We share kids. We share a house. We share a work life. It's as if Auntie Penny's will essentially married us without our consent."

"You know," Jack said, "I was just thinking along the same lines, but more that she gave you to me, without either of us consenting."

Bridget dried her hands and thunked dough to the counter. "You figure she gave me to you, no wedding necessary?"

Jack was so confused. "You don't want to go on a trip with me because it'll look as if we're married but you're annoyed with your aunt because she left out a wedding."

Bridget set to kneading the living daylights out of the dough. "You want to go on a trip as if we're already together. Which we aren't."

"I'd love if just the two of us went off together, but right now that's hardly fair to the girls, is it?"

Bridget gave the dough a few vicious pinches. "That's the whole point. It wouldn't be fair to them. And it's not fair to take me along and raise their expectations."

"You're worried that they'll want you to be their mom."

"Aren't you worried?"

He placed his hands on her shoulders and turned her to face him. "I would be thrilled if you become their mom, Bridge. I also think there is something more going on in your head than you're telling me. You don't want to go, I get that, but not for the reasons you're giving me because they don't make a whole lot of sense." She opened her mouth to protest. "But since this whole trip thing is stressing you out, we'll drop it. For now."

"What do you mean 'for now'?"

He had another idea, not worth bringing up in her state of mind. He released her. "I'll let you make up another batch of minicinnis while I check orders." At the doors, he paused and casually said, "So…our second date is Sunday, right?"

She didn't bother to look up. "Sure. Sunday."

He liked to think that by the end of their second date, she'd have a whole different take on their "marriage."

FRIDAY WAS THE last day of school orders. Jack and Bridget stood with a mic in the elementary gymnasium, the entire student population seated before them on the floor in grade-ascending lines, with teachers and parents taking up the perimeter in chairs on three sides.

Jack had located the girls. Sofia was in the front row with her kindergarten class and had waved as if flagging them down on a busy highway. Isabella had granted them a single wave. Pretty good for her.

Jack had been before crowds three times larger during his overseas events and ten times noisier. Bridget clearly hadn't. The mic in her hand trembled, and her smile, usually so laid-back and friendly, was strained. "I want to thank—"

Her voice cracked. The mic slipped in her

grasp and he reached out to grab it—or her, as the case may be. Her eye caught his motion, and he whispered, "You okay? You want me to take over?" She shook her head, drew in a breath deep enough to vibrate through the mic and pushed on.

"I want to thank Ms. Lever for coming up with the idea and taking the lead on this. And all the teachers for supporting the students." Her voice carried across the high and open space, strong and clear. *Good job, Bridge.* "And, of course, the students who spread the word so fast and made the Cinna-Bun Run for Crates such an amazing success. Give yourselves a big hand!"

The auditorium broke into jubilant, self-congratulatory noise. As the clapping died down, she said, "There's one more person I need to thank." She turned to him, tucking a strand of hair, almost shyly, behind her ear. "That's my partner, Jack Holdstrom. We couldn't have possibly filled the orders we have so far without his help. I couldn't do any of this without you. Thank you, Jack."

Looking for any excuse to make noise, the kids broke into applause again. All he could see was Bridget, her eyes soft and hopeful on his. She'd called him a partner. Told the public that they were in this together.

And the way she'd said it…with that dip and pause on his name—that spoke of an intimacy far beyond the warp and woof of running a business together.

If it hadn't been for the audience, he would've kissed her. He confined himself to a wave of thanks to the kids, and they responded with another round of clapping and foot-stomping. He felt like a fraud. He had helped for his sake, to clear his name, for Bridget's sake, for the sake of the publicity it gave the restaurant, not for the benefit of the community. He never wanted to see icing sugar again.

"Would you like to join me in announcing the winners?" Bridget asked him into the mic.

Now who was the con artist? She wanted to unload her public-speaking duties, and how could he refuse now?

Through his plastered smile he whispered, "Only if you kiss me tonight."

She thrust the mic at him. He raised his eyebrows. She gave him the stink eye and a single, sharp nod. He took the mic.

Sofia jumped to her feet. "That's my Jack-pa!" she said. Repeatedly. To her teacher, her classmates, the row seated behind her. Publicly claiming him as her father. He looked at Bridge to see if she'd heard, and her wide, congratulatory smile told him that it had happened for real.

He was a father on more than paper. He took the mic and lifted his voice. "Who likes Bridget's minicinnis?"

Applause.

"Who *loves* Bridget's minicinnis?" Unleashed, the students made even more noise.

As for Bridget, had she not just announced that he was her partner? In business and…yes, more. Life was…good, better than it had been in a dozen years.

Bridget whispered, "Jack, you need me to take over?"

Her smile was teasing. Brat. He said, "And the runners-up are…"

As he handed out minicinnis and gift certificates for Bridgie Buns, Jack felt strangely exhilarated. It was the high from Sofia's new name for him and it was the high from a successful campaign that stood to pay off a debt to the community. And it was the high from knowing that Bridget had told a crowd that she couldn't do without him.

Yeah, he planned to make their kiss tonight the best ever.

SATURDAY AFTERNOON AT the restaurant, Bridget inspected the bar counter in the light of day, rubbed at a smear until the light caught on the mahogany. Three stools down, Isabella wrapped a Christmas napkin around the knife and fork, just the way Bridget had explained. She tightened it with a band and then over top, she set a second decorative band in Christmas colors that read Happy Holidays. She took about ten times longer than Bridget would've, but it was perfect. Isabella had high standards. Unfortunately, she expected everyone else to follow them, as well.

"Jack-pa and Sofia are out longer than I thought they'd be," Bridget said. Bridget liked Sofia's name for Jack so much, she inserted it into every possible conversation. Isabella had so far held out.

"Christmas shopping for me is easy," Isabella said. "I told them what I want and where to go. They take too long."

"Yes, they are taking too long," Bridget said, correcting Isabella's English as she went. "She is probably showing Jack-pa all the things she wants."

"I told her not to make him give money," Isabella said. "He does not like to give money."

"Jack-pa thinks of you and Sofia differently

than he does other people," Bridget clarified. "He likes to spend money on you and Sofia."

"He adopted us," Isabella said. "He said the law makes him give money to take care of us. He told us."

How was a girl who'd only known a few phrases in English a month ago, suddenly able to form an argument in English that left Bridget fumbling for the right words?

"Did Jack-pa tell you that I was adopted, like you and Sofia?"

"Are you from Venezuela?"

"No, I was adopted here in Canada."

"Did your parents...? Did they...?"

"Sort of. I never knew my dad. I don't know if he is alive or not. And I was told years ago that my mother had died." From an overdose. "I hadn't seen her since I was six. She had problems of her own that were so big she couldn't take care of herself, much less me."

Bridget hoped Isabella wouldn't pry any further because explaining addictions to a child was way beyond her. It demanded Mara's skill set. "My point is I thought that my adopted mom and dad, and even my auntie Penny, were nice to me because they had to be. But they weren't, and it's the same for you.

Jack-pa told you that because he wants you to know your rights and not his obligations."

"What's the difference?" She said, banding another fork and knife with the precision of a bomb specialist. At this rate, they'd never open for the service tonight. Mano and his crew were already banging and clanging away in the back.

Bridget joined Isabella in her task. She didn't know how to explain in simple terms, so she opted to speak slowly and hope Isabella could sort out the correct meaning. "Having rights means you are important to everyone. No law says he needs to buy you Christmas presents, but he is. So I guess he's doing it because he—"

"Don't say 'love'!" Isabella scrunched her face.

Bridget had intended to flip out with "thinks you're pretty cute." But the sharp denial piqued her interest. "Okay."

"He does not need to love me," Isabella said. "And I do not need to love him."

"He knows that," Bridget said softly.

"Sofia wants to love him," Isabella said. "She said, 'Can I love him?' I told her I will think about it."

"I don't know," Bridget said, "that you can tell someone who they can love and not love."

"I can tell Sofia," Isabella said confidently. "If I do not, she loves everybody."

"Isn't it the season to love everybody?" Bridget said. She understood where Isabella was coming from, but she was interested in hearing Isabella's take.

"Sofia's too young to love everybody. Not even I can," Isabella said. "Not like you."

"Me?" Bridget said. "What makes you think I love everybody?"

"You love everybody in this town because you made all the crates."

"You're helping, so you must love everybody, too."

"It was your idea. The love comes from you," Isabella argued right back. "And you love your family and me and Sofia and Jack-pa."

"I didn't say I loved Jack-pa!"

Isabella fixed Bridget with a steady gaze, and Bridget wondered with unease if the girl had happened to overhear Jack and her exchanging a very attentive good-night to each other last night. Bridget had come to believe that Jack had forgotten about the kiss she'd promised him, but when they'd gotten into the house, their outerwear off, he'd pulled her into his arms, sunk his hands into her hair and claimed his reward. She had paid back several times over, thoroughly and perhaps not as quietly as she could have.

"But if you did," Isabella said in a way that showed she'd spent time thinking this matter through, "you can be Bridgie-ma. I told Sofia she can call you that, if you say it is okay. Is it okay?"

She had the same expectant look as Sofia often had. Bridget desperately wished she and Jack would show up.

"Oh," she began, the single breathy syllable calming her. "Oh. I am Bridgie, that's for sure, but I think the second part—the 'ma'— would be for whoever married Jack-pa."

"Okay," Isabella said, "I tell her to wait until you and Jack-pa are married."

Bridget's phone rang.

It was Tanya, and she wasted no time in getting to the point, her voice slow and firm. "Our records show you are moving into your third month missing payments on your residence."

"No, no. I specifically came in last month with payments," Bridget said, moving quickly out of Isabella's earshot past the clamor of the kitchen to the back office. "Don't your records show that?"

"On the restaurant you made a full one. On the residence, you made a payment but that applies to your first missed payment, so once again we're into your third delinquent month," Tanya said, her voice lowering as if ears on her end were pressed against the wall. "I mentioned how your account has already been flagged. There's nothing I can do to stop the process."

"Just to be clear," Bridget said. "Foreclosure."

"Yes."

"I see. What do I owe you?"

The amount, again delivered like a terminal prognosis, winded Bridget. She and Jack didn't have the money.

"When do you need it by?"

"The latest payment was due at the beginning of the month. The amount is due immediately, I'm afraid. I'd like to see it on Monday first thing and get it into the system."

She could hear Sofia's excited chirping and Jack's calmer voice at the back door above the din of Mano and his family crew. "Thank you for the call, Tanya. I'll be there," Bridget said quickly.

She slipped her phone into her pocket and met Jack and Sofia at the office door. "How'd it go?" Bridget asked, as they stepped into the narrow hallway.

"Brilliant!" Sofia said.

Bridget smiled at Sofia's display of her growing vocabulary. Jack wasn't fooled by Bridget's forced good cheer. "What's the matter?"

She directed her gaze at Sofia and gave her head a brief shake.

Isabella came through from the front, pulling on her jacket as she did.

"Did you get me my gifts?"

"That's none of your business," Jack said.

"But I don't want to get in the vehicle and see them through the shopping bag," Isabella said.

"You know what we're getting you, anyway."

"This way I can imagine it's something else."

"Hold on," Jack said. "You asked us to get one thing but you are hoping it's another?"

Isabella pulled on her toque and mitts. "You might have thought of something even better."

"If he did, it's small," Sofia said. "I had to

sit in the car while he went inside, and when he came out he had no bag so it is small."

"Or I went to the washroom like I said I was going to."

"You were there for a long time."

"Let's give Jack-pa a break, girls," Bridget said, "and let him take you home." To the house that at least for this day they still had.

"You coming with us?" Jack said in a way that suggested that would be preferred.

The sooner she told him, the...well, certainly not the better. This was definitely not the season of glad tidings.

JACK'S FIRST THOUGHT upon hearing the news a half-hour later was that Bridget wouldn't want to marry him now. She'd cite the financial mess as a reason not to enmesh their lives together even more. She'd tell him to return the ring that was right now in his jacket pocket. A ring he'd bought after coming off the best kiss he'd had since, well, since the one out on the lake.

Her next words did nothing to allay fears.

"We are screwed," Bridget said and plunked down on an overturned crate.

Jack refused to believe it. He couldn't. "I

will not have the girls eat from a garbage can again."

Bridget looked up with horrified eyes. "Is that what the girls—"

"Yes. And I will not have either of them even think that would happen."

"Canada does have a safety net."

"It doesn't have a safety net against trauma. Point is, we need to come up with about five grand fast. That shouldn't be too hard. I've got a thousand left. We'll drop in the money I'd set aside for the RV trip. That'll give us another five hundred. How about you?"

"I've got four hundred set aside for Christmas presents."

"Any room on your credit card?"

"No. The funeral expenses, remember? I'm barely making minimum payments. You?"

"Same. Not because of funeral expenses… but only making the minimum." He shoved his hand in his jacket pocket, his hand encountering the ring box. He loathed giving up on marriage to Bridget, even for a few months. The last time he'd delayed with getting a ring on her finger, of declaring his commitment to her, it hadn't happened. There had to be a way through this. "We need to go to the rest of the family, Bridge. They'd understand. And not to sound too uncharitable, but they are living here for free."

Bridget moaned. "Because I invited them."

"Circumstances have changed."

He used those exact same words when he explained the situation to Krista and Mara. "Basically we're asking for a loan of three thousand dollars."

Krista and Mara looked at each other in dismay. "The thing is," Mara said, "is that, if we'd known earlier, it wouldn't have been a problem. But we put our deposit on the rental for the first of January.

"And we're already cash-strapped from reno costs," Mara said. "I'm so sorry."

"Got it," Jack said. He scrambled to think of friends, even abroad, he could wire for a quick loan. He drew a blank. Among his co-workers, he was considered a man of means, mostly due to his inherited wealth, before he'd lost it all in the scam. "Bridge, you know anybody? Even if it was a few friends and you ask for a few hundred?"

Bridge called the three friends she considered close enough to ask the favor. Only one offered anything. Four hundred dollars. Bridget thanked her and told her to keep it.

Jack couldn't stand the growing despair on

her face. "Listen," he said, "we have work tonight. Work means money. Let's put it out of our minds for now, and do what we can."

It turned out that what they could do was beyond their wildest expectations. Together at the bar they tallied the results. "This is our best take ever," Bridget said. "As in the history of this place."

"Question is," he said, entering the numbers, "is it enough?"

"Enough to keep the restaurant afloat another month, for sure. The issue is the house."

But that wasn't his worry. He typed in a formula to get a projected take for next weekend. "Okay, cross your fingers." He hit the last button.

He read the number twice in case his wishing brain had intentionally misread it. He fist-pumped the air. "Yes!" And turned the computer for her to see.

"That is what we can expect next weekend based on the last two."

"Are you saying that we'll make enough money to catch up on our payments?"

"That's exactly what I'm saying."

"But Tanya said that the bank wanted full payments. By Monday."

"We'll give her what we got. We'll bring her the rest in a week."

Bridge gnawed the inside of her cheek. "Do you think they'll accept it?"

"What the system will see is that an account that has been overdue for the past year is suddenly paid up a week after issuing a warning. That should be acceptable."

Actually, Jack wasn't so sure, but for the slow release of Bridget's teeth on her cheek, he'd stick to this version.

"Thanks," she said. "I'm going to sleep better than I thought."

"You better get a good night's sleep. It's going to be another late one tomorrow."

"What do you mean? Tomorrow's Sunday."

Jack closed down his computer. "I know. Date night."

Her eyes widened. "Are you sure, Jack? You'd have to make dinner and you're tired, too. You shouldn't have to—"

"I shouldn't have to do anything I don't want to. Which is why tomorrow is date night."

She stepped up on the rung of her stool, leaned over and kissed him. A quick, tired kiss, but one that he hadn't initiated or had to win from her. "Okay," she whispered against his lips. "Date night."

CHAPTER FOURTEEN

KRISTA GAZED SOLEMNLY at Bridget's reflection in the dressing-table mirror. Behind them, on the bed that had once been Bridget's and was currently Deidre's, Sofia and Isabella looked on with the same absorption. At least, Sofia did. Isabella's expression, Bridget thought, held the same barely suppressed impatience she herself felt with Krista.

Her focus unwavering, Krista laid a hank of Bridget's hair across her front exactly as she'd done two minutes ago, then promptly flipped it back over Bridget's shoulder.

"Honestly, enough. Jack's waiting downstairs and I still have to find my shoes."

"Okay, okay," Krista said, "but you have no idea what a high bar your dress has set for your hair."

Her dress was gorgeous, a present from Auntie Penny three Christmases ago. Red with gold threading interwoven throughout, the off-shoulder number made Bridget feel…desirable. She might not have bothered to wear it except that Krista had remembered it, and Mara and Deidre had insisted, the girls had got in on the act and Bridget couldn't come up with any reason strong enough to overpower their pestering.

"Found them!" Mara said, pulling a shoebox out from behind Deidre's suitcase.

Krista abandoned Bridget's hair. She snatched the box from Mara, flung away the lid and gathered up the shoes with the tenderness she'd use to hold a newborn. "There you are, my gorgeous beings." She stroked the curved red uppers. "I released you from the nasty mall dungeon three years ago only to have you locked away in my evil sister's closet." She held them out to Sofia and Isabella. "Touch them and experience pure, distilled beauty."

The girls touched them with due reverence.

"Hand them over," Bridget demanded. "The reason I never wore them is because they go with the dress, which I've also never worn."

"Something I don't get," Krista said, doing as Bridget ordered. "Something must've happened in the past three years worthy of the dress."

"Nothing as important as going to a romantic dinner with Jack," Mara said.

Bridget decided to ignore both sisters and wiggled into her shoes. "Ouch, ouch, ouch. Your gorgeous beings have pincer jaws, Krista."

"Revenge for neglecting them. Now get downstairs and go get 'im!"

Bridget cringed at her sister's crassness, and left Krista and Mara with the girls and a ton of makeup.

Jack was talking to Deidre in the kitchen when Bridget cleared the stairs, her heels rapping on the hard floor. He stopped and stared at her from top to toe. He drew back his shoulders, expanding his already considerable chest, and said to Deidre, "Isn't she absolutely gorgeous?"

Not as heart-stopping as him. He wore a light grey suit with a blue shirt and tie—darker blue with silvery snowflakes that set off his eyes and light hair. And on top of that, he was looking at her with the same tender intensity as just before he'd kissed her at the lake. And on Friday night.

Flustered, Bridget turned to Deidre, who

beamed back at her with the same look of pride as Jack. "Yes, she most definitely is."

If only they'd stop staring. "Could we just go?"

Deidre held up her phone. "Pictures first. Here by the tree."

Bridget and Jack were obliged to pose, arms looped casually around each other by the Christmas tree and then by the fireplace and then—could someone come and take a picture of Deidre with Jack and Bridget? Which led to Krista and Mara taking pictures on their phones with all possible combinations of family members.

"How do celebrities stand it?" Bridget asked Jack as he held the door to the SUV for her.

"They don't have our family to contend with. Wave to your fans," he added, then closed the passenger door.

Sure enough, they were clustered at the front window—mother, sisters and…Jack's daughters. She returned their waves, which prompted Sofia into a flurry of two-handed waves.

Jack sent off a quick salute before pulling from the curb. "You know," he said, "when

I asked Auntie Dee if you were gorgeous, I already knew the answer."

Bridget squirmed inside the red dress coat Deidre had insisted she borrow. "Flattery will only get you so far."

He held out his free hand to her, palm up. "How far will truth get me?"

She hesitated, then slipped her hand into his. They were, after all, dating. Not like when they were high-school sweethearts, newly engaged, with the promise of a long future together. Still, their lives were far from over, and with the girls, and her sisters and Deidre back to stay, the future was fuller than ever. Even if it was missing Auntie Penny.

But that was the thing. Every time Jack had left on his short visits, she'd had to get over him. What if they got back together, and he left her again? This time, taking the girls with him.

If that happened, there would be not just one hole to stitch up in her heart, but three.

BRIDGET WAITED AT the front of Penny's while Jack rounded to the back door, insisting that he would be but a moment. A cold breeze off the lake curled around her legs, and made her fingertips tingle. A light snapped on in the back, and there… Jack appeared.

He opened the front door for her, his suit jacket and tie gone. "Welcome," he said, "to an evening at Penny's. I am Jacques and I will be your waiter tonight."

The place was transformed. To the white lights in the windows were added gold sparklers, and tea lights flickered at each table to create pools of soft light and from speakers came a holiday playlist sending out her favorite version of "Do You Hear What I Hear?"

At the best seat in the house, the curved bench with no cracked upholstery, shone three huge candles on a tablecloth that Auntie Penny had stored on the top shelf of her pantry. What would she have thought of her son laying it out for Bridget?

As she drew closer she saw that red and pink rose petals dusted the top. And a setting for two.

"Um, Jacques. These plates are heirlooms. My Auntie Penny never used them, and I don't think her mother used them, either."

"I am simply following orders."

"What if they break?"

"I was assured that they came from a setting for twelve. There'd still be enough for a full family sitting."

They were beautiful, trimmed in a pattern of gold ribbon with bunches of grapes. And her "waiter" was well-informed. There were more where these came from. Enjoy, she ordered herself.

"I see I won't be dining alone."

"Yes, your date will be joining you shortly," Jacques said, showing nothing but the same flirty smile Jack used to make middle-aged women order drinks beyond their limit.

Well, two could play this game. "I certainly hope so," she said with a flip of her hair that would make Krista proud. "I don't intend to go home alone tonight."

"Certainly," her waiter said. "We wouldn't want that, either." She took the proffered seat. "Would you like to view our wine list while you wait?"

"I come here so often I know your wines by heart."

"Ah, but we just brought this one in today." From the table over, he presented a decanted red wine, the exact one she'd mentioned offhandedly at the supper table once, weeks ago.

How long had he been planning this?

Her wine poured, he bowed. "Let me tell

you about our specials tonight. To begin, we have a fine lobster bisque, the seafood captured from the bay of Safeway, steamed and settled in a cream sauce and flavored classically with basil and a glimmer of oregano."

Next, "Jacques" described the entrée: the sirloin, aged and rubbed, and the vegetables, pliable yet robust.

"Hmmm…that's sounds delicious. Could I take a peek at your menu, though?" she teased.

His smile didn't fade. "By all means. One moment."

He disappeared through to the back. All this for her. Jack must've been planning the dinner from the second he won the bet, maybe earlier. She hadn't even started preparing until two hours ago. Well, okay, she squeezed in a haircut the other day, and rummaged through Krista's jewelry to bling herself up, but it was nothing compared to what Jack had done.

He meant it. He really meant every single word about winning her back. And she wanted him to win her. Wanted him to carry on making her feel as if she was worth winning.

From out of the back, Jack returned wearing his tie and grey suit jacket. He breezed to the table and gave her cheek a swift kiss.

"Sorry I'm late, honey. The meeting went longer than I thought and traffic was horrendous." He took the seat across from her. "I see you ordered a bottle of wine. Great choice." He glanced around. "I don't see the waiter. Should I just pour?"

"That's odd. He was most attentive when I was alone. I bet the women love to tip him."

Jack poured his wine as expertly as the waiter had done. "He better not try his so-called attentions with me around. Have you ordered?"

"No. He's gone to get a menu. I think I'll order the special, anyway. It sounds delicious. A lobster bisque to start, and then sirloin with grilled vegetables."

"I'll go for that, too." Jack raised his glass. "To us."

She touched her glass to his. "To us." And sipped. "Oh. Oh my, I'm melting."

"Only the best for you." A dud line, but it went down like her wine—smooth, warm, tempting.

"Besides," he said, leaning back, "business is good."

"Oh? I know you and your partner were struggling."

"We were," he said. "but I really think we've turned the corner. She's amazing."

"Should I be jealous?"

"Not at all. She watches me in case I slip up. I have to be constantly on my toes."

"Maybe she watches you because she likes what she sees."

He held out his hand, palm up. She set her hand in his. "Know that I only have eyes for you."

Another cheesy line, but she had to smother her smile with another sip of her wine. She made a production out of looking around the restaurant. "I'm hungry. Where has Jacques gone?"

"Burning his tip away. Here, how about I just go tell him?"

"You shouldn't have to."

"I know. It's as if I'm having to be the waiter, too."

Jack returned to the back. Two mellowing sips of wine later, he reappeared. "Jacques apologized. Apparently, they are short-staffed this evening, and he had to take on the cooking duties, as well."

"Oh, the poor guy. Well, if he cooks as well as he serves, we're in good hands."

Jack took her wineglass and set it down, then touched his lips to her hand. "It's official. I am jealous."

"Don't be. He just reminds me of you."

"That handsome?"

"Mmmm…" She picked up her glass and tipped back the last of the wine. "And the way he made me feel as if I was the only one in the room."

"As if he'd closed the whole joint just for you?"

"And gone to the trouble of decorating it." She picked up a pink petal. "Did you ask him to do this or did he do it himself?"

"It was my idea. You like?"

"I love."

His eyes sparked, then turned to alarm. "Could you wait a moment? I have to…make a call."

He dashed to the back, and from the kitchen such a clattering arose.

The noise settled and Jacques appeared at her table with the bisque. "My date came," Bridget informed him.

"I am relieved to know that you'll not go home alone," he said and refilled her glass.

"Though if he hadn't showed, I would have seen to it that you did not."

Bridget mock-gasped. "You better not let him hear you say that." She lowered her voice. "He admitted to jealousy."

Jacques replied back in the same hushed tone. "I don't blame him. Every man here has been staring at you." He straightened and spoke in a normal tone. "I will take the liberty of peppering the gentleman's bisque."

It wasn't long after Jacques left that Jack rejoined her.

"Where's your suit jacket?"

"Oh, I—I got a little warm while taking the call. How's the bisque?"

"Incredible. I mean it." She was tempted to ask if he'd made it himself, but she remembered in time that was a question for Jacques. "Compliments to the chef. Or Jacques."

"You have to hand it to the guy. Both waiter and chef. Man must have incredible talents."

"Be sure to tip him well. You never know. He may have children to feed."

"A mortgage. Or a loan."

She didn't want Jack thinking of money. At least, for this evening. Perhaps she could provide a little distraction.

She stretched out her leg, arched her foot.

"Do you like my shoes? I think Krista wants to marry them."

Jack's gaze dwelled on her foot, then ambled up her leg. "This is the most bare skin I've seen on you since the Canada Day charity event six years ago."

"I admit I wore that particular skirt deliberately."

"The Canadian flag had never been better displayed."

"I—I was trying to make you see what you'd missed out on."

His eyes met hers. "I knew. I've known since the day I broke off our engagement twelve years, seventeen days and eight hours ago." He paused. "Give or take."

"I wish you would've come back to me then," Bridget whispered, because she didn't have the strength to speak louder. Regret rose between them, making them slow their spoons. No, Jack had worked too hard to design this evening. She searched for a change of subject.

Jack took a pink petal, heart-shaped and veined, and touched its tip to a red petal. Not sure what was up, she played her part, placing red to pink. Back to soup. He slowly nodded as if she'd made a particularly ingenious move and, after careful pondering, set down his petal. She impulsively laid her petal next to his. The game continuing, the petals began to take a long, curved shape that she thought would produce a heart.

But in his last couple of moves, Jack had extended the arc outward into what she now saw was a circle. Her spoon scraped the last of the bisque from the sides of her bowl.

Jack excused himself and Bridget curled her toes in anticipation of the arrival of Jacques. He came, solicitous as before, inquired after her enjoyment of the soup and then whisked away the bowls. She hummed along to Michael Bublé as he serenaded about how it was starting to look a lot like Christmas.

Jacques arrived with the entrées, bright and sizzling and artfully arranged. She said she'd wait for her date to return before she started. Jacques looked gratified and assured her that no man with any sense would leave her alone for long.

He was right; Jack returned not a minute later, rolling down his cuffs as he did. After a few bites and assurances that each of their meals was cooked to perfection—Jack really did have a chef's flair—their game of the flower petals resumed. Jack seemed to have a very deliberate plan and Bridget was curious.

Through the rhythmic consumption of their meal, a largely silent duet of clinking cutlery and burbling of wine into glasses, the art piece was created. It was a circle, and when Bridget placed the last petal to complete it, she grinned in triumph at Jack.

But he continued, and at the top of the circle placed another petal jutting upward. He took up his cutlery again and ate his last piece of steak. Bridget wasn't sure of her next move. She cozied her petal beside his. He snuggled hers against his. She curved hers against his. He smiled and responded in kind.

Curiosity had her cutting through her vegetables without giving them the attention they deserved. She'd settled on a wreath when Jack made his apologies and it was time for Jacques. He swept away their plates and returned with dessert. Chocolate cheesecake from last night, when Jack had told her that they'd run out. He'd broken the hearts of a half-dozen cheesecake lovers, jeopardized his tips, so that they could share this pure, sweet heaven.

When Jack returned, he settled back into

the game. She felt like he was making art and she was filling in between his lines. When nothing except the melted chocolate patterns were left on their dessert plates, Jack took over completely and dropped petals in a rocky, crooked line on top of the wreath and then he sat back.

He smiled at her with a soft, yet intense expression.

"A wreath?"

He shook his head.

"A present with a bow on top?"

"Stand," he said, "and look at it."

She did and considered. A circle with a smaller, filled-in ball on top. What? What?

And then it hit her. "Jack," she whispered. "Oh."

From behind the candles—it must've been there the whole time!—he withdrew a small, unmistakable box and dropped to a knee before her.

He was really doing this. She needed to stop him.

He set the ring, a simple, elegant band with a strong and bright diamond, at the tip of her ring finger. "If I were to ask you again to marry me and tell everybody with this ring that we will be together for the rest of our lives, would you wear it?"

Every part of her screamed "Yes!" Every part except one. The one part that had gnawed away at her since he'd come back, apologized, shared shifts with her, wrapped minicinnis, slung coffee, joined her and the girls for bedtime stories, climbed up onto a roof for her—twice!—bragged to everyone about their date on the lake…and that one part had observed him the entire time and come to the same conclusion that now made her withdraw her hand from his.

"Jack, I don't believe you."

CHAPTER FIFTEEN

THE RING TREMBLED as Jack's fingers shook. Then he recovered, stood. "Do you mean because I spent money on the ring? Don't worry. Every jewelry store at the mall has a massive sale going on. This was a lot cheaper than it looks. Not that," he added hastily, "you don't deserve the best. I'm just saying that you don't need to worry. I've got this."

"No, not that. I mean, you shouldn't have spent the money now, but that's not my point." She played with the petals. The flower ring had occurred spontaneously to Jack, the perfect appetizer to the real entrée. "I feel as if this isn't real."

He held the ring between them. "It's very real. Let me put it on you, and you'll feel exactly how real it is."

She pressed her fingers to her temple. "No, Jack. I don't believe that you love me."

Of course, how stupid of him. He'd planned every detail, except the official declaration of his love. He tugged her hand into his. "Bridge. I love you. I've never stopped loving you. I've always loved you."

She leaned forward, their faces as close as if they were about to kiss. No contact tonight. "That all feels like a bunch of lines you've unrolled because you think it's what I want to hear."

"Don't you want to hear that I love you? Because I know I'd love to hear it from you."

"Why? Because if I say it and you say it, then it must be true?"

All evening, she'd been flirty and soft with him. Right up until he'd presented her with the ring. Now he felt as if he'd fallen to the ice and was lying there, cold and winded. "For me it's true. I can't speak for you."

She shook her head. "I haven't told you that I loved you in a very long time, yet you seem to think that we can carry on where we left off."

"I know where we left off and it was with us half a world apart and neither of us telling the other how we felt."

"I am telling you now."

Jack's confusion slipped into sheer frustration. "No. You're not. You're telling me that you don't believe that I love you. And you seem to be implying that you no longer love me."

"I didn't say that."

They were going around in circles. He took a steadying breath, rested the ring on the petals. "I believe that our hearts have been joined together for a lifetime." She fired him a skeptical look. "Fine. For longer than Isabella's been alive."

Bridge hissed, like when a water droplet hit a hot frying pan. "That," she said, "is part of why I don't believe you. It always circles back to me and the girls. To me as their mom. You completing your family."

"But think about it, Bridge. I wanted to marry you years ago, before the girls. If we'd both opened up to each other back then, we'd probably be married with two, three kids of our own. Yes, I think you'd be great with the girls. And, yes, I am happy that the three of you get along. If the girls didn't like you, then you can better believe that I wouldn't be asking you to marry me tonight. You and the girls are my top priorities. You're not going to make me choose, because I shouldn't have to."

Jack felt the rightness of his words. He didn't have to choose between her and his work. Her or his home. Her or his girls. They were all one. Why couldn't she see that? "What can I do or say to make you believe me?"

She gazed at the ring nestled in the red and pink petals, its facets glittering in the candle-light. "I think we need to wait. Let's see if you're still around in a year. If this place is still around."

Jack stared at her, but her expression didn't waver. He said, "You don't want to change, Bridge. You love your sisters. Deidre. You love the girls. I don't know, you might even love me. But what I do know is that you love staying exactly where you are more than any-thing. At this restaurant. In the house." A nig-gling puzzle suddenly clicked. "That's why you didn't want to come to the mountains with me and the girls. You're too scared to go anywhere."

Bridget jerked, flattened her hands on the table. "That's not true."

"It isn't? That phone conversation way back when. Remember that I asked you to join me, and you said you couldn't see what you'd do there. It wasn't me you wanted, was it? It was the life here."

"I shouldn't have had to make a choice,

Jack. You were supposed to come back here, remember?"

"You had promised to marry me, Bridget. I never backed out of that promise. You did because you chose this place above a place with me."

He picked up the ring, a petal catching in his fingers. He let it flutter to the table and inserted the ring into the box. "I think we're done here. I'll drive you home and come back to clean up."

Bridget hadn't moved. Her hands were still pressed to the tablecloth. "You go home. I'll clean up. I want to stay here for a bit."

"Of course you want to stay," he said, unable to keep bitter disappointment at bay. "Instead of being with me."

She dipped her head, with its mass of dark, glossy hair. And said nothing.

It was an admission of what had happened between them, or what had not happened. And there was nothing he could do to make it better. Nothing he could give, no words of great joy to pass along, no meal he could cook or business he could rescue.

"You're stuck," he said. "You're still up in your tree house, aren't you?"

She remained unmoved, silent.

"I'll walk home," he said, dropping the keys on the table. "You come when you're ready."

HE WAS WRONG. Wrong. Bridget forcibly relaxed her fingers. She only wanted to avoid an awkward ride back to the house and an even more awkward good-night. She had provided a way out, but he'd thrown it back in her face.

She'd climbed down from the tree house a long time ago. She began to gather up the ring of petals, his great romantic drumroll gesture to introduce his proposal. She now understood that the entire evening had been one long drumroll, all building to the moment he opened the ring box and presented her with their future together.

Why had he forced the issue? Why couldn't he have just left things as they were?

As they were. As they'd always been. She fingered a pink petal. By tomorrow, it would be wilting, without her doing a thing.

It was true that she didn't like to travel. When she was a kid, she'd always worried that when she returned, everything would be gone. Like how food had vanished from her biological mother's fridge, rarely replaced. She'd resisted every trip the Montgomerys took as a family, until it became easier for everyone involved to leave her with Auntie Penny while Krista and Mara left with Tom and Deidre. Then when she reached high school, she moved in with Auntie Penny. Eventually, Krista and Mara moved in, as well, when they reached high school. They'd moved on, and she'd happily stayed.

By then, no one expected her to travel, even though Bridget logically accepted that nothing was lost in doing so. She couldn't get her heart to make the same leap. By unspoken agreement, Krista and Mara visited her, and she welcomed them with open arms. That was how it was done. Even Jack knew that she didn't like going different places. Why else would he have said he'd come back after the year? And then found a way out of his promise by challenging her to come join him when he knew it was impossible for her?

Except she could have met the challenge all those years ago. By inviting her to join him out in the world, he had leaned a ladder against her tree.

But that was then, this was now, when things were far more complicated with the house, the restaurant, the girls. Especially the girls.

She wasn't ready to be their Bridgie-ma.

She had feared her first mother and then when rescued from her, she'd loathed her. News of her death came as a relief. It had damaged her relationship with Deidre to the point that she couldn't view her as a mother. Bridget herself was not fit to be a mother, despite what Jack and the girls kept angling for.

She dropped the pile of petals onto her dirty plate, clattered her plate onto his and picked up the works. With her other hand, she reached for the wineglasses.

Maybe the part of her brain on autopilot hadn't calculated for the difference in weight and shape of the plates compared to the sturdy restaurant-issue, but they skidded from her grip and crashed to the floor.

Bridget screamed. First, as a shocked cry. Then, with intent. "Jack! I told you that you shouldn't use the plates. I warned you that they could break. Don't worry, you said. There's plenty more where these came from. But look! These are gone. Forever. There will always be two less."

Ten more plates, he'd assured her, leaning another ladder.

Shards had scattered everywhere. She headed to the back for the broom, her shoes sawing into her toes. Par for the course tonight.

The tinkling noise of broken china as she swept made her think of another time when things had come apart between her and Jack. It was back at the Canada Day celebrations six years ago. Jack had remembered her red-and-white outfit. She remembered the afternoon thunderstorm.

They were manning a booth together as part of Jack's latest humanitarian project, this time to promote a newly founded partnership between Spirit Lake and a sub-Saharan village. She and Jack served up free cupcakes made from cassava flour and iced red and white with mini Canada Day flags. She'd been up half the night making them.

"Bridge, thank you for all the work you've gone to," he'd said, during a break. "When Penny had said you'd come up with something, I hadn't expected this."

"It's for a good cause." But she'd gone overboard. Transformed her feelings for him into twenty-four dozen cupcakes. She looked away, to the thickening rim of clouds on the horizon. "Looks as if we'll get a thunderstorm."

He'd followed her gaze. "You're probably right. At least we can see it coming. I've been in places where you're soaked before you know it's raining."

"Oh? Where was that?"

"Tropics. Sri Lanka, Bangladesh, Amazon." And between serving up cupcakes and his patter about village wells and market produce, he'd told her about his adventures and his vision to increase food security through reliable and safe distribution.

During a lull, he said, "There's a committee here in town. They plan to visit the village. See what's happening there." He paused. "You're welcome to join them. I—I'd love to show you around."

Her in Africa? With a bunch of strangers and him, her ex? "I can't see myself doing that."

"You wouldn't have to worry about a thing," he'd persisted. "Consider it payment for all the cupcakes."

"I didn't do it for you. I did it for the people in that village."

"Bridge." His voice dropped. "I guess I am having a good time with you, and I am trying to find a way for it not to end quite so soon."

By asking her to take off to a strange place. "Jack, that ship sailed a long time ago." A sharp breeze snapped the plastic tablecloth, shook the canopy uprights. "Storm'll be here in a half hour. We should do takedown."

"But—" A rush of people had come up and Jack had refocused. By the time they'd cleared off, the sky had darkened and they were scrambling to pack up.

A sudden gust swept up a couple dozen cupcakes and tossed them everywhere. Departing children had broken from parents' grips to chase after them. Jack had cracked up when a squirrel tried to lug away one.

His grin faded when he'd looked at her.

"They're gone," she said.

"You've made loads, Bridge. There's more than enough."

Pretty much what he'd said tonight about the plates. But she hadn't seen it that way tonight or six years ago. "Why don't you tell that to the women in your village?" she'd snapped.

His face crumpled. "I'm sorry, you're right. You know better than me what it's like to go without."

She'd only ever told him that her early childhood wasn't easy. On his own, he must've figured out how little food she'd had.

Maybe during his six-plus years working with the world's poor.

She could've told him then, could've extended their day together with her own story or two. Instead, she shrugged away his apology and they'd finished packing up in near silence. Back at the restaurant, Auntie Penny had fawned over Jack, and Bridget slipped away without having to say goodbye.

She hadn't told him the full story until this month, when he'd climbed to bring her down from the roof where she'd treed herself. He'd guided her down then, and countless times over the past weeks whenever she felt overwhelmed, tired, sad, lonely.

Tonight, he leaned up a beautiful, sparkling diamond ring of a ladder and she stayed frozen like when she was six.

Crouched on the floor with a dustpan full of broken plates, Bridget had no idea how to get her feet back on the ground.

CHAPTER SIXTEEN

TONIGHT WAS WATERMELON and kiwi bubble bath. Jack hadn't known that either fruit even had a scent until he poured it into the girls' bath.

"Watermelon or kiwi?"

Watermelon from both.

"Kitchen or bedroom?" Predictably, kitchen from Isabella and bedroom from Sofia.

"There's no food in the bedroom."

"Yes, there's the food in the drawer."

"That's for—" Isabella broke off. Jack knew it was for when food ran out. For when he could no longer provide for them. Could he blame her distrust when their livelihood wasn't secure?

"City or country?"

Both frowned. "What's Spirit Lake?" Isabella asked.

"A city for a mouse," Jack said.

"City!"

And Isabella agreed.

Before Jack could present another set of

choices, Sofia patted the pile of bubbles she'd built for yourself. "Look. I made a snow angel, Jack-pa."

Jack smiled. Days after she gave him his new name, he still experienced a shot of pride. He'd won her over. Isabella slipped on her rump at the other end of the tub, her foot shooting up through the skirt of the snow angel.

Sofia squealed. "Isabella! You wrecked it." Blobs of soap angel drifted across the bathwater.

Isabella righted herself. "It can be fixed." She set to patching the angel back together.

Jack reached to help.

"It was my fault," Isabella said. "I will fix it."

Isabella's trust was harder to earn. Already wired to take on far more responsibility than she should ever have had to, Isabella resisted attempts to get her to accept help.

"You're like Bridgie," he said without thinking.

Isabella frowned. "No, I'm not."

"I'm more like her," Sofia said. "Except shorter."

"No, you're not," Isabella said. "No one is like her."

Never a truer word spoken. "What I meant is that she doesn't like to accept help, either."

"Auntie Deedee and Auntie Krista and Auntie Mara are helping her right now with the crates," Sofia objected. "You can see them through the window."

Jack knew that very well. "Yes, but she doesn't like that she has had to accept their help."

"But she can't do it by herself," Sofia said.

"She knows that, which is why she has let them in."

"But that is because it is the Christmas Crates," Isabella said, patting bubbles in place. "It is okay to ask for help for other people. It is best to help yourself. It is good not to need people for food or a house or things."

Jack realized that even if he'd not lost his money and his venture had become successful, it would have done nothing to fill Isabella's scared emptiness. Would it be like Bridget's, and never fill?

The phone's alarm beeped "We Wish You a Merry Christmas," the agreed-upon cue for them to get out of the tub and into jammies. "Now remember I'm telling the story tonight because Bridgie is busy with the crates."

He'd planned to read them a Christmas

story about a boy and his penguin, but as usual, Sofia had a different plan. "Tell us," she said, climbing over the seven million objects on the bed, "about you and Bridgie and the lake."

No. That story was too raw now. He couldn't imagine a time when it wouldn't be.

"Tell me about the first time you ate her cinnamon bun," Isabella said.

She said it with such confidence, as if everyone would remember their first bite of Bridge's specialty. Oddly, he did remember.

"She burned them," he said. "A whole pan. Burned them black."

Isabella and Sofia gasped.

"I know," he said, clearing a spot on the bed. "Hard to believe. I had come over to go on a bike ride with her. Off we go, and we are on the far side of town when she jumps up and starts screaming about her buns, her buns, her buns. I have no idea what she's talking about. Everyone is staring. She forgot to take the buns out of the oven. She gets on her bike and I follow. We didn't have phones, and it wouldn't have mattered because Penny and Auntie Krista and Auntie Mara were shopping in Red Deer. And Bridge's parents weren't home, either.

"When we got back to the house—this house—the kitchen is thick with smoke. I open the windows and the doors. She opens the oven door and takes out the buns. So black and tiny."

The girls looked grief-stricken. "What did Bridgie do?" Isabella whispered.

He'd forgotten about this part of the story. It was…private. But he could tell part of it. "She turned to me and her brown eyes grew very big." Two sets of brown eyes widened in anticipation. "And she said, 'Jack, I don't believe it. You made me forget about food.'"

He'd laughed and taken her into his arms, and they'd kissed and kissed again, even as they choked on smoke. That part wasn't for the girls' ears, but they'd heard enough. Sofia threw her arms around him.

"I am just like Bridgie because you make me forget about food, too."

Isabella looked more dubious. "Did she ever burn another pan?"

"Not that I recall."

Isabella nodded and informed Sofia, "And that's why I am like Bridgie. I always do better next time."

And didn't that describe the woman he loved but could not reach. It was only when he switched off the overhead light and switched on the night-light that he realized something.

"Hey, we talked all this time in English."

"Yes," Isabella said, snuggling closer to her sister. "I think and dream of Bridgie in English."

Me, too, Jack thought. *Me, too*.

THROUGH THE WINDOW on the garage, Bridget caught the shapes of the girls and Jack as they passed by the upstairs bedroom window. Bath was over, time for jammies.

Bridget gasped. "Christmas jammies! I've forgotten to buy them."

Krista clapped a mittened hand to her heart. "Whatever will I sleep in on Christmas Eve?" She flung a scarf intended for the crate over her shoulder and pulled a mock moue. "Last year's?"

Krista and Mara were sorting through outerwear and matching them with a master list of requested items. At least, Mara was. Krista exclaimed over every pretty object, tried on toques, made Mara try them on, flung scarves over all their shoulders.

"Make fun of me now," Bridget said as she secured a ribbon on a crate and set it aside, ready for Deidre to layer the bottom with a large cardboard coupon from Spirit Lake's Auto Center. "But you will feel weird if you don't have a new pair to put on."

Krista shrugged. "It's happened before and I survived."

"But I've always given you a pair. Even when you weren't coming, I sent them to you."

"Yeah, but one year I went on a ski trip, and we left before the pajamas arrived. Bridge, you look as if I'd left behind a pet or something."

"But I asked if you'd gotten them in time, and you said 'yes.'"

"Because I didn't want to deal with you carrying on as if the world was coming to an end."

"I wouldn't have." But she saw Mara and Krista exchange looks.

Right. Another prime example of how she couldn't let go. "Okay, I guess I'm a bit obsessive about them. I'm sorry."

"It's fine," Mara said. "For what it's worth, I always like getting them."

"I'll buy them tomorrow, for sure. It's the least I can do, considering all the work you guys have put into these crates."

"And Jack's," Deidre said.

"I'm thanking you on behalf of him, because without your help, he couldn't have paid back the debt."

"We made ten thousand?"

"Pretty much, between the Brigade and the school sales." Now to square away the back payments on the house.

"Yay for us!" Krista said and glanced at her phone. "Shoot, the plumber. I have seven minutes before I show him around. Bridge, can I use the car?"

Mara followed. "I'm going with. I want to talk to him, and, anyway, there's a trick to turning on the lights."

After they left, the garage seemed quiet. Three ribbons were tied, three coupons inserted before Deidre spoke. "Isn't it time for stories with the girls?"

"Jack is covering for me tonight, so I can work on the crates."

"The girls won't like that."

Bridget didn't like it, either. She missed their scented smells, their squirmy snuggliness, the play of expressions on their faces as she spun out a story. But given the state of her strained relationship with Jack, she thought he would prefer the break in routine.

"Deidre, can I ask you something?"

"You can always ask. I'm not sure if I have the answer."

"Jack said I act as if I'm still stuck in the tree house. You know, the one that brought me to you and Dad."

"Stuck?"

"That I don't like change. Like always getting pajamas for Christmas and wanting to do Christmas Crates."

"I'm not sure why he thinks pajamas and crates constitute being stuck. They're more like traditions."

Bridget wasn't about to discuss the marriage proposal with Deidre, but there was one part she could hint at. "Isabella and Sofia, especially Sofia, are beginning to see me as their sort-of mother."

"You mean that business with 'Bridgie-ma'? Sofia explained it all to me. That when you and Jack get married, she can call you Bridgie-ma."

"And we're not engaged. Not even close." Bridget stapled on a ribbon, fluffed it and moved the crate to Deidre.

"Okay, but I'm not sure what this has to do with being stuck."

"Because I do love them, but I can't bear the thought of being their mother."

Deidre refluffed the ribbon on the crate Bridget had brought over. "Because you're afraid you'll be like one or both of your mothers?"

"No. Yes." Bridget sighed. "I know I'll never be as bad as that woman I share genes with, and I know Krista and Mara think the world of you, so I know the problem is with me."

"You?"

"Deidre. I think that you never stood a chance with me. By the time I came to you, I was already treed."

Deidre leaned on a crate, adjusted her shawl around her shoulders. "We took you to psychologists, you know. Time and patience were their top recommendations. And to treat your reactions as normal given the circumstances. But honestly, when you were a kid, only Krista and Mara could get you out of the tree house, as you put it."

"Do you think the girls should go see someone? Mara hasn't said anything. Maybe I should ask her."

Deidre arched her a look. "Is that for you to decide?"

No, it was Jack's call. By refusing him,

she'd also refused any claim on the girls. "Jack will tell me that it's none of my business."

"Don't know if he'll say that. I can imagine him asking why you're so interested."

It was Bridget's turn to eye Deidre. "More like that's your question. I don't know the answer. From the moment they walked through the door, it was like seeing my kids for the first time. As if they'd been taken from me and now just returned. Or maybe I was seeing the lost, lonely kid I once was in them. That first night, I might've signed up to be their mother, but now that they want me to be…"

"Ah, I see. You got scared and ran up the tree."

"I guess."

"I'm the last person to give you advice. I'm living in my kid's bedroom. I'm charity."

"You took me in."

"You were six, not fifty. I'd always prided myself on my independence. I wasn't going to be like my mother. Too scared to do anything for fear of disaster. And here I am, with nowhere to go."

Deidre's admission pained Bridget. No way would she tell Deidre about the financial state of the house, especially when there was a solid chance they could sail through it this weekend.

Deidre frowned. "What is it? Is there something else the matter?"

"No," Bridget said, and on a sudden impulse to hide her face from Deidre, she pulled her into a hug. "Just the usual stress."

Deidre's arms came around her and she whispered into Bridget's ear, "Those girls have chosen you to be their mother. You chose them. They're not perfect. Isabella is always hungry and Sofia is always hungry for love. But there's no one on earth who understands their needs better than you."

Bridget hoped Deidre could feel her nod because she wasn't ready to let go of this woman who had in her own way mothered her as best as Bridget would allow. "Deidre. You know your mother's dining set. The one Auntie Penny kept safe and is now yours?"

"Yes?"

"Last night, Jack brought two plates over to the restaurant and—and I accidently broke both of them."

If possible, Deidre squeezed harder. "Good. About time."

JACK DIDN'T KNOW how much more he could take. He had dropped off Bridget at the pajama shop, run five errands that took him to all corners of Red Deer, and yet he returned to find her still making her selection.

She had narrowed it down to four styles. One flannel with teacups, one with snowmen, another grey with red trim and reversible bottoms and a thin cotton pair in white and blue. She stroked the lapels, turned them this way and that on the display hangers. He suffered through her trying them on for size and then turning around in front of the mirror as she conferred with the salesclerk. She was twisting his brain around, too, because as hurt as he was, he also wanted to buy her every single one.

Wearing teacups, she turned from the mirror to him. "What do you think?"

"If I pick one, will you take them, no questions asked?"

She shoved her hands in her hair and gave an impatient scratch. "You can't pick only one because none of them have all the right sizes." She walked over to the selected styles, teacups tipping and sliding. "These two have only sizes for the girls, and only this one has for the sisters and girls but not Deidre, and with this one, I know Deidre feels better in the lighter weight—"

"We'll get the same ones for the girls, we'll

get another matching set for Krista and Mara and a third different one for Deidre. Deal?"

She set to gnawing her cheek. "They are my presents."

He'd said "we." How long would it take him to undo his dream of them as a couple? "Fine. You choose, then."

He had a thousand things to line up for the dinner service this weekend, the most critical weekend for the immediate future.

He'd text Mano about dark chocolate and steak.

"Jack?"

Bridget held up the two patterns. "You decide. It's for the girls."

Now she wanted his input? Right, so long as both their names weren't on the present. He pointed to one with snow people on skis. His choice was handed to the salesclerk to retrieve sizes.

She replaced the snow people one with another pattern. "For Krista and Mara."

The light blue ones with snowflakes and matching camisoles, hands down.

His aunt got the ones with teacups because as a promotion, she also got a teacup and saucer as part of a rewards program for belonging to Cozy Comforts. The restaurant should have a loyalty program. Did he have the time to roll that out for Friday's dinner service? If he had time to sit in a pajama shop, then yes. *Keep your eye on the bottom line, Jack Holdstrom.*

At the counter, he noted the number of pairs. "What about you?" he said. "You always get a pair, too." Penny—his mother—had always sent him a card with a picture of them in theirs. It was the only card he ever got anymore in this age of Christmas memes and gifs. He threw out the old photo when he received the new one.

"That was always with Auntie Penny," Bridget said quickly. "No need now, especially with money so tight."

"Did you know that Penny sent me a photo of you two in Christmas pajamas every year?"

From the surprised look on her face, he knew the answer. "Last year, it was red plaid, the year before, pink with stars, before that—" he shrugged "—you get the idea."

She'd probably refuse, but he plunged on. "Point is, you could start a new tradition. You have even more family for the photo this year."

"But I really—" She stopped, began to chew her cheek, stopped again. She fingered the snowflake pattern on her sister's pajamas. Was she seriously considering his change of plans?

"My present to you." He pointed to the snowflake pajamas. "Another one of these."

Dismay lengthened the clerk's face. "I'm so sorry. But these were my last two in this size. I have one in extra large."

He was not paying good money to see Bridget on Christmas morning in droopy pajamas.

The clerk clapped her hands. "I have the perfect solution!" She ushered them to a corner where two mannequins, man and woman, wore a matching pair. Hers pink with soft gray lines and his gray with soft pink. "What do you think?"

The pink one was cute. "That'll work," he said.

The clerk smiled. "And because you are buying so many, I can give you the men's one for half off."

"That's not necessary," he said.

Bridget reached to touch his arm, froze and let her hand hover there. "You might, as well," she said softly. "It'll look weird if you don't have a new pair and everyone else does."

"I've never worn a pair before," he said.

"Why start now? Besides, it'll look as if we're—" A couple. Parents.

"We are still partners of sorts," she said softly.

Of a restaurant, a house…and pajamas. "Are you establishing a new tradition for us, Bridge?"

She drew out her debit card. "The tradition has always been to buy pajamas for my family. That hasn't changed."

It had; it had worsened. Demoted to a kind of cousin, the girls cast even further out. He regretted suggesting the new tradition. He didn't want to carry around a photo where he and Bridge were both in it, but not together.

CHAPTER SEVENTEEN

LATER THAT AFTERNOON, Jack was discussing with Mano what to do if their supplier couldn't deliver their order of green beans when there was a heavy crash from Mara's unit.

"Bridget up there?" Mano asked.

"No, she's picking up the girls and dropping off the final order of buns to the school. It's probably Mara." They stared up. "I suppose I should go see if everything is okay."

A second thud and Jack swore he saw a ceiling tile quiver. "Good idea, before she breaks through."

Jack saw the problem as soon as he entered Mara's unit. Krista stood with a weight ball in her hands. Mara sat in the red recliner he'd found her and Bridget curled up in like kittens.

"There you are," Krista said and set down the ball. "See, Mara? I told you it would work."

"You dropped the ball deliberately?"

"You wouldn't have come up otherwise."

"Why not text or call?"

"Because we would've still had to come up with some bogus excuse about why we needed you up here, and that's just a big waste of time. We figured concern for the structural integrity of the restaurant would get you moving."

"What do you want?" He glanced around for something to be lifted, drilled, smashed.

Krista perched on the wide arm of the recliner. "Things between you and Bridget are still electric, but not in a good way."

"You could say that. What has Bridge said?"

"We tried last night but she won't talk. She's also the one that didn't tell us she was engaged all those years ago, either."

Which meant they probably didn't know that he'd proposed again. "If she's not talking, then neither am I."

"Except," Krista said, "we live with you two."

"Not for long, so it doesn't matter."

"Even when we move out," Mara said, "you and Bridge are family. You and the girls. It will always matter."

Jack shoved his hands in his jeans pockets.

Family. He'd already lost out on Bridget; he didn't want to lose his cousins or aunt, too. For his sake and the girls'. Especially for the girls. A thought occurred to him. "Do you think Auntie Penny finally decided to reveal that she was my mother because of Sofia and Isabella?"

"Certainly wasn't for our sake," Krista huffed. "I mean, what was she doing holding out on us for our entire lives?"

"She had promised my dad not to say anything," Jack countered. Was he actually coming to the defense of his mother?

"He died three years ago, and there's nothing to indicate she made some kind of deathbed promise to him not to tell all of us her secret," Krista said. "She robbed us of you and might have continued her deception if your circumstances hadn't changed."

Mara placed a warning hand on Krista's knee. "This is Jack's mother you're bashing."

"She doesn't feel like my mother. I'm going to need years of your therapy, Mara, before I figure out how to deal with her." He was only half-joking.

"All of us will," Krista amended. "You have group rates, Mara?"

"I don't think it counts if the therapist is part of the group."

"You're angry with her, too?"

Mara looked at her sister dryly. Jack felt a sudden kinship with these two women, bound together in their sense of betrayal by a dead woman. In his anger with Penny, he'd forgotten that his cousins had their own, too. "I guess the hardest part for me is that as angry as I am with her, I'm also thinking that she was scared."

Mara tilted her head. "Oh?"

"Scared of her entire family finding out the truth and freezing her out. Or who knows, maybe even the town turning on her. Maybe in her mind it was better to have something fake, than nothing at all."

"Wow," Krista said. "That's something Mara might say." She looked to her sister. "What do you think?"

Mara was studying Jack. "I'm wondering if you made this conclusion before or after your current falling-out with Bridget."

"After."

"Ah. You came up against our sister's tendency to hold on to whatever she has, instead of reaching for more."

Krista looked from one to the other of

them. "What am I missing?" She settled on Jack. "Were you thinking about marriage again?"

He shuffled his feet. "More than thinking."

Krista gasped. "You asked!" She turned to Mara. "I win."

"But that's finished," Jack said. "She refused."

"There's no chance of reconciliation?" Mara asked.

He'd spent every second since coming back to Spirit Lake trying to win her over. And in the end… He shook his head. "She doesn't believe that I want her for anything other than as a mother or a business partner, and since I come with the girls and the restaurant, we're kind of at an impasse."

He released a breath. "All I care about, all I'm allowed to care about, is that we make the last of the house payments on Monday."

His cousins drooped. "I'm so sorry we can't help you," Mara said. "If it was any other month, then I could throw something in the bucket."

"Me, too," Krista mumbled.

"Believe me, I understand," he said. "I'm optimistic it'll happen. If nothing goes wrong."

Mara gnawed the inside of her cheek.

Krista bit hers. It wasn't a Bridget thing; it was a Montgomery-sister thing. "You do know," Mara said slowly, "that a blizzard is forecasted for this weekend, right?"

No. Let Mara be wrong for once. He pulled out his phone, tapped on an app. Snow starting Friday noon. Continuing through the night. Accumulations of forty centimeters. Dropping to minus twenty-five Celsius. Blowing snow Saturday. All unnecessary travel not advised.

Skidding along streets in a blinding snowstorm to come to a restaurant definitely fell under the category of unnecessary. They'd be lucky to get anyone.

"Forecasts change all the time," Mara said. Krista nodded unconvincingly.

"Yeah," Jack said, unable to muster anything more profound.

Mara stood and hugged him. "Don't give up, Jack. Not on the house or Penny's. Or Bridge."

"Especially Bridge," Krista said softly. "Everything else can come and go, but she'll still be here."

She said it as if it was a compliment and not his greatest single frustration with Bridge. There was a higher probability that an Arctic high-pressure system would change direction before she would.

BRIDGET DEKED AROUND Jack with her two full plates and Jack ducked a shoulder to pass her with the coffeepot. He'd announced that morning he would enact his new policy to reduce the customers' refills in order to hustle them out the door sooner. She couldn't persuade him that the cents saved weren't worth the loss of the customers' goodwill. "I'll take my chances," he said.

She set the plates in front of the people at her table, ones who hadn't come in for a long time. "Eggs Benedict and the house special with eggs scrambled, a double order of bacon and potatoes." From the corner of her eye, she saw Marlene signal to Jack for coffee. He strode over to her, like out of a Western, his coffeepot cocked and ready to fire.

"Anything else I can get you?" Bridget asked. They smiled and told her everything looked great. Two happy customers and—

"I asked for a top-up. This is more like a top-down," Marlene said to Jack's retreating back.

Nothing wrong with the food at this establishment. Bridget eyed Jack. It was the service that was wanting. She edged closer in case she could mount an intervention.

"Sorry, new management policy," Jack said. More specifically, his. "Second refill is half the size of the first. Third is half the size of second, and so on."

"Since when?"

"Since the start of the week, but because you are a long-time customer, you got a three-day grace period."

Three days in which she and Jack had worked the front as if neither existed to the other. At least, that was the way Jack handled it. She'd taken his lead, and kept to herself. Gone was his banter, the intimate smile as he slipped past her, the let's-talk look. He talked to the customers. She talked to the customers. Jack talked to Mano; she talked to Mano. They didn't talk to each other.

Marlene looked over at Mel and Daphne. "Did you know about this?"

Mel shrugged. "First I heard of it."

"I order tea," Daphne said. She suddenly looked alarmed, and sprang open the lid of her teapot to check the water level.

Bridget swept over to another table of almost regulars. They had started coming in every Wednesday. Business partners who used breakfast as a time to regroup and re-charge. Their attention had drifted over to the exchange between Jack and Marlene. "Every-thing all right here?" she asked.

"We were thinking of asking for another coffee," the guy said.

"Oh, sure, not a problem."

On Bridget's way past Marlene, her long-time customer said, "Why would you ever come up with such a stupid policy?"

Bridget could flatly deny it. Tell her that the tight-lipped coffee slinger over there had decided to deprive Marlene, who dealt with abused children and a bungled system every day, all day, to save the restaurant four-point-two cents of coffee on a thirteen-dollar meal.

But, a united front and ull.

"Nothing's in stone, Marlene. All feedback is noted."

Marlene held up her cup, her piddle of cof-fee now weaponized. "Note this. While my coffee remains this empty, I will pay half of my bill and the third day I will pay half of that half, and so on."

"I hear you, Marlene," she said quietly. Jack had returned the coffeepot to its place and was watching her exchange with Marlene.

She came behind the counter and both she

and Jack reached for the coffeepot at the same time, their hands colliding on the dark handle. "I will take care of it," he said, his lips barely moving, Clint Eastwood–style.

"I think I'd better," she murmured. Two customers at the bar huddled over their brew, watching every movement.

"I made a customer dissatisfied, and I will fix it," Jack insisted.

They yanked on the handle at the same time. Their combined force sloshed hot coffee over the top and onto Jack.

"I'm sorry," she said. "I'm sorry. Are you okay?"

In answer, he set the coffeepot back on the burner very slowly and removed his apron, with its brown, spreading stain, very slowly. The coffee had formed a wet patch on the front of his jeans and down his right leg.

He exited to the back.

Bridget glanced around. Absolutely everyone, even Marlene, had found something else to look at. Bridget very slowly took the pot, wiped the outside dry and poured coffee to the brim for everyone, and everyone said their meal was good and no, they didn't want anything, just the bill, please and thank you.

When Mel and Daphne came to the cash

register to pay, Daphne whispered, "Is everything okay?"

"We're just stressed."

"Things do seem a…little tense between you two this week."

"I'll say," Mel said. "Warmer outside."

There was no way they were leaving without some kind of explanation, so she whispered, "We're experiencing some temporary cash-flow problems."

Mel leaned in. "This place in trouble?"

"No, no," Bridget said and quickly looked around. The last thing they needed was to have customers think that they were eating at a sinking ship, but the remaining customers were still cuddling their cups. "Not any more of a struggle than anyone else in town has with the bank."

Mel frowned. "The bank?"

She'd said enough. Jack's new coffee policy had nothing on her squawking aloud about the bank's involvement.

Mel looked as down in the dumps as all the Montgomery clan put together. "It would be a shame to see you have to close your doors. Been here for as long as I can remember. A good thirty years."

"And it'll still be here another thirty," she said, not believing it for a second.

Mel and Daphne didn't seem convinced, either. Bridget kicked herself for opening her mouth. What had she hoped to gain by telling them? Sympathy? Ten thousand dollars?

"Anyway," she said quickly, handing Mel back his change. "Thank you both for your support. And just to let you know that we're open this Friday and Saturday night. Our last dinner service of the year. I hope you can make it."

"You do know that there's a storm headed our way this weekend," Mel asked.

"It might blow over," she said, which was as likely as Penny's financial crunch blowing over.

Again, Mel didn't look convinced and, as always, dropped his coins into the tip jar. At the door, Daphne turned. "Will I see you at the school Christmas concert tonight?"

Right. "Sofia's singing solo," Bridget said. "She won't let anyone miss it for the world."

Sofia had exploded with happiness this morning when she learned that her first real snowstorm was arriving tomorrow. Jack had rallied and showed her pictures on his phone of what it would be like. He'd explained how the snow would sting and yet muffle everything, too. He'd made the snowstorm into an exciting wonderland, even as it spelled disaster for their finances.

He and the girls didn't deserve this, after all they'd gone through to come here. She had declined the offer to become wife and mother, but that didn't mean she didn't wish she could make it all better for them.

A CARNIVALESQUE VIBE rolled through the high-ceiling school gymnasium in anticipation of the Christmas concert—the first one for Bridget since being in one herself. Speakers played Christmas carols, tween girls dressed as elves did cartwheels up the aisle, a baby jingled a bracelet of bells, moms and dads drank coffee and burst into laughter with neighbors.

Bridget sat with Jack, who'd insisted on an aisle seat. Mara was on her left and Deidre's coat was on the next seat over, Deidre herself having gone to the back for a coffee and, from what Bridget could make out, had entered into a lively conversation with a circle of seniors. Krista had to work late at the Christmas shop, and had made Jack swear he'd video Sofia and Isabella.

"I'm going for coffee, too," Mara said. "Jack? Bridge?"

They'd both had enough of coffee for one day. Alone now, Jack said out of the blue, "I shouldn't have wigged out on Marlene in front of everyone. And you. I embarrassed you in front of your people, and I'm sorry."

"It's okay. She's built tough. Me, too," Bridget added.

"Yeah, Bridge. I know you." He looked straight ahead to the stage. Not too long ago they'd stood up there and Jack had the whole gym rocking. She had felt part of something intimate and something greater at the same time. The little bubble of Jack, her and the girls amid the larger and louder school population. "Do you think I scared Marlene off?"

"She knows we make the best coffee in town. She'll be back as grumpy as ever tomorrow morning."

"There you guys are," a familiar voice boomed out. Mel. "Ready for the kids?"

Jack stood as Mel came over. "Ready as ever. You?"

"You bet. I got a niece and nephew in the concert," Mel said. "The rest of us are over there. Oh, here's Daphne." His arm slipped around his petite wife.

A small child crashed into Mel's leg. "Amos, you monkey." Mel swung him up into his arms. "This is my latest nephew. He's one and a bit."

"Fifteen months last week," Daphne said and smiled at a teenager a good three inches taller than her. "And this is our oldest nephew, Matt. He's grade eight this year."

Hellos were exchanged. And Mel continued with his family rundown. "The youngest is with her class for the concert and the middle one, he's over…there! And oh, hey, did Daphne tell you our news?" He beamed at Bridget and Jack.

"How could I?" Daphne said. "We were only told at supper tonight."

"Two more on the way!" Mel held up two fingers like a victory sign. "Alexis and Connie are due. One in June, the other in July."

Grinning, too, Daphne wrapped her arm around Mel's waist and squeezed. "Mel. You'd think you're the proud papa."

"I'm the proud uncle, is what. Doesn't matter that I'm not the parent."

"Doesn't even matter if you're not related by blood," Matt said quietly and held out his hands to the baby, who pitched himself into his older brother's arms and allowed himself to be carried away.

Bridget vaguely knew Matt's story from Mel. Like her, he'd been adopted out of foster care. He was right. Bridget's first experience of love was for her sisters. She wondered how many more people like her and Jack and Matt and the girls were in Spirit Lake, products of bad beginnings and happy endings.

"The girls call me Jack-pa now," Jack said. A quiet admission of triumph followed by a congratulatory gush from Mel and Daphne.

"Funny how much power kiddos can have over you," Daphne said. "I swear the best part of my wedding day was when the kids wrote in their own card to us, 'Uncle Mel and Auntie Daphne.' That's when I felt married."

Deidre and Mara wandered up, and Bridget made the introductions. First, Mara and then…how to say this?

"Mel, Daphne, I would like you to meet… my mother." Strange, but true. "Deidre."

Mel reached out his hand. "Know of you. The Brigade's giving you quite the name," Mel carried on after a round of handshakes. "We were all sorry to hear the news about your sister. Penny meant a lot to Spirit Lake."

"Your daughter does, too," Daphne added.

"We wouldn't know how to start our morning without her."

Deidre wrapped her arm around Bridget's shoulders. "I am very proud of my eldest daughter.

"And—" she used her other arm for Jack's waist "—my nephew, too."

Mara tucked herself against Jack's other side. "He lost his mom, but picked himself up an aunt and some cousins."

"Well now, don't you all look set for a picture," Mel said and pulled out his phone. "Do you mind?"

Once Mel crowded everyone into a shot without a kid darting in front, Ms. Lever arrived at the mic to ask everyone to take their seats.

The concert started with kindergarten, which meant that Sofia's class was up first with her rendition of "All I Want for Christmas Is My Two Front Teeth." It was then that Bridget understood Jack's rush to claim an aisle seat as he took an unobstructed video of her with an extra close-up of Sofia flashing the audience her actual missing teeth.

As she skipped over to them once her act was done, Jack held out his arms. "You did great, Sofia," Jack said and gathered her onto his lap. Jack, Bridget thought with a pang of pride, made an awesome father.

They might've all left after Isabella's class finished—the school didn't want overtired kids the next day—except that Sofia insisted on singing along with every grade, regardless of whether she knew the words or not. "All is come, all is bright. Brown, young, verging Mother and Child…"

Isabella came and squeezed herself between Bridget and Deidre, pushing Bridget up against Jack, who had nowhere to go on his aisle seat. Bridget arranged Sofia's legs and feet on her lap and draped her arm across them. Isabella tilted toward her in order to see between the shoulders of the parents ahead and Bridget's arm settled across her shoulders. It was pure muscle memory. At this time of night, her right arm always came around one or another of the girls during story time.

She caught Jack looking at her arms draped over his kids. As if they were a family. Jackpa and Bridgie-ma with kids. But she had excluded herself by her own choice. A choice that meant living under the same roof was no longer possible. And since the girls needed a safe home and Jack was their caregiver, the outcome was straightforward.

She would leave, if not for her own sake, then for everyone else's.

She tightened her hold on the girls a smidge, felt the warmth of Jack, enjoyed them for the time remaining.

CHAPTER EIGHTEEN

THE FORECAST WAS dead-on. As the last of the coffee crowd filtered out of Penny's on Friday, the first of the snowflakes drifted down or, more precisely, sideways, caught up in a northerly breeze.

Jack tried not to look out the front windows as he set up for the dinner service. Tried to ignore Mano's glum predictions as he prepared sauces and marinades.

Tried not to wonder where Bridge had gone. She'd left right after the morning rush for an appointment, saying she'd be back in plenty of time to pick up Isabella from school. Now, with visibility diminishing by the minute and highway advisories flashing their yellow warning alerts on his phone, he was worried.

Except it wasn't his place to worry. He'd given up his place a dozen years ago. Still, when a text came in from her, he could breathe again. Back at the house. You want to pick up Isabella, or should I?

He texted that he would. He already had too little time with Isabella. The one upside to the end of the dinner services was he could spend evenings at home with the girls.

I will change and bring the vehicle over. See you in 30! She added a smile emoji. Wherever she'd gone had made her happy.

And kept her happy as she sailed into the office a half hour later, where Jack pondered how to wring out the last dollar from the budget. "Is it ever coming down out there!" She set the keys on the desk and shrugged off her coat to reveal her usual black cocktail dress complete with short boots.

In the few ticks it took for him to formulate a reply that didn't refer to how incredible she looked or to pry into her whereabouts earlier, she headed into the kitchen. "How can I help here?" Jack followed, caught up in the wake of her strange high spirits.

Mano threw up his hands. "We are beyond help. No one will come tonight."

Bridge grinned and kissed Mano on the cheek. "Quit fussing. Snow is falling, not the sky."

Mano and Jack exchanged stunned looks.

This was not the Bridget who'd sat beaten at the supper table six weeks ago, after grim news from the bank, or even last week when the bank had called about the house.

And he'd would be the last one to remind her of those worries. "I'm off to pick up Isabella, drop her off, change and be back in under forty-five, okay?"

Bridget waggled her fingers. "Take your time."

Here she was, safe and happy and gorgeous, and he was seriously worried.

SATURDAY NIGHT, AND Jack's worries, like the blizzard, had not abated. Friday night's take was half the previous week's, but considering the near whiteout conditions, not the disaster he'd expected. But the snow had continued through the night and all the next day. No sooner had Sofia winged out a backyard of snow angels than they were filled in, and she had to start again. She was in heaven.

Bridge had joined her there and flapped out a few of her own.

"It's good to see her like this. Just playing," Deidre had said to Jack as they watched through the kitchen window.

"I don't get it," Jack had admitted. "Unless

a busload of steak-craving tourists unloads in front of Penny's tonight, we face closing doors. And she's out there, making snow angels."

Deidre nudged him with her shoulder. "You could join them."

"I don't think Bridge would like that."

Deidre had laughed. "Who's to know? For Sofia, at least, the more the merrier."

No. He was stressed enough without adding the stress of not appearing that way. But then Bridget swept into the restaurant twenty minutes before opening, wearing the red-and-gold dress, the one she'd worn to their date, the one he'd gone down on bended knee before.

Krista must've got to Bridget's hair. Her dark masses were swept up into soft coils of a labyrinthine complexity. She wore makeup: her eyes were extra bright and soft, her lips red and glossy.

She wrapped an apron, a skimpy red thing with jingle bells, around her waist and grinned at him. "I figured I might as well pull out all the stops."

He dropped his gaze to her red shoes. "You'll be crippled tomorrow if you're in those all tonight."

She shrugged her bare shoulders. "I've no-where to go tomorrow."

It was when she fastened a sprig of holly to the lowest dip of her dress, drawing attention there, that he couldn't hold his tongue any longer.

He closed the office door. "Bridge, listen. I know you and I are not together. I get it. But you in that dress, it hurts."

Her fingers stilled on the sprig. "I don't understand."

"And I don't know if I can explain it. I don't even know if I have the right to tell you, but not saying how we feel is what has brought us to this point, so I'll get it out there and then we'll leave here and get on with our work."

"Okay."

"When you wore that dress, not even a week ago, I had the best time of my life… and then the worst. And even though it ended badly, it was significant. It was an evening I—and I think you—won't ever forget."

She flicked at a holly leaf. "Yes," she whispered.

"But you coming here tonight in the exact same dress means that you now figure it's a work dress, not a special one."

Her beautiful brown eyes widened. "No,

Jack. That wasn't it at all. I mean… I knew from the way you reacted that night that I looked good in this dress, so if you liked it, others would like it, and that would help the bottom line. For the sake of the restaurant. For you, the girls, for all of us. I wore it because it is an important dress. One that I'd like to change into a good memory."

Good memory. Like making snow angels with Sofia. Just as he figured. He'd messed it up. The dress was a sad reminder for her, one she was trying to make better, and here he'd dragged her out of her newfound optimism. "Sorry, Bridge. Forget I said anything."

He kept away from her for the rest of the evening, parking himself behind the bar. Not that there was much to do. At the height of the evening between the first and second sittings, the restaurant was only at a quarter of capacity. Mano's eldest daughter pushed around saucers and bowls pointlessly. Jack would send her home, except that she was counting on a ride with her parents. Bridge easily covered the front, the few plates swept away within seconds of completing. The usual hum had muted to the level where individual voices could be identified.

One of them rose suddenly from a booth.

"Is it just me or is everyone in here single and without a date on Saturday night?"

Jack vaguely recognized the speaker, a man about his age seated alone. He'd come a couple of Saturday nights with his buddies and their girlfriends. He'd been the odd man out, and tonight he was even more so, sitting alone in the giant booth. The same one Jack and Bridget had sat at for their date.

The scant population turned to him. Even Mano took a gander from the order window. Bridge crossed to his table and spoke too low for Jack to hear.

His reply came through loud and clear. "Doing just fine. No place I'd rather be. How about I buy you a drink?"

Bridge quickly extracted herself from him, and met Jack at the bar. "We can't let him drive home," she said.

Jack checked the order screen. "He's on his sixth."

"He usually holds his liquor pretty well, but I think he'd already knocked back a few before coming here."

"Okay, I'll see if I can get him to hand over his keys."

The man looked up unsteadily as Jack approached. "Am I in trouble?"

"What kind of trouble are you thinking?"

He thumbed over to Bridge at the bar. "I shouldn't have hit on the staff. That's a no-no."

He was glad the customer realized his mistake, but for extra insurance Jack added, "I understand, but she's already spoken for."

"Congratulations. You drew a high card."

Jack's first instinct was to correct him, but the point was to deflect attention away from Bridge. He simply replied, "Thanks."

The customer nodded. "The good ones usually get snapped up."

His voice had lowered, and the rest of the customers had returned to their meals, or in the case of one, an intense game of Candy Crush

If conversation kept the drunk in check, then that was what Jack would give him. "I'm not your ideal dining partner, but mind if I take a seat?"

"Sure, but I'm not buying you a drink."

Jack sat across from him. "Couldn't accept it. On the job." He held out his hand. "Jack."

The man took careful stock of Jack's hand and lined up his own hand with it. "Carson."

"Your meal okay?" More food into the man might soak up the alcohol.

Carson contemplated his half-finished plate. "Best steak I've ever had. And I've had steak across the world."

"Oh, yeah? For business or pleasure?"

Carson shook his head. "Who gets on a plane packed with strangers and barely any food for pleasure? Of course, for work."

"What do you do?"

"Oil-and-gas exploration. I'm an important muckety-muck."

"But a tough schedule."

"Yeah. My buddies, they changed jobs when they got serious with their girlfriends. I should've done the same."

Even muckety-mucks had regrets. "Things didn't end well, I take it?"

"Things never end well. Long distance does a number on relationships."

"I hear you."

"Hard to get a decent girl. No, let me correct myself. It's not the getting, it's the keeping. That's where I always trip up."

"Me, too," Jack said.

Carson turned to the bar, where Bridge was dressing a martini. "You think you'll mess up with her?"

"I already did once."

"At least she gave you another chance."

"There's that," Jack said noncommittally.

"Me, I keep better to a diet than a woman."

"You find the right woman, and you'll come around," Jack said.

"Yeah." Carson picked up his fork and knife, set them back down. "I should give you my keys before I do anything stupid."

Jack shelved the keys behind the bar and Bridge shot him a grateful smile. "Thanks. That's a weight off my mind."

"He's just sad. Woman troubles. By the way, if he makes a comment on how we're together, it's due to a misunderstanding."

"No worries. At least there's no misunderstanding between us."

She walked away, leaving Jack to wonder not for the first time where all her sunniness had come from. Across the way, Carson raised his water glass to Jack. A sign of encouragement. Keep it up. Keep her.

Carson, buddy, I would if she'd let me.

IN THE END, even with Bridge's dress and Carson's high drink bill, it wasn't enough. The tally stopped fourteen hundred dollars short. Jack rested his elbows on the bar. "It's a measly amount in the grand scope."

"Exactly," Bridget said, on the other side,

rubbing her feet. "Which means there's room for you to negotiate with the bank."

"It's not the house money," Jack objected. "Or not just it. Next month, we'll have our backs to the wall trying to make payments on the restaurant and the house again. And forget about the other essentials like food and toilet paper."

"We could run a dinner service next week. For New Year's. The weather will be better by then. Cold but not snowing, and everyone will want to go somewhere to celebrate. I could decorate the place. What do you say?"

Her determined optimism was breathtaking. "Okay, what has got into you? A few days ago you were stressed to the gills, and now you act as if you're sitting on a winning lottery ticket." He paused. "You're not, are you?"

"You think I would've worn these heels tonight if I was?"

"Truth? I have never seen you so carefree, and that includes when we were dating as teenagers."

Bridget's gaze drifted to the dark outdoors. In the hazy glow of the streetlights, snow swirled and hit like scatter shot against the windows. He should get out there and warm up the vehicle. "I—I… You were right, Jack.

I am stuck. And a lot of that is because of my fears. And you saying it made me realize how worn down they've made me."

Was she saying she wanted to change, and for him?

"I know things are serious. I know the problems haven't gone away. But I also know that you and girls will land on your fect. You've brought them through much worse already—and you'll do it again. If you want, you can find work. Might not be saving a restaurant, might be something even better. And with help from your family. They helped rescue you from the Christmas Crates fiasco, and they'll be there for you again whenever you need them."

Jack didn't like how she was missing one critical factor. "What about you? Where will you be in all this?"

She gave him a soft smile. The smile that in the past always came before a long, sweet kiss. "Don't you worry about me, Jack. The world always needs a good cinnamon bun."

He leaned closer, inviting her to come within kissing range.

"Jack?" she whispered.

"Yeah?"

"Could you go warm up the car?"

He pulled back. Bridge might have changed, but things between them hadn't.

CHAPTER NINETEEN

"I NEED TWO coffees over here!"

Bridget tossed two packages over an assembly line of crates to Krista.

"A tea and three bears!"

Bridget did an express ground delivery of the goods to Mara at the far end of the bench. She redirected over to Isabella and Sofia, who were tasked with slipping gift cards from three stacks into tin cardholders. A quick count revealed that under half of the required fifty-three were completed. Not good.

"Keep it up, girls," Bridget said, trying to sound upbeat and not panicked. "Stay focused. You don't want General Deedee on your case." She gathered up fifteen holders and scrambled back to her station. She'd drop them in and then start the final step of cellophane-wrapping the crates.

The garage door opened, letting in a blast of cold air, and Deidre with clipboard and phone. "We're at T minus forty-nine minutes before launch. Where are we at, Bridget?"

"Turkeys are in place. I'm going to tuck the cardholders into these, then start wrapping them."

Deidre hissed. "We should already be in the wrap stage. There are still the tags to put on and then the final cross-check."

"Do you want me to help her?" Mara said.

"I can't afford to pull you from there, or else we'll fall behind on the second delivery round which is scheduled for T minus two hours and—" Deidre consulted her phone "—forty-seven minutes. Has anyone heard from Jack?"

As if the saying of his name invoked his presence, a vehicle outside gunned up to the garage door which rose to reveal Jack opening the back doors to a utility van. Bridget blinked against the noon light.

"About time," the general said when Jack appeared in the garage. "Jack, please tell me that you've kept the temperature at a minimum. We cannot have the turkeys thawing at all."

"I am fully briefed on food-handling procedures," Jack said. "The van is cold enough to give a snowman frostbite."

"Good. We're a full twenty minutes behind schedule. Leave the van doors open, close the garage door, get in here and help Bridget."

Jack completed the first three instructions in seconds and peeled off his jacket to start the fourth. "Okay, how can I help?"

Bridget dropped in the last cardholder and came to the other end of the bench—well, a plywood sheet secured to sawhorses. "We need to wrap and tag these crates and load them, all in forty-five minutes."

"Forty-four," Deidre said, "and don't forget to clear final check with me." Her phone rang. "I need to get this. Everyone, go, go, go!" She departed, her voice suddenly sweet as she talked to one of the crate recipients.

"I bungee jumped with less adrenaline pumping through my veins than I have now," Krista declared. "Mom's gone all power-hungry."

Isabella's head came up at *hungry*. "When are we eating?"

"How much longer do we have to do this?" Sofia said.

Jack pointed at Sofia. "Until your job's done." Then he pointed at Isabella. "After your job's done." To Krista, he said, "Can it, cousin."

He turned back to Bridget. "How about we measure out the first one, I cut the rest while you wrap and then when I'm done cutting, I tag?"

Bridget felt her stress reduce from the size of a crater to a…crate. "That'll work. Remind me to text Deidre when you start tagging, so she can start her final inspection."

He gave a short nod and instantly they fell into their pattern of fitting together to take on whatever task they set their minds to. Crisscrossing paths during breakfast service, working shoulder-to-shoulder on two thousand plus minicinnis, voices merging during bedtime stories, lips coming together… as they very nearly had the night before last. She had put on the brakes because it wasn't fair to him to rekindle their relationship when she planned to leave it all behind.

Yes, she would miss him and the girls and Deidre. But neither could she stay in the house and pretend to herself that she had moved on.

She exhaled. Jack shot her a look. "Don't worry. We got this."

And just as she'd raised him up when he felt down Saturday night, he was doing the same for her. Perfect partners in all ways except the one she could only give him by moving on. But for one more day they could be their best. "We got this," she repeated, and meant it.

KRISTA'S COMPARISON TO bungee jumping ran through Jack's mind time and time again during the delivery of the Christmas Crates. Pack the crates, pack up the girls, negotiate the snow-filled side streets with Bridge riding shotgun with addresses and Google Maps, deliver the crates and then back again for the next round. A burger eaten behind the wheel, bathroom breaks timed for when Deidre could cover tagging, bedtime for Sofia rushed between loads.

By the time the final delivery rolled around, the frenzy of the day had burned into a kind of mellowness. He glanced over his shoulder. Isabella had insisted on accompanying them on every delivery, even though she had the option of staying behind, as Sofia had. Although either he or Bridge could've easily crossed off names as crates were delivered, it mattered to Isabella to do this job. Who was he to deny her the opportunity to give to the community she now belonged to?

And that he belonged to. The Christmas

Crates program had started off as a kind of penance for the wrongs of his mother, but it had turned into a profound act of gratitude to the people of Spirit Lake and to his new-found family. This place was now more than his hometown. It was his home. All because of the woman beside him checking out duplex numbers as they rolled along a darkened street. "Here," Bridget said.

Jack parked, and together with Isabella, they delivered the crate. This was always the awkward time. Today he'd been hugged, kissed, and even licked by a Lab who smelled dog treats in the crate. There had been tears of gratitude and kid-loud cheers. There'd also been the occasional quiet handshake, the murmured thanks, the hurried rush to close the door to hide their shame.

Behind this door was a senior couple in pressed clothes, the man leaning on a cane. Jack set the crate on their kitchen table and was asked if they'd like coffee and cookies. Jack and Bridget assured them they couldn't stay. Out on the sidewalk, Jack heard crunching.

Isabella was eating a cookie. "She put one in my hand on the way out."

He and Bridge exchanged smiles. "What is this—your fourth treat today?"

"Sixth," Isabella said.

Three deliveries later, Isabella asked if she could wait in the van. "Are you sure?" Jack asked. "You might get another treat."

Isabella snuggled down into her seat. "I'm full."

No sweeter words had fallen from her lips in all the time he'd known her. "That," Jack said over his shoulder to Bridget, as he carried the crate up the walk, "is the first time she has ever declined a chance to get more food."

"Two months of my cinnamon buns don't make up for one day of takes from delivering Christmas Crates," Bridget said, coming up beside him as she rang the doorbell.

Jack shifted the crate around so he could look her straight in the eye. "This one day is because of your buns, Bridge. You were her meat and potatoes. Today was just the icing."

Her face lit with amusement. "Mix metaphors much?"

"Yeah, yeah. But I hope you know... I thought this was going to be the worst time of their already horrible year, and you made it into something great."

She tilted her head. "You played no small part."

"Then let's say that because of us—because of all the Montgomerys— their presents are bought, the turkey is in the fridge, the tree is up, new pajamas are there. Everything for them is good."

The door opened, the crate passed along with an exchange of Christmas greetings. Back on the sidewalk, Bridge touched his arm. "Thank you, Jack. It means a lot, an incredible lot, to know that I could love them and it didn't end badly."

She meant their brokenness. "Listen, Bridge, you and me—"

"No. It's okay. We're okay. Jack, I just want you to know that I think I found a way to climb down."

He felt tingles, and it wasn't the cold. "What are you saying, Bridget Montgomery?"

Isabella stuck her head out the window. "C'mon. Let's do this."

"I'll tell you tomorrow," Bridge said quickly and hopped into the van.

There'd been a dozen years of unspoken feelings between them. He supposed he could wait one more day.

TUESDAY MORNING, Jack confined himself to the kitchen with Mano. Since his spectacle with coffee rationing, his new policy was to stay out of sight and let Bridge run the show.

He arranged twists of orange slices on four plates, parsley on the two omelets, whipped cream and strawberries on two others, and voilà. Ready for Bridget to deliver.

He set them on the serving window and it hit him just how full the restaurant was. Beyond full—brimming. Bridget was darting among the tables, like a bee with flowers, delivering sweet nectar of caffeine with two pots. But she clearly needed help. Workers in blue coveralls and kids in ski gear and seniors and families kept coming in, squeezing into booths already occupied. There were nine in one booth. Too bad they hadn't had these numbers Saturday night.

"Mano, is this normal?"

"I do not have time to think about what is normal. Get this to Marlene." Mano indicated a full house special.

Marlene had come in ten minutes late and said that she needed to hit the road as soon as possible. To his relief and surprise, she had returned the day after their run-in and he'd apologized for his behavior, but her answer had been a tight-lipped glare. He'd steered clear of her after that. Here was his chance to help Bridget and try again with Marlene.

Bridget registered Marlene's plate and the direction he was heading. He gave what he hoped was a reassuring smile and weaved between the tables to Marlene. "Good morning. Your usual. Bridget will be along shortly with more coffee. Will that be all?"

She looked at her plate, looked across the restaurant at where Bridget was slinging coffee with two pots and then glanced over to where Mel and Daphne sat. Mel and Marlene exchanged nods.

What?

Marlene pushed back her chair and stood, the scrape across the wood floor like a bow on a violin string.

Marlene was about to make a scene. His second thought was how he had to convince Bridget that—*please believe me*—he'd done nothing, absolutely nothing. Bridget must've sensed impending disaster because she paused to watch.

Marlene stood and drew breath. Ready to blast him one.

At the table by the window, shoulder-to-shoulder with college students and seniors, a young woman lifted up her phone. The newspaper reporter he'd done his interview with, about how his recently discovered mother had defrauded the people of Spirit Lake of ten thousand dollars. This was being recorded. The altercation was going to end up smeared all over social media. All over town.

Bridget didn't deserve this.

"Marlene, please—"

She held up her hand for him to stop and sang with perfect pitch, "On the first day of Christmas, Spirit Lake gave to thee, a toonie in a Christmas Crate." From under her table, she lifted out a crate and tossed in a two-dollar coin. Jack looked at Bridget. She shook her head, looking as dumbfounded as he felt.

Two more chairs scraped back, as Mel and Daphne joined Marlene for the second verse. "On the second day of Christmas, Spirit Lake gave to thee—" Mel gestured to Jack as Daphne took the crate from Marlene "—two twenty-fives and a toonie in a Christmas Crate." In dropped two twenties, two fives and a toonie.

On the other side of the restaurant, at the booth with nine, the trucker with his oversize mug rose. "On the third day of Christmas," he sang in baritone to Bridget, "Spirit Lake gave to thee, three crisp tens—" and he was joined by the entire restaurant as Mel crossed the restaurant with the crate "—two twenty-fives and a toonie in a Christmas Crate."

Into the crate was dropped thirty bucks plus twenties, fives and a toonie. It was a flash mob. A Spirit Lake flash mob for Bridget and him. Somehow word must have leaked out about the restaurant's finances, and this was a fundraiser.

Bridget had also clued in. She rotated in spot to the next singer. Tanya, the bank manager.

"On the fourth day of Christmas," she sang solo, ending with, "four twenties lured…" And in floated four twenties. Bridget's fingers began to loosen on the coffeepots—Jack reached her side just as a man in a suit stood for his part. Carson, the drunk muckety-muck.

Bridget paled, and Jack took the pots from her failing grip. He stood close in case he had to catch her next.

Carson shuffled in his polished shoes, then cleared his throat. "On the fifth day of Christmas, Spirit Lake gave to thee—" he looked Jack straight in the eye as he dug in his pocket "—five bro-o-ow-wn ka-chings!" He pulled out five one-hundred-dollar bills and let them drift into the crate.

Bridget gasped and raised her face to Jack's in wonder.

Everybody joined in. Even Mano appeared at the serving window to follow along.

The revised carol continued, the newspaper reporter rose from her spot and filmed the singers, the other guests, Bridget and Jack. The crate dipped and bobbed along like a boat on the choppy sea of hands around the restaurant as toonies, tens, twenties and five brown ka-chings rained into it.

On the seven ones are twinning, when a modest fourteen dollars landed into the crate, Bridget broke into tears, and napkins fluttered along hands to her, their arrival giving more rise to their need.

The song grew to its rousing conclusion of twelve hundred coming, a sum that had Bridget waving her hands in amazed refusal, laughing, crying, blowing her nose.

As the carol concluded with the rowdy volume of a stadium singing the anthem, Mel came over with the loaded crate. "We heard about your troubles," he said, "and a bunch of us got together to help. The same way you've helped out the town over the years, Bridget.

You and your aunt. And I guess your mom, Jack. Though I'm still getting used to that, I got to admit.

"Point is, here's what we collected. It's not just from us. We're just the ones who could make it this morning. Daphne's got a list going. She set up on the web a—" He looked over at his wife.

"A GoFundMe page," Daphne said. "I'll manage it for you. I used the picture from the Christmas concert of you two with your family. Our goal is twelve thousand dollars, and—" she waggled her phone "—we are set to hit it by noon."

Bridget touched his arm. "You talk to them," she whispered, "I can't."

Jack set down the coffeepots on a table, a flurry of hands sweeping aside plates and cutlery to make room. Jack shook Mel's hand as he accepted the crate.

"Could you look here?" The reporter snapped their picture. Raised phones everywhere also immortalized the moment.

"Thank you," Jack said to Mel and then again, louder for the whole restaurant to hear. "I swore I'd given up making speeches when I left my job, but this one needs saying.

"I think I speak for both Bridget and myself when I say that this is a complete surprise. I mean, look at her."

The crowd laughed good-humoredly at Bridget's teary state. "I know what she's thinking. She's thinking that she doesn't deserve what you've done this morning." He nodded his thanks to Daphne. "Now, we all know that while she makes the world's best cinnamon buns, she's wrong about this."

Laughs and murmurs rippled through the restaurant. "She loves this town. Loves the people. It's her story to tell but I will say that our cinnamon girl had a rough start in life. A start that would've shriveled many of us. Instead, she chose to open her heart over and over again. She would do anything for Spirit Lake. She has done everything. There's no one more deserving of your generosity this morning than this crying mess right here."

Applause crackled through the restaurant. Bridget was indeed a mess, but something in her posture, a softening and a quietness, like she was an observer of a beautiful scene, caught his breath, made him hope.

"It's me you might have your doubts about." He paused. "I know Marlene does."

"Teach him what topping up means, Bridget, and we're good," Marlene called.

More laughter.

"I'm the new kid on the block. My mother—Mel, you think you're having a hard time wrapping your head around Penny having a kid, try being that kid. She willed me her half ownership in this restaurant. I saw it as a way to make money to support my two girls. That was it. But the restaurant came with Bridget. The woman who agreed to marry me twelve years ago. But then I chose my career abroad over her. Stupid, right?"

"You're telling me," Carson muttered to general murmurs and claps of approval.

"But I'm back, and I've got my head screwed on straight now."

More claps, a couple of hoots. "I guess what I'm trying to say is that I know I don't deserve your generosity, your goodness. I don't deserve her generosity, her goodness. But she deserves ours."

All eyes turned to Bridget. Jack had hoped to save her from having to speak, but the crowd seemed to expect something.

He edged to her side, ready to do whatever she asked of him. She wiped away her tears and slipped her arm around his waist, holding him tight against her. Perfect.

To the hushed crowd, she said, "I didn't

know—I had no idea. But now, now—" she smiled up at him "—now I totally, absolutely, forever get it."

She turned her smile to the crowd and waved to them like the small-town hero she was. "Thank you. Thank you, all."

Jack had one more thing to add. "Coffee is on the house!"

CHAPTER TWENTY

THAT AFTERNOON, THE entire Montgomery household headed down to the lake to skate. Or, as in the case of Mara and Deidre, to watch the others. Bridget knew Mara felt nervous on the crowded ice with skaters sweeping along the edge of her vision, though she said that she'd rather keep Deidre company.

Their mother hardly lacked for company. Skaters sliced to a stop to speak to her, others called and waved, young and old. Her leadership with the Christmas Crates campaign had opened up old and new acquaintances, and her outgoing nature had thrived. She'd already signed herself up to captain the campaign next year, if Bridget didn't mind. And at lunch, she'd even chattered about a part-time position at the seniors' center that had her name written all over it.

Bridget knew there was no better person to inherit Penny's community legacy than her sister. Deidre's eyes had welled up, and

Bridget felt tears prick her own eyes, and she might have slipped into her second crying jag of the day if Jack hadn't burst through the front door with a large cardboard box, declaring that he had the best news ever.

Better than a crateful of money from caring people? Better than fifty-three families assured of a Christmas celebration? Yes. Used skates for the girls and a couple of pairs for Krista and Mara. And brand-new *Frozen* helmets for Isabella and Sofia!

And since it was Christmas Eve and the rest of the day was theirs, they'd trooped down to the lake. Isabella and Sofia took to the ice like it was in their blood, which was good because Jack wibbled and wobbled, and was of little instructional use to the girls beyond posing as a living example of what not to do. Once the girls had firmed up their ice legs, Bridget searched out a distant corner of the ice for herself.

She wanted to try something she hadn't done in a very long time. She glided backward, did three back crossovers and gathered her momentum into a tight spin.

As she twirled out of it, Jack crashed into her and they were obliged to grab hold of each other to stay upright.

"That was pretty," he said, his hands lingering at her waist. "You spinning. All legs and hair and…pink."

She was wearing her pink sweater, pink toque and mitts from their first date. The good date. "Thanks."

He pulled out his phone. "The paper uploaded a story about the flash mob this morning. Krista's with the girls so I can show you."

The glare of the sun and snow made the screen hard to read, and they had to cave their heads and shoulders together to create enough shadow. It was a picture of her when she'd slid her arm around Jack's waist. He had the crate in one arm and was smiling down at her. They looked…together, every bit the happy couple.

And here they were, still looking the part. She needed to keep her promise to him from last night and tell him her plans. She tried to glide away, but he snapped her back to his side.

"And here's Daphne's text," Jack said. "'We just hit fourteen grand! We will keep the page open until the New Year to allow everyone the opportunity to give.'" He grinned at her. "Remember three days ago when I would've called it a miracle to have come up with fourteen hundred?"

She gave a second determined push away, this time opening enough space for his arm to fall away from her waist. "That's wonderful. I couldn't be...happier for you."

His smiled faded. "Bridge. This is for us. For all of us." He glided to her on shaky legs. She glided back and held up her hand.

"Last Friday, when I told you I had an appointment, I did something."

His eyes, blue as the sky above, stayed fastened to hers. She forged on. "I went to my lawyers and I arranged for them to sign over my share of Penny's and the house to you."

He reached for her, stumbled, steadied his footing. "No, Bridge. No. Why?"

"Because I was stuck up that tree house. Stuck at the house and the restaurant. I always made my family, my sisters, come to me. And when you didn't want to come to me, Jack, I cut you out of my life."

"I was at fault, too. Can't we agree that we were both to blame and leave it all in the past?"

"That's what I want, but I can't just say that and not do anything."

He shook his head. "Isabella was right. You're dead set on fixing your mistakes."

"I don't see anything wrong with that."

"It's wrong when you give up everything you have, and give it to me. I didn't ask for your every worldly possession, Bridge. I don't want it. I don't accept it."

She had expected his resistance. "Jack, listen to me. I decided the night of the Christmas concert and moved on it the very next day before I lost my nerve. But it was easy. I didn't realize how…sore I was always feeling. How much I was holding on to for most of my life. I don't *have* to do this. I *want* to do this."

"But you earned your share. I got it for free. How can you ask me to take what you've given money and time over for?"

She glided to almost within reach. "You will if you love me."

His eyes widened. "You've got to be kidding. That's the dumbest expression of love I've ever heard."

She folded her arms across her chest and waited.

"Forget it," he said. "I'm not accepting your share of anything." He stripped off a glove and shoved his hand into his jeans pocket. "If you are really unstuck like you claim you are, you'll let me put this on you." He pulled out the ring, the diamond glittering bright in the sun.

"Please don't tell me you've been walking around with that in your pocket."

He grinned. "After what you hinted at last night and this morning's fortune, I intend to capitalize on the momentum."

"You plan to propose here on the lake in front of everyone?"

"Get while the getting's good. Or, as in our case, while the taking's good."

Bridget's heart leaped. "I will take your ring, if you take my shares."

"You don't have to pay for this ring, Bridge. It was always yours for the taking."

"My offer stands."

He stood solid, the ring glinting. Beats of silence passed. Skaters passed. From the other side of the skating area, Bridget could hear the Montgomery women cheer on Isabella and Sofia. Could they see the sparkle of Jack's ring from across the way?

"It's your turn to make a move, Jack."

"What do you mean?"

"You offered the ring to me a week ago. I've come back with an offer to give you shares in exchange for the ring. You come back to me again with your original offer. You need to counteroffer, if we hope to move negotiations forward."

A glint to match the ring appeared in his eye. He gazed out over the lake. Slowly smiling, he turned back to her. "Fine. I will accept your shares as a condition of our engagement, providing you accept my shares as my wedding gift to you."

"*That* is the dumbest expression of love. We'll just be back to square one."

"No," Jack said softly. "Square one is us saying goodbye twelve years ago. We are so many squares beyond that."

They were. And no going back. No staying put, either. Not a change of address, but a change of heart.

He wiggled the ring. "Whaddya say?"

She bit her cheek to keep from smiling. "That all you got, Jack?"

"I'd go on bended knee again except I'm afraid I'll trip, break a bone and lose the ring."

"I'd better take it quick, then."

"Definitely."

She removed her left mitt and offered her hand, then pulled back. "You told me you loved me. And I never said it back."

"You want to give me everything of yours. I figured as much, Bridge."

"You shouldn't have to figure it. I love you."

"I believe you." He brought the ring to the tip of her finger. His fingers, like hers, trembled. He slid the ring to her last knuckle.

"Do you believe me?" he whispered.

"Yes," she said and kissed him, long and slow, where nothing, absolutely nothing, was held back. She felt him slip the ring on all the way, felt his words drop from his lips onto hers. "Love you, partner."

ISABELLA WOKE EARLY on Christmas morning as she did every morning, the room pitch-black except for the greenish glow from the night-light over the bedside table. It gave off enough light for her to glide open the bedside drawer and gather up the contents into her school backpack, which she'd stowed by the bed last night. Jack-pa and Sofia didn't stir, though Sofia wouldn't last for too much longer. She wasn't good at sleeping alone.

Isabella crept down the stairs past Bridgie's sofa bed. Bridgie-ma's bed, now that she promised to marry Jack-pa. From the back-door closet, she put on her coat, toque and mitts, and pulled on her boots. She stuffed the bags of sunflower seeds, unshelled peanuts and cereal from her backpack into her coat pocket, and opened the back door. Cold rushed at her, stabbed through her brand-new pajamas. She'd wondered how she'd get used to the cold, but she had. Anyway, she wouldn't be out for long.

In the glow from the deck light, she crept down the stairs and stamped through the crusted snow to Gabriel, misshapen and ready to lose its head. From her bedroom window, Isabella had watched birds pluck at the clothing, nestle on the soft shoulders of the jacket. Once she'd seen a sparrow pop out of the jacket pocket. She opened up her bag of sunflower seeds and cereal, and tossed them at Gabriel's feet. She pressed unshelled peanuts into the snow angel's head, laid them along the shoulders, dropped a few into the pockets, then scattered the rest.

The kitchen light flicked on. Ah, good. Bridgie-ma was up. She was kneading the bread dough at the kitchen island when Isabella stole back in. "Heard you leave. Are you ready to help?" Bridgie-ma whispered.

Isabella nodded. She had wanted to make this alone, but she couldn't find a way to pull it off without Bridgie-ma's help. Isabella was glad she'd asked because it made planning easier and Bridgie-ma seemed as excited to be part of it as Isabella had been to deliver the Christmas Crates.

While Bridgie-ma rolled and flattened the dough, as she always did when making her cinnamon buns, Isabella took the jar of olives and raisins from her backpack. She tapped the jar lid to break the seal. It still didn't open and Bridgie-ma leaned over and twisted it open without Isabella having to ask. She didn't need help to slice up the olives. Bridgie-ma opened the ham and cut off a thin slice. "Like this?" she whispered to Isabella. It was thicker than Isabella remembered from last Christmas. Better.

Bridgie-ma layered on the ham. She'd be done soon and Isabella had yet to finish with the olives. Footsteps on the stairs. Sofia and Jack-pa. Ha, Isabella thought, neither could sleep without her.

"What's happening?" Jack-pa whispered.

"Pan de jamón," Sofia whispered excitedly. "Ham bread. From where I come from."

"But you would've had to get up hours ago to make the dough," Jack-pa said to Bridgie-ma.

Isabella had not thought about that. She had caused trouble. Bridgie-ma grinned. "Nah, I couldn't sleep, anyway. Too excited thinking about today, tomorrow, every day."

She and Jack-pa shared another of their endless secret smiles that more than once ended with embarrassing kisses. "I need help with the olives," Isabella said quickly.

Together Jack-pa and Isabella did the olives, while Sofia scattered the raisins on the ham. Isabella spread the olives. And then they all watched Bridgie-ma tightly roll the bread and slice it onto a pan and brush on egg white. She slipped it into a hot oven and set the timer.

She turned to them. "How about we all have a little cuddly nap in my bed while this bakes?"

They all crawled into Bridgie-ma's bed like all the mice in the storybook. Jack-pa and Sofia dozed off easily enough, but Isabella couldn't. And neither could Bridgie-ma who gazed at the brightly colored tree.

"It's my first time making *pan de jamón*," she whispered.

Isabella understood completely. "You don't want it to burn." She left the bed and tiptoed to her backpack in the kitchen. She took out the last of her stash, juice boxes and granola bars, and returned to Bridgie-ma.

She held out the juice boxes, and Bridgie-ma

chose one. The same with the granola bars. Isabella knew Bridgie-ma had picked for herself the flavors she thought Isabella didn't want. Isabella did the same with Sofia all the time.

Not that it mattered what Bridgie-ma had chosen. She could tell from the bready smell filling the air, the presents under the tree and the four of them underneath the same blanket, that there was more, far more to come.

* * * * *

Get 4 FREE REWARDS!

We'll send you 2 FREE Books plus 2 FREE Mystery Gifts.

Love Inspired books feature uplifting stories where faith helps guide you through life's challenges and discover the promise of a new beginning.

FREE Value Over $20

Get 4 FREE REWARDS!

We'll send you 2 FREE Books <u>plus</u> 2 FREE Mystery Gifts.

Love Inspired Suspense books showcase how courage and optimism unite in stories of faith and love in the face of danger.

FREE Value Over $20

YES! Please send me 2 FREE Love Inspired Suspense novels and my 2 FREE mystery gifts (gifts are worth about $10 retail). After receiving them, if I don't wish to receive any more books, I can return the shipping statement marked "cancel." If I don't cancel, I will receive 6 brand-new novels every month and be billed just $5.24 each for the regular-print edition or $5.99 each for the larger-print edition in the U.S., or $5.74 each for the regular-print edition or $6.24 each for the larger-print edition in Canada. That's a savings of at least 13% off the cover price. It's quite a bargain! Shipping and handling is just 50¢ per book in the U.S. and $1.25 per book in Canada.* I understand that accepting the 2 free books and gifts places me under no obligation to buy anything. I can always return a shipment and cancel at any time. The free books and gifts are mine to keep no matter what I decide.

Choose one: ☐ **Love Inspired Suspense Regular-Print**
(153/353 IDN GNWN)

☐ **Love Inspired Suspense Larger-Print**
(107/307 IDN GNWN)

Name (please print)

Address   Apt. #

City   State/Province   Zip/Postal Code

Email: Please check this box ☐ if you would like to receive newsletters and promotional emails from Harlequin Enterprises ULC and its affiliates. You can unsubscribe anytime.

Mail to the **Reader Service:**
IN U.S.A.: P.O. Box 1341, Buffalo, NY 14240-8531
IN CANADA: P.O. Box 603, Fort Erie, Ontario L2A 5X3

Want to try 2 free books from another series? Call 1-800-873-8635 or visit www.ReaderService.com.

*Terms and prices subject to change without notice. Prices do not include sales taxes, which will be charged (if applicable) based on your state or country of residence. Canadian residents will be charged applicable taxes. Offer not valid in Quebec. This offer is limited to one order per household. Books received may not be as shown. Not valid for current subscribers to Love Inspired Suspense books. All orders subject to approval. Credit or debit balances in a customer's account(s) may be offset by any other outstanding balance owed by or to the customer. Please allow 4 to 6 weeks for delivery. Offer available while quantities last.

Your Privacy—Your information is being collected by Harlequin Enterprises ULC, operating as Reader Service. For a complete summary of the information we collect, how we use this information and to whom it is disclosed, please visit our privacy notice located at corporate.harlequin.com/privacy-notice. From time to time we may also exchange your personal information with reputable third parties. If you wish to opt out of this sharing of your personal information, please visit readerservice.com/consumerschoice or call 1-800-873-8635. **Notice to California Residents**—Under California law, you have specific rights to control and access your data. For more information on these rights and how to exercise them, visit corporate.harlequin.com/california-privacy.

LIS20R2

THE WESTERN HEARTS COLLECTION!

19 FREE BOOKS in all!

COWBOYS. RANCHERS. RODEO REBELS.
**Here are their charming love stories in one prized Collection:
51 emotional and heart-filled romances that capture the majesty
and rugged beauty of the American West!**

Get 4 FREE REWARDS!

We'll send you 2 FREE Books plus 2 FREE Mystery Gifts.

Harlequin Special Edition books relate to finding comfort and strength in the support of loved ones and enjoying the journey no matter what life throws your way.

FREE
Value Over
$20